Praise for Raven c.s. McCracken

I EAT BUTTERFLIES

"Unique and very well thought out and I admire the author for having such an amazing imagination… *I Eat Butterflies* definitely includes some sexy and darker stories, and I wouldn't hesitate recommending it if it sounds like something for you! It gives you what it promises, no doubt about it." —*Rebecca, Kindle Fever*

"In this collection of two novellas and one novelette, McCracken—who is best known as the creator of *The World of Synnibarr*, a cross-genre role-playing game—gives us fresh takes on the core themes of power, independence and domination that so happen to ride the rails of vampire horror, magical fantasy and science fiction, respectively." —*James Gormley, HorrorWorld.org*

THE BRIDES

"Dark, sinister and clever…" —*Cherie, Goodreads.com*

Other Works by Raven c.s. McCracken

The World of Synnibarr
The Ultimate Adventurer's Guide
Crypt: The Pharaoh's Curse

I Eat Butterflies: Tales of Vampires, Mages and Mutants
(Anthology)

Novellas (Originally Published in I Eat Butterflies):
The Brides
Merlin's Knot
Velocity Syndrome

Coming Soon – The Worldship Chronicles
(Based on The World of Synnibarr):
Mage Warrior
Temporal Illusions

IT'S ALWAYS SPRING BREAK SOMEWHERE IN THE GALAXY

Raven c.s. McCracken

Swooping Grizzly Publications

Edited by Kelly DeWitt

Cover illustration by Meg Norris
Cover design by Kar-Dix Graphix
Author Photo by RJB Photo

Published in the United States by Swooping Grizzly Publications. For contact information go to the author's website ravencsmccracken.com. The publisher does not have any control over and does not assume any responsibility for author or third-party websites or their content.

ISBN-13: 978-0615560533
ISBN-10: 0615560539

First Trade Paperback Printing
(10 9 8 7 6 5 4 3 2 1)

To my mom, Carol Roberts, my inspiration and giver of life.
I love you.

Two vessels flew a twisted path through the last of the asteroid field. The lead ship, smaller and therefore more maneuverable than its adversary, was barely managing to keep any distance. Like hungry teeth, it seemed as if the ever-moving boulders sought to devour any chance of escape—which, in fact, they did, as they were sick and tired of annoying trespassers who came and went as they pleased without so much as a 'How-do-you-do?'

At every opportunity, the trailing craft hammered its foe with plasma-sheathed projectiles. This, too, was seen as quite rude by the asteroids, who took severe casualties as the smaller vessel continued to be annoyingly successful in its attempts to evade them both.

The interior of the smaller craft shook.

"Whoa …" muttered the young woman seated at the controls as she turned the wheel to avoid the last of the large asteroids. "I'm too wasted for this …"

Another volley shook the vessel, and one of the crew levered herself across the seats. She had short, dark hair with a red streak and a solid athletic figure. Dropping into a seat in front of a laptop, she closed one eye in an effort to see clearly and said speculatively, "I definitely think that we are being followed …"

"What was your first clue, Lisa?" laughed another of the vessel's occupants, a young man with a spiked Mohawk.

"Dan, honey … are you sure we're safe?" The question came from a beautiful young woman seated next to the man with the Mohawk. She had short red antennae emerging from her blond hair and eyes like pools of gold and blue.

Dan blearily looked at a series of six miniature traffic lights set above the pilot's head. One light was red, one was yellow, while the remaining four were green. He pointed at the display and gave her the thumbs-up sign.

"As long as we have at least one yellow light up there, we are good to go, Blixa!"

Lisa pointed to her laptop and focused through one eye. "I bet they just want our autographs!" A following blast made the craft shake, and Lisa threw up her hands defensively and added, "… or maybe not."

"Dan ..." The irritated voice came from the largest member of the crew. "I told you we should have armed this crate." Despite the shaking, the man was attempting to pour a cup of tea. Another concussion and the small teacup was lost on the floor. Obviously fighting frustration, he attempted to refill the seemingly tiny container.

Dan braced himself. "Completely. Shoulda set the laser printer to stun."

After a small hiccup, Dan, in a mock British accent, added carelessly to the pretty woman at his side, "Pony can't 'old 'is tea."

"We are almost free of the star's gravity well." The announcement came from a three-foot-tall floating metal egg in a voice that sounded as if hundreds of excited girls spoke simultaneously. "Christine, once clear, it might be prudent to hit it!"

"Just tell me when!" shouted Christine.

Unexpectedly, the shuddering ceased for a moment, and with a happy mechanical 'ding,' the yellow streetlight changed to green and the red light to yellow. Pony took the opportunity to quickly finish pouring his tea.

Dan gave a chuckle. "Bet they've run out of ammo—" His words were followed by a severe concussion that threw the small tea service to the floor, and the cabin into darkness.

Into the scant illumination cast by the traffic lights, Pony said disappointedly, "Aww, man, now I gotta make another pot!"

--

Earlier ...

It was an absolutely perfect Saturday evening for the outdoor show, the type of balmy Massachusetts night that one wished would last forever. The noisy crowd of college students gathered on the edge of the campus around the foot of an old school bus that served as a stage for the evening's entertainment. The audience laughed and enjoyed life as only they could, the careless vivacity of youth funneled into a moment of time that was so precious and yet typically wasted, along with those who enjoyed it.

The announcer held the microphone and shouted down the rowdy college students. "The next group is led by our very own Dr. Daniel Towne, whose post doctorate work on quantum power sources has a better chance to 'make it' than this group of losers better known as … 'The Misplaced!'"

The stage was set atop the psychedelically painted school bus, complete with lights. The band opened up, and the singer, clutching his bass, sauntered up the microphone, his stiff Mohawk blocking the light behind him like a shark's fin. Dressed in black leather jacket and tight black vinyl pants, he was transformed into a silhouette in the white light. Standing stock still, he began nodding his head in rhythm with the drummer.

Pounding the tiny kit like a madman was a giant almost seven feet, two inches tall with a mane of coal black dreadlocks that matched his skin. The long dreads, bound with rings of silver and gold, reached down to his chest; they caught the lights and looked like sparks as he played. With power and precision, the giant poured energy into the drum-set while the singer simply nodded, letting the intensity of the music build.

As the guitar player began the first intro riffs, light suddenly sliced down from above like the eyes of the gods of rock, and she appeared in a corona. Dressed in a short black skirt and red leather corset, she strode forward in thigh-high boots and commanded the audience's attention with eyes of the deepest blue set in a pale face. A large red streak in her short black hair matched the corset as graceful fingers gripped the fret board like a lover. Upbeat melody joined the drums, and the crowd roared their drunken approval.

The bass joined the guitar after a few moments, counterpointing the melody and wrapping around the beat. Once the intro was complete, the bass player's voice began to soar out over it all like a titan.

With non-stop energy, The Misplaced drove the crowd wild as they smashed their way through their set of eleven songs.

Near the end of the performance, a well-dressed man appeared, standing just out of the lights. He pressed his fingers in his ears and winced each time the drummer hit a cymbal. When The Misplaced finished their set, and the band was moving their gear, using the ladder, he climbed up the side of the bus.

Dan recognized the long-time friend and family attorney and pulled him up with a warm handshake and a hug. "Tom, what a surprise!"

The older man struggled with his footing, but managed to return the warm greeting. "Wow, you guys are loud!"

Cupping his ear, Dan said, "What?"

The attorney started to repeat the question, but then he stopped and frowned. "I'm afraid this isn't a social call, son."

Dan looked at the old family friend and tried to guess what he could have to say that would make his expression so grim. Nearly all of his encounters with the attorney had been positive, and as he was the executor of Dan's trust fund, his unexpected appearance usually meant good news. The first time Dan had ever set eyes on the attorney was when Tom was dangling a set of keys for Dan's first car.

Dinner at the folks' last week had been routine. His father hadn't mentioned anything forbidding, and so Dan was at a loss to explain Tom's compressed frown.

Dan tried to sound lighthearted as he walked away, winding a cable around his arm. "Can't it wait?"

The attorney cocked his head. Dan swore he saw tears flash in the stage lights as Tom withdrew a bulky envelope and said succinctly, "Your father's company been charged with tax evasion. As is standard practice in such cases, the IRS has seized his assets. I'm here to notify you that your trust fund was among those assets." Tom handed the envelope to Dan. "This was all we could manage to liquidate of it before the seizure, son. It's a little over fifty thousand—your last paycheck so-to-speak."

Dan looked at the envelope like it was a bomb. He blinked for a moment and then asked, "Where is he?"

The expression on the lawyer's face took an even worse turn. "That's the final bit of very bad news."

Dan scoffed, "What could be worse?"

"Dan … son … how can I put this? The strain must have—" Tom fought to remain professional and finished as his eyes overflowed with tears. "It must have been too much for him. Your father had a massive stroke and died this afternoon. I'm so sorry, son."

The quiet statement stopped everyone on the stage. Dan heard the words echoing in his mind, and as the ache began to well up, the emotion shutting out everything around him, he was suddenly engulfed by the drummer's and guitar player's arms. Dan could vaguely remember hearing himself crying out, "Daddy! No! Not my Daddy Choo-Choo!"

--

Sunlight slanted into the dust-filled room from between the thick curtains. The only sounds came from the miniature railroad and the diorama that was its universe. The whistles, hauntingly nostalgic, created a happy atmosphere, and for a moment, there was no place else in the world but here.

Dan stood on his stool and watched the progress of the main engine as it crossed the big bridge. His father seemed as tall as a tree as he leaned over Dan's shoulder, took Dan's small hand in his own, and placed it on the control box for the big engine. His dad's hand was warm and soft, yet stronger than everything.

The boy looked up at his father and leaned against him. Mom always said he had inherited his father's eyes; they were a soft brown and full of kindness. But Dad said he had inherited his mother's bright smile and disposition. For this reason, his father had dubbed him "Sunshine."

The big engine approached the curve, and his dad asked, "Faster or slower?"

Dan eyeballed the train and gauged its speed; much more and the big model would tip over and maybe break. "Slower, Daddy, and then faster!"

"Good boy." His father made Dan's little fingers reduce the speed, and the heavy train coasted around the curve securely on the tracks. As it emerged, his father put the train back up to its former velocity, and Dan threw his hands up in the air screaming "Yay!"

"Daddy, me and Mom had a good time last night."

"Mom and I," his father corrected. "You two always have a good time when you go out and sing."

Dan nodded his head enthusiastically. "Last night I got enough tips to buy myself a lot of Roy Rogers."

"And, as your Mom told me, you threw up because of it." Dan's father suddenly had the image of his nine-year-old son in the bathroom just as sick as some of the drunks. It was amusing and disturbing simultaneously, and he thought, *maybe he should switch to Shirley Temples.*

"Daddy?" Dan's voice was far away as he watched the train.

"Yes, Sunshine?"

"Why did Mommy quit singing?"

"Well, Son, she had bigger responsibilities, and she chose them over her career."

"But why? She really loves singing."

Dan watched the railroad crossing bar drop.

"It was 'cause of me, wasn't it? She quit to take care of me?"

"Whoa!" Dan's father picked up his son and hugged him. "This had nothing to do with you or me, Son. Just her, and nothing can change the way she felt back then."

"But she talks about it all the time; I just want her to be happy."

"So do I, Son, so do I! And so you guys go out and sing. I know that makes her happy."

Dan rested quietly for a few moments on his father's shoulder while his dad rocked him gently back and forth in rhythm to the train. Dan's soft brown eyes fell on the "Special Books" as his daddy called them.

"Daddy?"

"Yes, Sunshine?"

"Tell me again. Why are those books so special?"

Dan's father turned and glanced at his life's work and said, "Most books, like the books you have in school, will teach you something. But, in order for them to teach, you have to be able to learn. And these are the only books in the world that are supposed to be able to do just that: teach you how to learn. There are three basic parts to the process. And when you are old enough, I need you to read them, to see if they really work."

"When will I be old enough?" Dan's gaze was fixed in an expression of wonder.

His father's voice took on a mysterious tone, and he laughed as he said, "You will be old enough when you say you are."

Dan quietly rocked back and forth in his father's arms and said, "Maybe tonight? After dinner?"

"But you were going to watch TV—Star Marshal is on."

"I'd like to learn how to learn, Daddy. Then, maybe one day, I can become a Star Marshal."

"As you wish, Sunshine."

--

"I think he is building a game," announced Pony, as he tapped the keyboard with his large fingers. "He has been locked in there for two weeks now, Lisa. So far he has asked me to code up some simple routines, with only enough information to do the job. One of the applications was for maneuvering in three dimensions with a video game controller. That's what clued me in. But the other was derived from the controlling parameters of CERN's super-collider, and I have no idea why he would want that. This is getting a bit out of control, don't you agree?"

"Yes … yes." The young woman closed the dog-eared copy of Gray's Anatomy and removed her reading glasses. Her hands were strong, with nails cut short. The efficiency matched everything about her, from her soft blue scrubs to her white doctor's coat. "He missed my last tournament—I placed third incidentally. He asked *me* to get him basic information on life support systems, spacesuit construction, and everything released by NASA—and the Soviets—on the space station's radiation protocols. From the amount of packages delivered by UPS, I can only assume he is focusing on this new project to keep his mind off his dad's death. You might be right about this game thing. Some type of new virtual reality system?"

"You placed third!?" Pony took a slow swing at her with his right fist. Lisa set down the Gray's Anatomy while gently redirecting the punch, and struck low with a chop, this time at his femoral artery, just above the knee.

Pony's balance was off, and Lisa barked like a drill instructor, "Dude, keep your foot straight. How many times do I have to tell you?" Lisa tapped Pony's inner thigh again and then continued with her fight story. "Yeah, the other bitch did not know what to think! And when I took off my helmet, my hair fell into place perfectly!"

Lisa let loose with her favorite combination, her fists a blur, seven strikes designed to confuse, weaken and eliminate. "Dude, it was so cool, I was like, hey there, yeah, I'm a bad ass. Yeah …"

"How long did the other girl last?"

"Two rounds—hardly enough to work up a decent sweat."

"And speaking of sweat …" Pony wrinkled his nose and made a distasteful face. "There is no shower in the lab, and that is not healthy. You know that as well as I do, Doctor."

"Stop it."

Pony only continued. "What, Doctor? Stop what … Doctor?"

"Oh, thank you, Doctor, as well," laughed Lisa.

"I'm only a software doctor, with a minor in engineering, while you on the other hand, are a medical doctor. He hasn't even come out to eat!"

Lisa shrugged. "Probably had food sent to him in the overnight FedEx stuff; you know Dan—he is very thorough."

Pony stood to stretch his gigantic frame. Through the yawn, he said, "But we do have a show tomorrow night, and we haven't practiced."

"Are you suggesting we make an 'intervention'?"

"I just wanna see what he is working on!"

There was a jingling of metal in Lisa's hand. "I've got a set of keys to the lab—"

--

Pony remembered the day he met Dan Towne. It brought back a craving for Dr. Pepper and Cream-sicles. The warm morning had rolled into a very hot afternoon, and when school let out, Pony always hit the local Stop 'n' Shop for a can of ice cold Dr. Pepper.

Dan, just a year older, was almost always at the comics stand looking for something to read whenever he came in. Dan was already somewhat of a minor celebrity in the small high school, reputedly a genius. He also played bass and sang in the Terrace High jazz band. Rumor had it that he had graduated, along with a friend of his—a girl named Lisa Parks—when they were twelve, and that they only hung around school to take electives.

Pony headed for the store, partially to have a soda and partially to escape the heat. Dan's expensive Mustang was parked outside as always, the paint job covered in dust and the inside of the car littered with pop cans, assorted fast-food wrappers, intermixed with school and comic books.

Today, Dan was perched, legs crossed, on the hood of the car, his pink Mohawk standing straight up, a comic book and a college physics manual in his lap. As Pony approached, Dan set the books aside and slid off the hood. Reaching quickly into his car, he pulled out a soda and offered it to Pony.

"Dude, I see you here every day, and you get the same thing I do: Dr. Pepper. Figured I'd save you the trouble this time."

Pony looked at the can and reluctantly took it. "Your name's Dan, right?"

Dan slid back up on the car and cracked his soda. After a big gulp, he answered, "Yep. And you quit football and tried out for drums in the jazz band this year, didn't you?"

Pony took a drink, belched loudly, and said, "Yeah. Had to—hurt my frickin' back."

"Bummer … Dude, listen, Mr. Kennedy's an ass. You didn't get in jazz 'cause you're black."

"Figures. I knew he was a frickin' racist!"

Dan laughed. "No, dude, you don't get it. Most of the kids in jazz are like, ultra-white. You'd make 'em look sooo *bad*!"

"You think so?"

"Absolutely, to the *Max*!" Dan loved to emphasize the slang word whenever possible. "I prayed he would pick you. I'm a white boy. I barely gots me some rhythm!" The off-beat clapping gesture made Pony laugh. "You, on the other hand, sound like you've been playing for a while."

"Sorta; off and on, since I was ten." The sincere compliment from one of the coolest kids in high school erased the remembered embarrassment of the failed audition.

Pony eyed the comic book and asked, "Who's your favorite?"

Dan shrugged. "Changes all the time. Right now I like Starburn 'cause of the science-based storyline and the ship. Who do you like?"

"The Hammer. Not just 'cause he's black! Dude, Bam is massive!" Pony made a hammer gesture with his fist.

"*Maximum!*" Dan was suddenly excited and fished out the latest copy from somewhere within the mess in his car. "I loved it to the max when he used Bam to beat his way through all the crystal demons to rescue The Dove."

"*Totally!*" Pony looked over Dan's shoulder, and they glanced at a few of the pages together.

"So," began Pony after a few panels of the comic, "the rumor around school is that you're rich and a genius. Just like *Thomas Forge with his Gladiatron Force Five Power-Armor!*" Pony said the last few words like an announcer.

Dan inwardly winced. Embarrassed, he turned the page and gave his patent reply. "My family's rich, not me. And I'm not exactly a genius, just kinda clever. All I want to do is rock and read."

A strange emotional sensation of comfort swept through Dan as the large boy stood next to him. The powerful feeling reminded him of his father for some strange reason. Probably his mass, reasoned Dan, and on impulse he asked, "So, what are you doing? You got a job after school?"

Pony shook his head and finished the soda. "Just the usual: homework, practice, and then dinner. After, I don't know—maybe read or watch a movie, hang out with friends, whatever. What are you doing?"

Dan tossed the comic in the back of the car. "We are forming a band." Then he added, "And, in honor, I'm dying my Mohawk black!"

--

"But Daddy! I love her and we are going to get married!"

"Young lady, I don't ever want to hear that out of your mouth again!"

Lisa stomped her foot and sat down in a huff, her guitar clutched like a teddy bear. "You can't tell me who to marry, Daddy."

"Lisa." She could see the pain in her father's face. "Enjoy yourself, honey. But don't go run off and actually marry the girl!"

Her dad sighed in defeat.

"I know you're nearly eighteen and will soon be legally old enough to make your own decisions, but you have your future to think about. Like it or not, if you're 'in the open,' there are some admission boards that will reject you."

"And some that won't … I've got a nearly perfect MCAT," Lisa countered, her anger melting to frustration.

"Yes … yes," he placated, "but the best schools prefer discretion amongst their medical students. Not to mention the best hospitals. Like it or not."

Lisa hated to admit that her father was right. The fact that he was right was not right. But as Plato once said, *There is the way things are, and the way we would like them to be.*

Her father chewed his lip. "Why don't you and Dan give it another go? I really like that boy."

"So do I, Daddy, just not in that way," she insisted. "We've been friends for too long for that; that window has closed … tightly. Besides, Dan doesn't want a girlfriend."

Her father scoffed, "Well, those tricks he taught you sure seemed to have worked out. Quick: what's the answer to 264 times 739, divided by 78."

Lisa blinked and rapidly answered, "2501.2307692 ... 3."

Her father checked her result on a calculator. It took longer for him to key in the numbers than it did for Lisa to come up with the correct answer.

"Right again. That's absolutely amazing, honey. Before you met that young man you hardly ever read a book and could barely finish pre-algebra. Now you read two books a day at least and are challenging pre-med classes! You could be a doctor in no time."

"Yeah," admitted Lisa, "too bad our stupid school system doesn't bother teaching us the same 'tricks.' Americans might stand a chance if they did."

Lisa began absently fingering a scale on her guitar.

"I heard 'Locomotive' got a new drummer. How's that working out?"

"Pony's great, and we changed the name to The Misplaced, but right now Dan is teaching him the 'tricks,' and until he gets 'em down pat, we aren't practicing. Dan figures rehearsal will be Pony's reward."

"How's the big kid doing?"

"He's mastered the speed reading and the memorization stuff; it's just the math that's giving him trouble. Pony was good at math before and is having a hard time, like, letting go of his old ways. I'm sure this has cool implications toward neuro-plasticity. Dan is essentially trying to get Pony to rewire his own brain very late in the game."

"Wish I could learn these tricks," mused her father.

"You're too old," she sneered good-naturedly. "For some reason, the training has gotta happen when you're a kid. By the time you reach eighteen to twenty, it's too late. And Pony just turned sixteen."

"Well, it worked for you!" Her father sounded proud. "Everybody says that you're a genius."

Lisa snorted.

"Right." She looked at her father pointedly. "As Dan likes to say, 'I'm just a bit clever, that's all.'"

"So," her father insisted, "are you still planning on marrying Heather?"

Lisa's voice was flat as she replied, "No, Daddy, we will just live together in sin!"

"Clever girl."

She was shocked at how easily her resolve melted. But when her father gave her that happy smile, she abruptly realized that she needed still her father's approval more than society's acceptance.

--

"You are so close, Pony, just bear with me, dude; trust me, it will come, and understanding why it works will totally help to the max."

Pony looked at his new friend, and a hot flash of anger cut through him. They had been at this for a few months, and he was tired and not a little frustrated. All he wanted to do was play drums, not be tutored. "Man, I'm getting sick of this."

"But you've almost got it."

"Doesn't feel like it." Pony mind was awhirl. "Sorta feels like I'm going crazy."

"You have to admit it works," Dan offered. "You read and memorized this year's history book in under an hour and haven't failed a test since."

Exasperated, Pony countered, "Crazy as that sounds, that seems easy compared to this. This mental arithmetic is freakin' kickin' my ass! I feel like my head is going to explode."

"Just practice and practice. Repetition is the key, just like music."

Dan pounded the arm of his chair. "Just think about how cool it will be. We're like the beginnings of a superhero group. Once you've got it, things will change quick, trust me. To date, I have read and re-read every science and physics book in several libraries, and just like you, I did it in under an hour each. I'm not any smarter than anyone else. I just now know a ton of junk!"

Pony reluctantly admitted to himself that Dan was right. Ever since he learned the first tricks, his grades took a dramatic jump up, and he was getting a lot of positive attention.

But fatigue, mixed with low blood sugar, was still an insistent alarm. "I'm freakin' tired! Dude, I just need a small break."

"I'm starting to think that you're lazy," Dan sneered. "You're at the one yard line and giving up?"

"Feels more like the fifty," admitted Pony. "And I didn't say anything about giving up, just taking a little break."

"*Wuss!*"

Pony stood up and the big boy towered over Dan. "What?"

"Guess I'll stay smarter than you … *wuss*."

"*Whatever!*"

Dan rolled his eyes. "I frickin' hate that word!"

"*Whatever*— I can still kick your ass!"

"Oh, and the Neanderthal reverts to physical means to assert his dominance. *Wuss*! Come on, you've almost got it, just try again!"

Pony glared down at his friend. He could see endless possibilities in Dan's expression, profound and difficult challenges ahead. He didn't know if he was up to them.

Dan saw the distant look in his friend's eyes and casually asked, "Hey, dude, what's 367 times 34?"

Pony felt abrupt astonishment as the result flashed into his head with perfect clarity and precision. It was as if the answer was part of the question, and his anger was swept away in wonder as he replied, "12,478."

"By George, I think he's got it!"

"*Whatever*," dismissed Pony with a laugh. "Now can I have a freakin' Dr. Pepper?"

--

"Dude!" blurted out Dan. "Let's stop in the pet store. They just got in a bunch of ferrets!"

"Man, why do you like those things?" Pony then wrinkled his nose and added, "They smell."

"Just a little." Dan shrugged indifferently. "I'm thinking about getting one. Easier to take care of than a girlfriend."

"You'd have to name it Stinky."

Dan wrinkled his nose. "I would never date a girl named 'Stinky.'"

Pony laughed good-naturedly and held the door.

Dan made a beeline straight to the bookracks and picked up the first manual he saw with a big picture of a ferret on the cover.

To the casual observer, it looked as if Dan was scanning each page. But Pony knew otherwise, and while he took time to look at the cockatiels, Dan finished reading and memorizing the thin book and was trying to get the cage full of slinky bodies to pay attention to him.

The group of rambunctious creatures was in a constant state of motion. Wrestling and playing, they seemed to be a solid knot, a single furry entity intent on nothing more than each other. Try as he might, Dan could not get their interest.

Pony sauntered up and asked casually, "So. You still want one?"

Dan poked his finger into the cage slightly.

"You don't want to do that." The pet store's employee wore a red crisp vest with a Terrace PetPet logo on it.

Dan jerked his hand back and shoved it into his pocket. "Sorry."

The employee took a closer look at Dan and asked, "Hey, you guys are in that band, aren't you?"

They both nodded.

"Wait just a second." The employee started off. "I've got something to show you."

The employee was gone for a moment, and Dan and Pony returned to the cage full of ferrets.

"They're pretty easy to take care of, and the book said they are a lot of fun," said Dan.

The ferrets' cage sat at the end of a wall of cages that were stacked high above their heads and formed into a corner. When the employee returned, Dan and Pony spun around and were trapped as he nonchalantly dropped most of a nearly seventy-pound anaconda into their surprised arms and grunted, "Here's something to write about!"

Pony caught the business end of the snake. Rightfully agitated, the reptile opened its mouth and hissed at him. His face suddenly pale, Pony held onto the muscular neck with all his might. He took a single step back and felt the wall of cages wave dangerously back and forth above his head.

The bulk of the snake had been deposited in Dan's unsuspecting grip, and his jaw dropped as instantly all the information he had ever read about anacondas flashed through his mind. The data surged in a wave that paralyzed his ability to react.

The snake decidedly did not like him and naturally undulated in panic. Dan knew its defense in such a situation, but was completely unprepared for the snake's uncanny ability to aim the thick stream of urine directly into his gaping mouth.

Coughing and gagging from the unbelievably foul taste, Dan sputtered, "Oh gods … snake piss, dude!" He spat some more and fought for control over both the snake and his stomach. "The snake pissed in my mouth!" cried Dan.

Turning away, he glanced at Pony, his friend locked in a hilarious death-stare with the snake, but for some reason, Dan's gaze came to rest on the cage of ferrets.

The previously furiously undulating mass was now absolutely still. Each and every member in the cage sat in perfect position, as if an audience at a theater. Not a single little black eye blinked as they watched the humans wrestle with their most hated enemy, the snake. Dan stared in astonishment and swore he saw one of them eat a piece of popcorn.

When the snake began tightening its grip, Dan looked back and noticed that the store employee's arm was beginning to turn purple. The man grunted in surprise, fear growing on his face.

"What the hell do you think you're doing?!" The manager for the store was suddenly on the scene, and with his aid, they managed to wrestle the anaconda back to its cage. When the reptile saw its home, it seemed to leap from Dan's arms into the tank.

While they exited the store, they could hear the manager actually firing the new employee on the spot, and Pony asked, "So, do you still want a ferret?"

Dan, spitting and wiping his mouth, answered over a burst of disgusted laughter, "No! *No pets!*"

--

The test results were a clear indication of their predispositions. Dan placed highest in physics, Lisa in chemistry, and eventually Pony surpassed them all in mathematics. Following a whirlwind of successful challenges, all three were accepted at M.I.T., riding on grotesque amounts of grant and tuition money. Lisa's compassion drove her to medicine; Dan, of course, selected physics as his path, while Pony let the engineer in his heart create magic out of structure. And together they continued to make music as The Misplaced.

--

The door opened, and Lisa and Pony saw a bedraggled Dan Towne shuffling around a cylindrical device built of quartz coils, roughly the size of a large kitchen sink, that emitted the strange purple-blue glow of a live plasma field. Dan smiled at his friends like a sleepwalker and continued about his work. Dreamily he started explaining, almost as if talking to himself.

"You know my father and I used to build model trains, and they would go round and round. Daddy Choo-Choo I used to call him."

Dan made a sleepy circle with his finger.

"And the train concept led me to the CERN super-collider—what is essentially the largest machine in the world, created for the sole purpose of 'banging rocks together.'"

He circled his finger, then put his fists together, imitating the sound of a small explosion. He then picked up a large articulating model of Gladiatron Force Five and a laser pointer, along with a brand new laptop, and placed them all inside the device with the quartz coils.

Dan tapped a keypad set on the side of the device, and a strobe flashed within, splashing the ceiling with bright light. He dropped into a chair, rolled to a computer screen just out of sight, and grunted as if hardly impressed.

Dan then tapped the terminal's keyboard. There was a pulsing sound as a light rolled along the device's coils, and from within the strobe flashed once more. Dan stood up with a groan and reached into the strange device with both hands to withdraw, not the Gladiatron figurine or the laptop or laser pointer, but a largish model train engine.

The model bristled with high tech leads and out-of-place wires that made the replica look like an invention of Jules Verne.

Dan activated a few switches on the model to the sound of his slippers shuffling across the cold linoleum and set it on the lab table. On a computer screen behind him, a train icon appeared, and Dan announced dreamily, "IC Drone on line." He then depressed a few buttons on a keyboard, picked up a game controller, and then started a video recording.

"External security field in place, and this is drive test—" Dan looked at the log and continued, "One hundred and forty seven. Smoke modifications to the drive code for controlled deceleration. Gotta have brakes!"

Pony and Lisa glanced at each other, noting the number of the test, and then looked eagerly at the model train as Dan worked the controller. Abruptly there was a micro sonic boom, and the model vanished from one side of the table and appeared on the other.

Dan grunted his satisfaction as he looked at the readouts. "Inertia levels within the drone were at point zero three during drive operation, barely noticeable." He tapped the controller and continued. "That was the drive at one percent capacity; I am now dialing it back to one hundredth capacity." Dan then used the controller, and the same purple-blue plasma field that was around the device with the coils appeared beneath the model. Guiding the drone with his thumb on the analog control toggle, Dan made the train slowly levitate across the table and off.

Pony made to catch the model, but it did not fall. And, as if the train were a remote-controlled helicopter, Dan made it fly around the room.

"No way!" gasped Pony.

"It seems you've discovered a new form of propulsion," admired Lisa, passing her hands beneath the train when it floated past.

Dan shook his head. "Not exactly. The secret of this is more like 'Pullpulsion' or what I call Tension drive. The IC field is able to generate beams of coherent gravity waves that I tune to apply tension, used to pull the drive unit. In essence, the drive falls in any direction the beams are aimed, at the speed of gravity, which come to find out is considerable, especially when you extend a gravity tension beam to a single point in space and increase the g-force itself. When you create multiple tension beams and focus them on a single point, it appears that space breaks similarly as does the atmosphere when you achieve disambiguation, or breach the sound barrier. You know it as a sonic boom. At these velocities it becomes a 'Spatial Boom.'"

Dan guided the model train over the device with the glowing coils and gently lowered it within.

Pony looked over the rim of the machine. Inside it sat the train, nothing else. "What is this thing? A charging mechanism?" Pony was trying to take all of this in stride, but was having difficulty, especially when he realized that the items Dan placed in the strange device were no longer there, just the train.

He was about to ask where the items went when Lisa touched him and asked Dan, "You said IC field is able to generate … gravity." Her eyes went wide as she contemplated the implications: artificial gravity systems.

"It is capable of much more than that."

Dan sat in a chair and rolled himself to another keyboard.

"The Induction Coil, or IC as I call it," he pointed to the device, "analyzes any aspect of existence placed within its array and is able to replicate what is analyzed utilizing the very same energy that powers time itself."

Dan suddenly became aware of his friends as if he had just woken from a dream.

"For instance, right now I can detect every aspect of existence within the coils down to the quarks." Dan pointed to the screen where a staggering list began to scroll down. At the top of the list were the terms Fulcra, Time, Space, W/S Forces, Gravity, Inertia Vectors, EM Pressure, Tesla Waves, and items such as Thermodynamic Constants, Spectroanalysis-Mass, Gas, Atmospheric Data. Following each of the headings was a host of numbers that changed constantly.

Dan reached over and tapped a key on the coil mechanism. There was a familiar strobe light, and the train was gone. As if the effect was now commonplace, Dan pointed at the screen and continued.

Lisa thought she was going to wet her pants.

"So, here is the data that represents the model train: its mass, the energy required for the atoms to maintain their atomic shell, and a host of other properties right down to the gravity waves the mass of the train itself emits. You can see I have actually shunted the raw matter, in quantum form—what I now call fuel—to micro-dimensional bottles within the device. I haven't quite figured out how to efficiently create matter, or whatever. So far I can do it, but it requires a lot of energy to make something from scratch, so to speak, and much less to take that something apart—be it light, matter or whatever—and put it back together."

"Although ..." Dan raised a finger to make a point. "Once I analyze a pattern, I can assemble anything into that shape, just so long as I have the fuel." Dan then flicked the menu, and an image of a bottle of wine appeared on the screen. "I've been using the coil as a trash bin and have stored enough fuel to make a ton of stuff." Dan touched the controls on the IC device, and after the strobe effect, withdrew a bottle of chilled red wine and three glasses.

"Pony, I know you prefer beer, but under the circumstances ..."

"This is the greatest breakthrough in scientific history," gasped Pony, suppressing the urge to shout. "And quite probably the most dangerous thing ever created!"

Dan smiled darkly. "It gets worse."

"Nice …" said Lisa sardonically.

"With one of these you can make another. And I was surprised at how cheaply and simply a coil unit can be built in a pinch." Dan pointed to another of the IC devices constructed with what looked like hula-hoops for the coils. "That one let me build this one. Nobody can mold quartz seamlessly like this."

Dan opened the bottle and poured the red wine in the glasses.

"To a new world."

Lisa took a sip of the wine, and it exploded perfectly across her pallet. "This is nothing short of miraculous." She took another sip and said, excitement building in her voice, "Just think of the medical applications! You can take someone apart and fix them at the most basic level and then put them back together. Eventually this will lead to teleportation!"

Dan shook his head sadly. "Unfortunately, that is the one major drawback I have yet to get past. Once you take apart a living creature, it does not reunite—alive." Dan glanced sheepishly at a spot on the window sill. "Not even a plant. Let alone an amoeba."

Pony stared at the glass in his hand, swirling its contents in the light. "Then how do you explain the perfect taste of this wine? It's basically organic, and at the microscopic level, alive."

"That is not entirely accurate, Doctor," said Lisa. "The state of wine is closer to a state of decomposition. Organic decomposition, but it is totally dead, nonetheless."

"Ah!" Dan was excited. "That explains why I can make food, but not a living animal."

"Perhaps it's the Heisenberg principle?" offered Pony. "Indeterminacy and all that crap."

"No, I've coded a compensator application, which you have to take a look at," dismissed Dan.

"It seems to be something I have missed in the basic precision of the IC field's quantum mechanics or maybe my current method of focusing the reunion matrices. At any rate, I will keep at it. But for now, there is a lot to play with that does work."

Pony walked over to the prototype and squatted down. "This thing looks relatively simple." Pony did not touch the device, but gave it a thorough onceover. "You said 'time' is the power source?"

"Yeah, I call it Fulcra: the fulcrum upon which all existence pivots. It's ticking away all around us," replied Dan through another sip of the wine. "I tap into the temporal 'dis-state,' the place between material realities, and siphon what I need from the apparently limitless power source that drives the engine of time."

Pony took out a small Zig-Zag paper and commenced to roll a cigarette. All the while, his eyes never left the prototype Induction Coil. Dan and Lisa looked at each other with disgust. As Pony carefully licked the paper and finished, he stood up and whistled. "Dude, I thought you were building a game."

"In a way, I am … but wait! There's more. And Pony, don't you dare light that thing in here!"

Lisa and Pony raised their eyebrows simultaneously.

Dan continued. "Let me show you how to make this thing. It's much simpler than you would think. And once you can build one, you can build others."

--

The modified French engineering program CATIA was linked to the IC unit. Developed to build jetliners and used by Boeing, it was the most advanced software of its type, and it allowed engineers to completely construct an aircraft within a computer and fabricate it robotically. Pony spent hours modifying the locomotive within the program and was proud of the results.

The chair groaned beneath Pony's weight. Dan and Lisa eagerly watched over his shoulder as he activated the coil. With the now-familiar strobe effect, the locomotive appeared. Pony flash-read the rapidly scrolling data and slapped his hands together. "You see there!" With his massive forefinger, he pointed to the screen well after the actual line had passed. "I've cut the fuel usage sixteen percent."

Both Dan and Lisa contemplated what they had seen for only an instant. The numbers were compared to data they had memorized from over sixty tests. And both arrived at the same conclusion nearly simultaneously: he was right on.

Dan slapped his friend on the shoulder and linked the locomotive to the control station. When the train icon appeared on the screen, Dan handed the game controller to Pony as if it were an award. Pony stood and made a short bow before proceeding to triumphantly fly the train around the room.

"Perfect," said Lisa, her doubts transforming into calculations and extrapolations as she contemplated the future. Ever the physician, Lisa was most proud of the 'healing protocols,' or repair sequences she had forced the boys to adopt. Redundancies in the coils made it possible to have the ship rebuild damaged systems on the fly. Just as long as a single coil unit functioned, the primary systems would 'heal.' In her mind, she ran through the details of the other systems she was responsible for including sickbay—thanks to the hospital and university, she had duplicated every piece of medical equipment she could get her hands on including CAT, MRI and PET scanners—life support, and radiation shielding, etc., and was as satisfied with her results as Pony was with his. She looked at her best friend and shook her head in wonder. Clever indeed!

Dan's expression was undoubtedly the same as any explorer poised on the edge of the unknown and unable to resist its siren's song. His voice was pragmatic and sharp as he insisted, "Now to build something we can ride in!"

--

The private four-seater Cessna neared the airport at the perfect angle.

Christine's friends ignored her entire approach and had not ceased a constant stream of dialogue the entire time concerning everything from their shopping trip to the poor state of animals in cosmetic research.

The sound of her friends' voices faded into the distance as she neared the runway. Within a few hundred feet of the tarmac, the wind shifted, and she compensated expertly with her rudder. Keeping the nose in a straight line, she fell into what she called, 'The Zone,' and with hardly a bump, the wheels touched the tarmac.

Christine remembered the first time she ever attempted a landing. She was fourteen, and completely caught off guard. The training flight had been going well. Christine had set, or trimmed the plane's control surfaces to ensure the best flight angle and had maintained her heading precisely. She flew entirely by the small two-seater Cessna's instruments as the solid cloud cover below blocked any landmarks. There, above the clouds, it was almost painfully bright and clear, while on the ground it was a high overcast day.

Constantly keeping track of time versus her airspeed, the clouds rolling below her like a road, she counted the minutes until she had to make a starboard turn to 230 degrees. When the moment came, she looked left, then right, and dipping her wing to the port, she then stepped on the starboard rudder and turned the control yoke with one hand to the right. The plane smoothly turned, and she watched until the compass read 230 and then straightened the rudder and yoke and leveled out.

The instructor, his eyes obscured by his aviator sunglasses, checked the GPS as he adjusted his hat and headphones and smiled. "Excellent." He made a note in his logbook. "Now, maintain this heading for two more miles, and then drop below the clouds."

"What's the ceiling?"

"We're at eight now; the report says the ceiling is near five thousand feet, zero precip."

"Plenty of clearance." Christine checked her airspeed as she counted the minutes. When her mental mark came up, with a gentle nudge of the control yoke, she pointed the nose at a downward angle, reduced thrust with her right hand, and began her descent through the thick clouds.

The windows went gray. The real trick about being a pilot is knowing the weather. Meteorology determined almost everything about flying. Even the best pilots have been killed by a sudden shift in the atmosphere.

Once they were free of the gray, Christine hit the wipers and cleared the windshield. The dense clouds rolled by overhead as she leveled out, the sensation always delighting her. It was like driving while standing on one's head.

Christine looked down and noticed they were over the water, a small island a few miles ahead. The San Juan Islands of the Puget Sound were dotted with private airports, and once they were within sight of one, her instructor pointed to the thin strip and announced casually, "Put her down there."

Christine's insides froze. "You never mentioned anything about landing today."

Her instructor simply shrugged and pointed with his pen before he returned his attention to the logbook.

Christine adjusted her angle, lined herself up, and started her approach. What looked like a thin strip grew into a wide runway that was lined on either side by tall trees, the solid forest cleared for just this purpose. Christine worked her rudder and reduced thrust as she deployed the landing flaps and the gear.

The plane's first stall alarm began to groan, the tone a warning that she was close to falling out of the sky. Christine fought with her tail and kept her nose straight as she dropped to three hundred feet. That's when the crosswind hit.

A strong breeze from the side forced her tail to swing to the right. She adjusted, and despite the unexpected crosswind, managed to straighten her nose. That's when the crosswind died, and she passed below the level of the trees.

The effective windbreak combined with the crosswind's sudden absence caused Christine to lose control over her rudder. Like a drunken hooker, her tail began to swing back and forth, and no matter how hard Christine tried, she could not regain control.

"We're going to hit and roll!"

"No, we're not," said her instructor calmly. "Just put her down."

The second stall warning started its urgent tone. Still Christine could not get her tail in alignment; when they were within one hundred feet, it still swung back and forth like a pendulum.

"We're gonna crash!" Christine started to hit the throttle, and her instructor stopped her.

"You'll shear off the flaps!" He released her hand and insisted, "Just put her down!"

Christine's panic forced her perspective into a form of tunnel vision. The runway constricted into a tightrope, and she was losing her balance. At fifty feet, the third stall warning hit.

Christine released the yoke and cried, "You put her down!"

Her instructor grabbed the controls and set the plane down on one wheel. The moment the single wheel hit the runway, the plane straightened out, and they were safely on the ground.

Christine had her face in her hands and was fighting tears. "Why didn't you give me any warning I was going to try landing?!" cried Christine, her voice quivering.

"I thought you were ready for it." Christine looked up between her fingers and noticed that her instructor, his sunglass-obscured face unapologetic, was composed and appeared to not have been bothered by the brush with death.

Christine dropped her head and let out a long sigh. "I failed."

She cried, "*I totally blew it!*" Her voice dropped to a whisper, "I could have killed us!"

Her instructor did not say a word in agreement, but gave her a very pointed gaze as he turned the plane around. When they were once again in the air, Christine also realized that, had she 'put her down,' this little airstrip would have been the site of her first take off. On the flight home, the Straight of Juan de Fuca passing away beneath her was as gray as her mood while she battled within herself. Christine rallied against her own justifications for childishly abandoning control and vowed to never give into fear again. The next time she found herself approaching a runway, she forced everything from her mind, and trusting herself unlike anything she had done before, she entered 'The Zone' and set that plane down.

The memory of that second landing made her smile as Christine pulled her private airplane into the hangar, killing the engine before she took off her headset and fluffed her curly brown hair. "So, you guys … like, let's split up, go change, and meet back at my place to 'pre-party' for tonight. I've still got some homework to finish. I take the Bar next month."

One of Christine's friends, a girl with coal black hair littered with white highlights, said, "If we get there early, we can beat the cover charge."

Christine took off her sunglasses, revealing a set of shockingly green eyes, and shrugged as she opened her seat belt. "I don't mind paying, Katie; the bands deserve it. Some of them use the vacant hangar to practice and need the money for rent."

Katie jumped the subject and grabbed Chris excitedly by the shoulder. "Oh! When you mentioned the Bar exam, it reminded me. Did you guys hear about Dan Towne's father?"

"No," said Christine, "what happened?"

"His dad went like, ballistic in a courtroom and killed the judge and then shot himself! And that Dan locked himself in his room for like … a year or something!" Katie slapped the back of the seat for emphasis.

One of the other girls argued, "I heard his father got arrested and had a heart attack or a stroke and like … just died. And it was only a couple weeks, Katie, not a year!"

"Who told you that, Courtney!?" asked Katie.

Courtney smoothed her meticulously dyed auburn hair and slyly admitted, "Pony. He told me at the first show they played, just a month after it happened."

At the mention of the drummer's name, each of the girls sighed.

Christine clenched her fist and lightly pounded on the plane's control yoke. "That's one good looking man." Then she added with mock sarcasm, "Too bad he's a doctor! Yum!"

Katie laughed. "Can you say: *take this one home to the parents*!?"

"I got Dan, once ..." Courtney admitted slyly. "He wasn't bad at all." She bashfully made a measurement gesture with her two hands.

Christine looked incredulous. "You did not! I thought he didn't like girls. I've never seen him with a girlfriend."

"He doesn't want a girlfriend." Courtney dropped her hands into her lap and pouted. "He said between school and the band that he didn't have the time."

"Well, he found the time for you, didn't he?" laughed Katie. "Slut."

Christine brushed Courtney's hair aside and said, "Men will always find time for a gorgeous girl like you, Courtney. I know I would." Christine hastily added, "If I were a guy."

Courtney blushed, but couldn't suppress the wicked expression that crossed her face with the memory of their one drunken night together. Courtney flicked her eyes across Christine's, saw that she was remembering as well, with a very big smile on her face.

Christine finished her post-flight inspection of the plane as the last of her friends drove off. Saving the logbook entries, she was surprised to see the outrageous colors of The Misplaced bus flash by the open mouth of the hangar. The graffiti-colored vehicle was a school icon.

Christine stuck her head out of the door just before the tail of the unmistakable bus vanished into the vacant hangar, and she whispered to herself, "I bet they're going to practice before the show tonight."

There was a strobe of brilliant light from within the hangar as Christine approached. When she looked around the corner, Pony was busy coiling up a long white plastic tube while Dan pushed some type of gear toward the back of the bus. The guitar player, Lisa Parks, was busy coiling up a piece of plastic tubing similar to Pony's.

Christine took a close look at the bus. For some reason, it looked bulkier and maybe a little bit bigger than it had a moment ago. The wild paint job was the same, as were the obscene decorations in the windows, but somehow the vehicle looked different. Maybe it was the wheelbase, or the proportions, but one way or another, this did not look like the familiar old party bus. The only truly noticeable difference was a new luggage rack fully loaded with gear. That definitely was not there when the bus had rolled in only moments ago.

Pony was the first to spot her. His expression was a mixture of embarrassment and then a sudden flash of anger that melted to his typical smile. "Uh, guys, look—it's Chris Tester."

"This year's *homecoming queen?*" Lisa, still focused on wrapping the coil, sounded incredulous.

Pony pointed with his chin. "None other."

Lisa looked up and couldn't believe her eyes. Christine Tester was the type of young woman that belonged in a fashion catalog. She was a perfectly proportioned girl with full lips, upturned, lightly freckled nose, and the look of the spa about her creamy tan skin. She stood about five foot six and wore sandals that matched a simple one-piece white dress, belted loosely in the middle, that appeared comfortable as well as very stylish. Even this simple outfit matched her reputation as a 'party girl,' along with her eyes of green that flashed with a light uniquely their own.

She wore no makeup—Lisa could tell by the look on her face that Christine seemed acutely aware of it—and her brown hair, kept in a short curly fashion that just brushed her shoulders, looked like it was begging to be touched.

"Hi." Christine shyly walked in, waving. "I saw you guys pull in, and I thought you were using the hangar to practice. I wanted to listen in." She looked at the band and followed with, "But you're not practicing, are you?"

"No, Chris, we're not." Dan finished stowing the equipment and said, "We made some changes to our ride. Come and check it out."

"What type of changes?" Christine eyed the bus with a mixture of excitement and suspicion.

"A new mini-bar, Pony-sized reclining seats, leather couches, and wait till you hear the stereo!" Dan opened the side door of the bus via a remote key and gestured. "After you."

"Like, really? Oh, wait till the girls hear I partied on the bus!"

As Christine bounced up the steps, Dan cast a glance at Pony and

Lisa, and they quickly finished with the coils and followed him on-board.

Pony muttered under his breath into Lisa's ear, "I am certain this is not a good idea."

Lisa winced and cocked her head speculatively. "Maybe, but if she saw anything, we really have no choice. Lucky for us, she's a fan. I would hate to have to drag her on-board, kicking and screaming."

Pony eyed Christine's figure and smiled, "I wouldn't mind so much." Lisa smacked him as they boarded.

Christine was appreciatively admiring the interior of the bus. The flat screens, set strangely over the windows, leather couches, and the mini-bar all glistened, as if brand new, which, in fact, they were. Dan dropped into the driver's seat and turned on the stereo. The band's latest recording started. It worked!

Dan looked at Pony and Lisa, and they silently echoed his expression with big smiles and disbelieving shakes of their heads. When the bus had rolled into the hanger, it was nothing more than an empty shell. Now it had been rebuilt, down to the smallest detail by the IC unit, just as they designed it.

Above the driver's seat was an array of six antique streetlights, each hung vertically and bolted to the slanting ceiling, and all of them were showing green. Dan looked at the front windshield. It was really a solid piece of armor, like the rest of the bus, with monitors mounted in place of transparent, and very flimsy, safety glass.

Dan pressed a small button on the windshield washer switch, and the viewscreens became active. When he closed the door, he could feel in his ears when the pressure seal engaged, and he heard the whirr of small fans as fresh air, created by specific IC units, began to circulate. With a sigh, Dan scanned the modified dashboard filled with status gauges, represented by a strange collection of antique TV screens, mechanical aircraft avionics, and wind-up clocks. All were exactly as they should be. Excitement made his hands shake, and he gripped the steering wheel for a moment and took a deep breath.

While Pony stowed the coils in an overhead bin, Lisa moved behind the mini-bar and activated the coil mechanism that looked like a refrigerator with a microwave keyboard on the front. She selected 'bottled beer, quantity: six' and pressed 'Enter.'

There was a quiet 'ding,' and Lisa took out 3 of the bottles, passing one out to everyone but Dan. Christine seemed oblivious and took the offered beer without any comment other than a quick "thanks."

Lisa and Pony silently toasted Dan with the bottles as he stared at Christine in the rearview mirror and contemplated the next move. They didn't have long to wait.

Dan turned the key, and the engine rumbled to life. At least it sounded as if the engine rumbled to life—however, everyone on-board, except Christine, knew that this was only for appearances' sake. The true engine of the bus was absolutely silent.

Dan saw a tiny glittering of energy cross the doors, and the eyes of a troll doll on the dashboard glowed green.

Christine laughed when the engine started.

Dan turned to her, asked, "You got time to take a short spin with us to test her out?"

Christine checked her cell phone reflexively and then answered, "Nice, hell yes. Turn up the music and let's roll." She patted the seat next to her indicating Pony should sit down. Pony eyed the beautiful woman, and considering what they were about to do, thought it an excellent suggestion.

Amidst their music, Dan guided the bus free of the hangar just at sunset. With deliberate care, he typed a predetermined set of coordi-nates in on the old-fashioned ten key fixed to the driver's armrest, suppressing his excitement with the routine.

Once free of the hanger doors, Dan depressed the clutch, shifted into the first gear of Tension drive—bare minimum velocity—took a deep breath, looked at his friends in the mirror, and released the clutch.

There was a minor, almost imperceptible feeling of acceleration, as if they were rising in an elevator, the microscopic press lasting per-haps three seconds. When it stopped, everyone felt the air pressure fluctuate slightly in his or her ears. Earth now filled the star-encrusted blackness of outer space on the side view panels.

Dan checked the overhead signals, and all were in the green. Every gauge read what it was supposed to.

That was when Christine started screaming and passed out.

Pony cradled their unconscious passenger and said to Dan, "Nice driving job."

Lisa fought down a glimmer of trepidation as she flipped open a laptop and glanced at the readings.

"Everything looks good," she said professionally.

"What hap— " Christine slowly opened her eyes and covered her mouth with her hand as she started blankly out the window. In a muffled voice she asked, "Like, is that … real?!"

Pony resignedly replied, "Yes, hon. I do believe it is."

"We're in space?" She shook her head. "*Nooooo way!*"

Lisa played with the laptop and blanked the side 'windows,' then called up the view on the large flat screen at the front of the bus. "We are well out of the orbit of any satellite debris. Exactly forty thousand miles."

"Just like that?" Christine scoffed, "We flew forty thousand miles, *just like that!?*" She snapped her fingers.

Lisa noted that the girl had a very expensive manicure and looked at her own nails as she called up the readouts of the trip. Her fingernails were clean and short, just like a doctor's should be. The necessity did nothing to reduce her abrupt flash of envy as she displayed the navigational vector on the diagram with a marker for their present location in orbit blinking happily.

"Not possible." Christine shook her head. "I've been flying all my life. Nothing is that fast. This is some kind of joke. Come on, you're planning on showing this to everybody at the show tonight, right? It's a trick of the panels. You have flat screens in place of the windows, right. Am I right?"

Christine started for the door. When she reached the yellow line, a force field crackled and blocked her passage like a sheet of thick glass. She gave an astonished yelp, jumped backward and rubbed her hands.

"For your own safety, miss." Dan's voice was cheerful. "Please stay behind the yellow line while the bus is in motion."

Christine traced the field with a fingertip. It sparkled and buzzed with electricity to the touch. She pushed, and it was as if she pressed into a steel wall. Dan sat on the other side of the yellow line, his expression shifting from apologetic to mischievous.

"I was afraid that you had seen us using the coil."

Dan sighed.

"I couldn't risk you telling anyone what you might have seen before we're ready to make the announcement."

"No kidding …" Christine turned and pleaded with Lisa and Pony. "This is insane!"

"An Internet video would have spoiled the surprise," whispered Pony protectively.

Christine looked out the front viewscreen, her panic subsiding somewhat. Halfheartedly she cried, "I should go home!"

Dan's surprise raised his eyebrows, his Mohawk riding up his forehead with his astonishment.

"Chris, do you really want us to take you home?"

Christine eyed the controls, and as the pilot in her heart eclipsed her dismay, she asked, "Do you know where you are headed?"

Dan looked at Pony and Lisa, and they all shook their heads. "Haven't a clue. We figure it's always spring break somewhere in the galaxy."

Christine looked at her cell, the 'no service' message only further confirmation.

"We aren't going to come back and all our friends are going to be old or dead?"

They all shook their heads in unison.

"We don't think so," said Lisa. "All our Tension drive gears pull us at ratios of three times three of the speed of light. That way the fold-back of time allows us to fall in a consistent pocket of relative time space."

Christine sat back down and took a long pull on her beer, panic moving toward curiosity.

"Pull us …? No thrust? Fold back …?"

Pony gave a big smile. "Yep, we 'fall' toward our destination. The Tension drive opens space around us, and the forefront of the rift draws us along after it, in a nice, nearly inertia-free pocket. We cannot run into physical objects in this state, as there is no space for matter to occupy. Likewise, no one could shoot at us or vice versa."

Dan shifted in his seat. "The fold-back is a fact of relative space-time connection. The faster you go, the slower time flows. Reach the speed of light and time stands still."

Pony interrupted. "That's why delicate photons survive the travel across vast distances. They travel at the speed of light and are unaffected by relative time."

"Anyway, as I was saying …" Dan laughed. "So, when you go faster than the speed of light, time begins to flow backwards. As you approach twice the speed of light, the backward flow begins to slow down once again, and then, voilà, at three times the speed of light, time begins to flow forward once more. We skip velocities in units of three times three and remain in the normal space-time continuum."

Lisa finished her beer. "We are in more danger of collision at slow speeds than at Tension velocity."

Christine's eyes began to focus as the shock appeared to be wearing off. "But it's too fast for short distances …"

"Exactly," said Dan. "Plus we don't know if a full pocket can be created in close proximity to a star. I just used first gear, and this is a three speed, manual transmission, of course. 'First' lets us go up to nine times the speed of light, 'second' up to eighty-one times, and 'third' up to six thousand five hundred and sixty one times the speed of light—at these velocities, the Galaxy shrinks dramatically!"

Lisa blanked the flat screen and reestablished the view out the side windows. "The experiments say no, we can't safely establish a full drive pocket for short trips; however, once one is up, it will function. So, we have to go out of range of the sun's … excuse me, Sol's gravitational influence. Then we can 'fall' in second gear. However, we should be able to fall into a solar system, under full Tension drive, and pass through or decelerate within, safely."

Pony finished his beer with a gulp and started rolling a cigarette. "That will work good for dramatic entrances … or surprises!"

The Earth hung massively in the windows of the bus as the group stared out into the void.

Dan turned and gripped the wheel. "We were going to play it by ear. As long as everything was working as expected, we would just go for it. This is a hell of a lot more interesting than school!"

Christine balked and stomped her foot. "But the government … people should know about this!"

"We've already discussed this." Pony lit up his cigarette. "The government would mess this up. People would mess this up. Can you imagine some corporate monger, with his advertising cronies in tow, blasting into space!?"

Lisa opened another beer and handed it to Pony. "Not to mention religious zealots."

Christine finished her bottle and took Pony's before he could grab it. "Pony, put that cigarette out! But this is like, really dangerous, you guys. We should have two ships, some sort of back up. We could die out here, and no one would know!"

Dan shrugged, his resolve tightening. "True. But if we get anyone else involved, it will take forever, and we will be squeezed out, not to mention locked up."

Pony took back his beer and reluctantly snuffed out his cigarette. "It's better to ask forgiveness than permission."

Christine slapped her hands down on the leather couch in frustration. "I've watched sci-fi movies—what if we get attacked? How are we going to fight?"

Pony took a hit off the beer and handed it back to Christine. "That's my department. We've got an interesting strategy. We rely on our defenses and try not to be aggressive."

Christine put her hands on her hips. "What defenses?"

Pony smiled at her and stood up, grabbing the ceiling and leaning into her menacingly. "We establish a Coil field around the bus and take in whatever is fired at us. If the shields don't stop the attack, we will simply absorb whatever it is and convert the effect, or weapon, into power. Heck, in theory, we could fire the effect, or weapon, right back at—whatever."

Dan was considering destinations, looking at star charts up on his screen, and said absently, "The Coil field traps any type of matter or energy."

Christine sat back down in defeat. "It sounds too simple ... there must be a catch."

Dan, still scanning the star maps, shrugged. "The simplest things do not have catches, Christine. They just work. Like the wheel, electricity, my hair."

Christine's resolve faded, and with one last effort she cried, "What about insurance?!"

Lisa snorted through her drink. "Insurance companies steal freedom and money. They ruin lives and profit by keeping everyone afraid of liability and the unforeseen. Forget liability, we have freakin' responsibility." Lisa's voice took on a Mexican accent as she finished with, "We don' need no steenking insurance ..."

Christine stared out into space. "Ok, say we are safe, just for a second, and that this 'bus' isn't going to kill us. There are still a million things that can go wrong. It's just crazy—we should go back!"

Dan stopped his search, selected a destination, and turned to Christine. "You can't tell me that you are not the least bit curious as to what is out here, Christine? I've been waiting for this my entire life!"

Lisa's tone was infectious as she dared the girl, "Who knows what we are going to find … if anything at all …"

"I just hope that whatever we run into out here is friendly," said Pony indifferently. "The thought of space Nazis is a bit frightening."

"Nothing like a good roadtrip." Christine sighed and bit her lip. "Well, I just hope that whoever, or whatever we find out here, that they are well dressed. Oh, one last question: do you have a shower on this thing?"

Dan hit the clutch …

--

Christine stared over Dan's shoulder at the rainbow lights that formed the walls of the Tension drive pocket. Dan turned the bus' large steering wheel slightly, and their position adjusted, just like driving down a normal road. The corridor began to gently turn, and Dan kept the bus perfectly in the center of the 'lane.' Christine noted that exactly like her airplane's yoke, the wheel moved up and down as well. Dan pressed down on the accelerator, and the bus seemed to increase speed slightly as he pulled them up what appeared to be an incline. Dan focused on the 'road,' and said, "As our destination is always in motion, I think this twisting and turning effect compensates for the dynamic orbital mechanics, thus necessitating constant course corrections."

Christine understood immediately. "I wonder what would happen if you, like, let us slide into the wall?"

"Probably the same thing that happens when you drive off any road at speed: it's one hell of a bumpy ride."

They passed through a bright flash, and Christine gasped, her eyes smarting as she asked, "What was that?"

Dan shrugged. "I think they are stars, and that we are passing through, or very near to them." Dan pointed to a computer simulation of their progress, and the sphere was dropping away along their trajectory. Moments after they passed, the 'road' began to twist once more. In the forward view, another star was rapidly approaching, and with a bright flash it was behind them, as if they had passed another driver in the night.

Christine noted that the computer was recording their progress as they made the trip.

She announced, "You're building an accurate starmap."

Dan glanced at the simulation and grunted agreement. "Yep, we have NASA's star charts, but they are completely inaccurate. By the time we can see the light from any star, it is no longer in that place." The diagram on the computer adjusted slightly as they flew by another star.

Christine noted that the number of the star was displayed. "So, as you pass by where each star really is, at this point in time, you can create an accurate map to the stars around it as well. That's why the road keeps changing. With each correct position we pass, the extrapolation moves on to the next star along the way to our destination."

"Nice … good work, Chris. Yep, freaking stellar extrapolation."

Christine watched Dan for a few more moments in silence, memorizing the controls. Whenever he made an adjustment, or looked at an instrument, she asked for an explanation of its function and usage, an unexpected desire to pilot the craft growing as she learned.

Lisa was tuning her guitar. Pony sat across from her, and they both watched Christine as she seemed to flirt with Dan.

"Cozy quick," said Pony.

Lisa gave a menacing look and then sniffed with halfhearted sarcasm, "It vexes me greatly."

Pony leaned in like a conspirator and gave Lisa a hungry leer. "She would look better next to you." He softly growled, "A whole lot better than your ex, Heather, or … what was his name … Brad? What ever happened to Heather, anyway? I thought you two were going to get married? I so would have loved to have gone to that wedding!"

"Pervert." Lisa let her eyes linger on Christine's figure. "I'd still be with Heather, but she turned out to be straight, and Brad hates to party, and I'm the 'Party Panther.'"

Lisa strummed an intro riff. "Honestly, though, I would have thought little Miss Prom Queen would be in your lap."

Christine picked that moment to glance back at Lisa and give her a sincerely flattering leer before turning back to Dan.

Pony and Lisa glanced at each other, and they both suppressed their astonishment.

Pony said, "Looks like there's more to little Miss Prom Queen than meets the eye."

"I would never have believed it," whispered Lisa. "She's such a girly girl."

"Lipstick included no doubt," rumbled Pony.

"You sound disappointed."

Pony only smiled and shook his mane of dreadlocks. "Nawww, not really. I'm more interested in seeing if there are any girls out here."

"... and whatever ..." Lisa winked.

"Now who's the freaking pervert?!"

Pony's loud laughter was followed by a strange sound that almost resembled someone speaking in a garbled language. The noise issued from every speaker, overriding The Misplaced's music.

Christine pointed to the side monitors, and a large shadow could be seen through the Tension field wall. It shifted and shimmered as if it were a submarine riding alongside them underwater in bright sunlight. The sound began again and repeated itself.

Pony flipped the armrest of the couch open and used the touch screen controls. "Whatever it is, dude, it's matched velocity and is broadcasting on a simple EM band through a ... a ... no freaking way! That looks like a moving Einstein/Rosenberg bridge. Oh, you have got to be kidding me ...?"

Christine sounded panicked. "What is it?"

"The wormhole is the size of a neutron!?! Wow! Oh, I gotta copy that be'och." Pony touched the controls rapidly. "Come on ... *come onnnnn* ... there! Dan, I've got it; you want I should destroy their bridge? I can."

The sound began once more, and Dan cocked his head. It was definitely a language. "I think we may have just made first contact. I'm dropping out of Tension drive." Dan hit the brakes, and the rainbow road tore. Suddenly they were surrounded by an endless sea of glittering stars.

Pony watched his screen and laughed. "You took 'em by surprise. They are turning around whoever they are. I'm 'raising shields,' just to be cautious." Pony touched the key pad, and a purple glow enveloped the entire bus.

With the long trail of their 'spatial-boom' dissipating in the darkness, the alien spaceship decelerated to vector toward them on a direct intercept course. Spherical, the gigantic ball's surface was crisscrossed perfectly along the equator by a repeating series of signaling light flashes: a deep purple, to a bright white, followed by a deep blood red.

In the distance, the startled crew of the bus could see that the metallic surface of the craft was covered with every kind of sensing device they were familiar with, plus many other types of which they weren't. From vast arrays of dishes and clusters of domes, to forests of antennae and much more, every foot of the hull was covered, as if the ship had only a single function: 'to listen.'

The large vessel slowly approached, and Dan fought with himself, struggling between mixtures of calm and excitement: after all, how many times had they watched spaceships on TV and in the movies? The ship didn't look all that different from something he had seen before. Then the realization washed over him once more, and with absolute terror, he thought, *but these were real aliens*.

Dan glanced in the rearview mirror at Lisa and Pony and regained a measure of self-control. He was the lead singer of The Misplaced, the frontman of their band, a doctor; he showed no fear. The show must go on.

The alien ship moved closer—it was the size of a small city. Soon all they could see was the side of the craft and its horizon. A yawning portal opened, and several points of light rushed out and seized the bus, like radiant tugboats, smoothly pulling the vehicle within.

"I don't like this at all!" whispered Christine harshly.

The stars disappeared, and the massive hangar door closed. Pony watched his controls and whispered, "Dan, all's clear on the Tension field. We can drive out of here right now, if you want to. Whatever this crate is made of, it can't hold us, bro."

Dan looked at Pony, then Lisa, and finally Christine and folded his hands in his lap happily. "I want to meet our hosts."

Christine looked pale. "I have to go pee!"

Lisa sat quietly running the mantra over and over in her head: *Real aliens, real aliens, real aliens … oh my!*

--

The buzzing lights drifted around the perimeter of the bus' shields. Pony noted that there were small variations in the amount of energy the field used when the lights swept across it.

Pony took his eyes off the readouts and said, "I think they must be scanning us. Right now our field is set to absorb and assimilate any energy so we probably look like a shadow."

Lisa slid next to Pony. "Can't you isolate what they are using to scan us?" She playfully slapped him on the arm. "Sort it out, man!"

Pony pressed the limits of the hastily coded filter application and adjusted it to differentiate anything the bus projected versus the unknown. On the screen, a simulation of a wave flowing from the tug-lights to the surface of the IC field became visible.

"Psychedelic," admired Dan, "but do you think whatever it's spitting will hurt us?"

"Not much of the scan is getting through. Our field is pretty efficient." Lisa looked at the data they were gathering with the eye of a medical doctor. "No, nothing that will harm us. Not that I can see here. Anyway, the energy levels are too low." She pointed to Pony's screen. "It's definitely not any kind of hard radiation like x-rays." Lisa moved Pony's hand and set the field to reflect the sensing effect back at the tug. Abruptly the lights winked out.

"Peekaboo!" she said playfully.

Dan felt a subtle movement of the bus through the controls. He looked at the laser interferometer and noticed that the external gravity pressure was increasing to a perfect one g as the large alien bay's lights came on.

Outside, Dan saw the small American flag on the antenna droop and then flutter slightly in a breeze. "We've got gravity, lights and atmosphere, people." Dan pointed to the flag, and looked at the antique gauges. "Normal barometric pressure and it's breathable. I'm shutting her down." Dan turned the key, and the mock engine noise fell silent.

The bus sat in a white featureless expanse, when on a far side of the chamber they saw what appeared to be a file cabinet, at least six feet in height, moving directly toward them.

Dan turned down the stereo and motioned the others to look. "Hey, you guys, check this out!"

Pony leaned his forehead above the side window-like monitor and said quietly, "I've got a bad feeling about this."

Christine laughed. "I think if they meant us any harm, they would have already done something nasty."

Lisa was surprised, but found herself agreeing with the prom queen's logic.

"Christine's right, I mean look at this size of this ship! Why would they make gravity, light, and air, if they intended to kill us?"

"Maybe they just want to lull us into a false of security and then, *assimilation*." Pony grabbed his throat as if being strangled.

Dan waved them down as the device approached the side of the bus and stopped. Across the front of the cabinet, a panel began to oscillate between white and black, and the device slowly moved backwards. After a few feet it stopped, the panel quit changing color, and the cabinet moved forward again. From this position, the device appeared to spray something into the air, and then it slowly backed away from the bus. After a few feet, it returned once more to its original place alongside the bus.

"What on Earth is it doing?" whispered Christine.

Lisa laughed. "Chris, I don't think 'Earth' fits into this."

A small door opened at the base of the cabinet, and a thin chord snaked out with a metallic-looking sphere-attachment at the end. Slowly the device moved backwards, wiggling the line. The ball on the end began to glisten and sparkle, the rhythmic pattern almost hypnotic.

Once again, when the device reached a particular point, it retracted the line and rolled forward, as if to reset.

This time a mechanical arm extended directly from the chest and with an unmistakable gesture, beckoned the occupants as it backed away, as if to say, "Follow me."

Pony finished his beer and shook his head, the bottle catching the alien ship's illumination with a flash. "No way!" Pony stabbed at the floor with his thick fingers and announced emphatically, "I am not getting off this bus."

Dan agreed and started reaching for the key when the cabinet moved forward once more, the formerly oscillating black and white panel now depicting a large bottle of beer, exactly like the one in Pony's hand. Slowly it began retreating once again.

Pony took in a sharp breath. "Is that what I think it is?"

Lisa let out a resigned sigh. "Yes, Pony. It looks like a beer."

"No one ever meant any harm offering a drink." Pony, a smile plastered across his face, stepped past Christine. Toes to the yellow line, he said, "Driver, this is my stop."

"Are you sure about this, Pon?" Dan arched a single eyebrow in question as he reached for the mechanical lever to open the door.

Pony's tone was pleading, and he pointed at the cabinet slowly rolling away. "Man, that is a beer."

"It's just an image of a beer," corrected Christine.

Pony waved her statement away. "The thing just made an image of a beer. Dude, a beer!"

"Alright, but if this gets us killed …"

Dan released the internal force fields and opened the outer doors.

Pony was the first to step out of the bus. The moment his feet hit the deck, he saw couches, a table with chairs, and other furnishings spring up out of the floor nearby, all molded from the surprisingly soft deck plating, and all furnishings designed for a biped. Without warning, one of the light-tugs appeared above Pony's head, and before he could react, winked out, leaving only the residual flash burning in his retina like a camera's. As they disembarked, they each were 'photographed' in this fashion.

The cabinet rolled toward the furnishings. Pony's image—a full-bodied duplicate right down to his gigantic trench coat—replaced that of the bottle of beer. Like a congenial host, the cabinet took a position in the makeshift conversation pit and beckoned them to join it.

Last off, Dan turned to shut the doors, and temporarily blinded by the flash, failed to notice as a pair of small light-tugs zipped past him and into the interior of the bus.

Lisa, clutching her guitar for security, perched on one of the chairs and gave her companions a speculative look. Pony dropped onto one of couches and rested his elbows on his knees. Christine took a seat next to Pony, her mouth open and her eyes wide.

Dan casually flopped into a chair and put his boots on the table as if he were comfortably at home. Taking out a pair of sunglasses, he squinted at the bright white light and settled them into place. As if in response to his desire for less light, the room's illumination softened somewhat, and the image of Pony on the file cabinet gave a very mechanical smile.

When Dan did not remove his eye covering, the illumination continued to fade. As it approached darkness, Dan snapped the sunglasses off of his head and shouted "Whoa, whoa. Ok, ok." Pointedly he replaced them in his jacket pocket, and the illumination increased to half its former strength.

"Observant, aren't they?" remarked Lisa.

The cabinet moved to the table, and the mechanical arm emerged. In its manipulators were four items that looked precisely like transdermal nicotine patches. The image on the cabinet depicted Pony removing the backing of the patch and affixing it to his forearm. The image repeated itself, each time followed by the mechanical smile.

Dan looked at the patches. "Lisa, you're the medical doctor. What do you think?"

Lisa inspected a patch, fingering the backing and smelling the interior. It had a vaguely familiar antiseptic aroma. Sliding the guitar to her back, she peeled off the backing and firmly attached it to her forearm. Nonchalantly, she pulled up her guitar, and gripping the neck like it was the lever of destiny, she dramatically strummed a chord.

The alien sound started the moment the guitar chord faded, and Lisa gasped, "I can understand them!"

They're translators." Dan jumped to his feet and quickly affixed his patch.

Lisa looked at her arm with wonder. "They probably send us the desired information via neuro-chemicals or maybe a virus. Freaking brilliant!"

Christine eyed hers with suspicion. "A virus? Hope I'm not like ... allergic."

She looked afraid as she applied it. "I'm really sensitive to medications."

Pony rumbled something disparaging about patches versus beer and sat back down, stuck his on, his eyes affixed on their host.

The voice from the cabinet was melodic, soothing and completely artificial, void of any emotional inflection or inference.

"Welcome, Ambassadors," it began. "Let us start by offering a formal greeting to those of your world or community. As we have not previously encountered your particular planet's peoples, you four are hereby granted special galactic ambassadorial status, as are the first additional ninety-six of your world's sentient beings, biological or non-biological. It is your duty, as first contacted, to communicate all of this information to your place of origin."

The voice went on speaking with Pony's image, although it appeared slightly out of sync, the movements of the mouth trailing the words with a tiny time lag. "As ambassadors for your specific place of origin, you are treated with special protocols long ago established to ease the joining of the Galactic Dominion, the first of which are the translator patches: Inocu-p's. These patches provide specific language data as well as inoculations for each of the worlds you may visit. Each world, or even in many cases space stations, may require its own In-ocu-p. You may now remove this first patch as it has already implanted the galactic standard language, Galstan."

The cabinet rolled forward. "For identification purposes, individually state your specific nomenclature of recognition."

"You mean our names?" asked Pony as he peeled off his patch.

"Correct!" The cabinet went around to each of them and collected the desired information. Then the device asked, "And the name of your place of origin?"

Dan replied, "Our home world is called Earth."

The voice was official. "There is some difficulty with that specific designation. We have thousands of worlds whose names translate to the word Earth. It seems that natives seem to often relate the name of their world with the soil required to grow their food. Do you have an alternate designation, such as Earth plus your star's name or names, if more than one? Even perhaps the name of an orbiting geological satellite?"

Everyone looked at Dan, and he waved them away. "Don't look at me, I only open my mouth to change feet."

Lisa shook her head. "This is the type of thing that will get us into a lot of trouble eventually."

Christine put her hand to her mouth. "Like … wars!"

Pony coughed and said, "It's like we are the first to, like … discover our planet. Oh, Dan, this is a golden opportunity …"

Lisa grabbed Pony by the coat. "Oh, no, you two. This is important. None of your shenanigans."

Pony almost had tears in his eyes. "But Lisa, dude … this will last, forever!"

"We could go with anything … the name someone gave a planet in a famous movie or book," whispered Christine. "It's like a cosmic domain name."

Christine's words set off a thought, and Dan looked at the cabinet. "Can we change the name in the future? I mean, you have got to understand, this is a big decision, one that everyone on our world will want to debate. It could take decades."

The image of Pony appeared to be learning human physical mannerisms. With its hands in an apologetic pose, the mechanical expression of Pony's face still in a smile, the cabinet replied, "The Administration does not compensate for such trivialities: select a designation for your home world so that we may proceed with the induction. You are the first of your kind to make contact. You have earned the honor of renaming your world." And then, as if commenting to someone else in the room, the voice added, "This matter always takes a bit of consideration on the part of the new entries."

"We are going to be in such trouble," groaned Christine.

Pony, ever the programmer suggested, "Can you use our language and have our true word for Earth come out as, say, Everest, so when we speak the word 'Earth,' it is translated into 'Everest' and vice versa?"

"That would entail reprogramming every Inocu-p with that specific syntax variation for each separate language in the galactic community—for a single word. Please choose a designation for your home world."

Dan broke down. As the lyricist for The Misplaced, he couldn't help himself as he blurted out, "Hell." Dan looked at the image of Pony on the cabinet and shrugged. "Will that do?"

"That designation is nearly as popular as your first suggestion Earth."

Pony adjusted one of the rings on a dreadlock. "This is harder than naming a band."

Lisa stomped her foot. "Whatever we choose, it has to sound cool. We do not want to come from a world with a lame name."

"We could go with Gaia, or a Greek or Roman god," offered Christine.

Lisa brightened at the suggestion. "Yeah, planet Athena or Aphrodite. I like the sound of that."

Pony shook his head in frustration. "Can you imagine us telling everyone we had to rename the planet? No matter what we choose, it's going to be a real problem."

Dan suddenly announced, "Pangaea!?" Dan brightened as he repeated the name. "Pangaea! It's what we called the Earth before the continents split up. Nobody can get too pissed if we use that term. It's not religious, not gender specific, and widely known. What do you wrenched lumps of humanity think?"

"Wretched lumps?" Pony clicked his tongue. "When did we get an upgrade from absolute waste?"

Lisa crossed her arms defiantly. "I thought I was the slut!"

"So you've all been promoted, just barely, up to Christine's level."

Dan pointed to the prom queen with his thumb. "Now, what do you think?"

Christine gave him a sideways nod, as if to say *could be better, could be worse, but it will do.*

Pony and Lisa echoed the expression through the million-mile-stare of astonishment. When Dan turned to make the announcement, Lisa winced as if in pain, and then mouthed the word, "wait." Dan ignored her as if she were his little sister.

"We have decided that from this point on, the rest of the galaxy will know our planet as Pangaea." Dan crossed his fingers, and they waited.

The image of Pony was silent and then gave a mechanical smile. "Accepted. And the name of your vessel?"

Dan hadn't thought about it. He looked at the graffiti and offered, "I'm thinkin', maybe … The Misplaced?"

The eager nods from his friends were like silent applause.

While Dan and the group answered questions, the light-tugs flashed around the interior of the bus, rocking it back and forth. In her peripheral vision, Christine caught the movement, but the vehicle ceased moving when Dan turned to look.

The image of Pony on the cabinet gave its mechanical smile once more. A compartment set near the base of the device opened, the image of Pony's knees folding away. The mechanical arm extended four plastic-looking cards in its robotic grip. The manipulator placed these on the table with a surprising dexterity that resembled a casino dealer's flourish. Each of the cards had their pictures and displayed a host of other unrecognizable data.

"These are your identifications, as well as an intergalactic communications device complete with a link to your financial accounts now on file and accessible anywhere in the Galactic Order Dominion. As ambassadors, you have each been granted one hundred thousand galactic standard commerce units or 'G's.' This is a once-only grant and will not be repeated."

"Future currency must be earned by citizens through their own merits. Each world has its own exchange rate, and subsequently its own currency, based on the Gross Planetary Value of the world. In your case, Pangaea, the exchange rate will be derived by a host of complex factors that have yet to be determined."

Dan sucked in his breath and tried to not lose focus as a million questions suddenly flowed into his mind with that last statement. Shoving his thoughts aside like a stubborn screen door, he continued to listen and memorize every word the unit was telling him.

The image of Pony's lips were now moving in perfect sync with the unit's words as apparently their hosts had learned their speech patterns. "Whenever you make planet-fall, all monetary units are automatically adjusted as required."

When Dan picked up the card, an animation started with his image and ended with a host of arcane script that only barely made sense on a strangely familiar subconscious level. It was like reading in a dream; he could understand what it said, but could not place the script in any normal reference. This suddenly frustrated him. He was used to flash-reading and memorizing everything he read. This unusual dancing script seemed to somehow thwart the process that was now as familiar as his sense of touch. It was like becoming blind suddenly.

Dan looked at Pony and Lisa and saw the same realization dawn in their expressions. Pony actually shook his head and opened and shut his eyes before holding the card in his hand and looking at Dan, as if betrayed somehow.

"Your vessel was inspected and found wanting in several areas such as navigation, identification beacons, and gravimetric communications. Your star charts, and aforementioned systems, are now updated and integrated into your user interfaces. You have also been provided with a standard Inocu-p fabrication unit. As the patches are used up, the unit will need to be refreshed occasionally. Refreshers are available on all inducted worlds and habitats, free of charge."

"None of your craft's systems were compromised, or duplicated, in any way, with one exception: all cultural data was archived to preserve your race's identity. Note: your drive system, and the technology it is based upon, is considered unique, even by Administration standards."

Dan laughed and said, "Noted—and cultural data?"

The voice intoned, "Data such as arts, picture images, and audio files. If your race is not encountered again, your species' cultural information has been preserved by the Administration for all time. Your planet status has been switched from closed to open, which indicates your world is now a member of the Dominion."

Dan shook his head in another attempt to shove aside a billion questions and crossed his arms over his chest to retain some of his composure. "Well, okay then. Thanks, you've totally set us up. Now, what do we owe you?"

"We are an ancient facility, whose origins are lost to antiquity. We exist to fulfill the purpose of assistance, administration, and peace-keeping to all known worlds and races."

"We require no compensation; we are self-maintained and vast. There are, however, four important laws which we enforce, and as you now know by this meeting, we are always watching."

"Oh, boy, here we go," whispered Pony.

"First: your race may not deliberately annex, or in any way delib-erately contaminate any 'closed' world. As most non-con star-systems have yet to be placed on charts, this is seldom an issue. There are tril-lions of inhabited worlds."

Pony's expression on the cabinet modulated to a rather severe scowl, as if the Administration wished to strongly emphasize the se-verity of this discourse. "Second: your home world of Pangaea may not launch any military forces into interstellar space. We do not allow military, religious, or economic-based interplanetary conflict. You may police the region within your planetary system, but no further."

"Third, when you are within the dominion of any specific world or habitat, you are to abide by the laws of the local government, then the laws of the Administration, and lastly the laws of your home planet. When in open space, the laws of the Administration apply, followed by the laws of your home world, unless the laws of your home world contradict the laws of the Administration; then, Admini-stration policy supersedes."

The blank screen was replaced by a close up of the entire Milky Way galaxy spinning in a deep void. "And lastly, your planet's in-habitants, each and every one of them, are now members of the Galactic Order Dominion, and like it or not, responsible for preserv-ing, protecting, and nurturing life's continued existence–and happiness—throughout the galaxy. Until Pangaea can be trusted, you are on … probation. Note: remember your ambassadorial status. Welcome to the frontier."

Christine could not resist as her attorney's mind seized on the 'Laws.' "What happens if we were to break any of these laws?"

"Dependent upon the specific type of infraction, and its relative severity, we take appropriate actions that range from limiting the number of vessels, or in some cases, specific individuals and their constituents that may utilize intergalactic travel, to placing an embargo on all intergalactic contact of a specific world and its constituents, temporarily or permanently, dependent upon the severity. In rare instances, we will deal with a specific individual directly."

Christine twisted her mind around the enforced benevolence and found her lawyer's reason rebelling. But then it was pretty clear. The realization almost made her cry with relief. The galaxy might be a good thing to be a part of.

Dan, his heart pounding in his chest, slid the new Administrator ID into his wallet. "Well, then, what should we do now? Any recommendations?"

"What was your original intent upon leaving your home world of Pangaea?"

The crew said in unison, "Road trip!"

"If exploration is your mission, then based upon your specific zoological type—Peri Descendant—the nearest comfortable planet is listed as Wildrahnae."

Lisa stepped toward the cabinet, a strange intensity in her expression. "Peri Descendant?"

"Yes," said the voice succinctly, "by your reckoning, millennia ago, your basic genotype type was seen to arise independently on many planets throughout many systems. The first encountered race called themselves the Peri." An example was shown on the panel.

The cabinet went on, returning to Pony's image. "It appears that nature fills the zoological niche with the same combinations that, in general, seem to manifest themselves with your particular species as the result, or slight variants thereof. Some based on chemo-synthesis, others replace arsenic for potassium. Your basic peri bipedal, opposable manipulators and enhanced intelligence design is quite common actually, as are other various genotypes you will encounter, all based on the specific type of planet of origin. The more common the planetary type, the more common the genotype. This is why we are so easily prepared to make you comfortable."

Lisa strummed a string on her guitar thoughtfully. "So, we will meet others that look like us?"

"Yes, you will meet others that are exactly like your species, right down to DNA."

Christine looked off into the distance and said dreamily, "A galaxy of cute boys and girls …"

Pony looked disappointed. "Aww, man, I was hoping for some bug-eyed monsters. But I guess a few cute girls will do!"

Christine eyed their host as it rolled away and was swallowed up by the wall. Once it was out of sight, she blurted, "Oh my god! We should totally go back and notify Earth. I mean, like, legally, we should not even be out here!?"

"What—'legally'? Where did *you* come up with that?" Dan laughed and asked suspiciously, "So, just what *is* your major, Christine?"

The band cocked their heads expectantly. Lisa even went so far as to begin tapping her foot.

"Come on," Dan chided, "Christine, what's your major?"

The girl looked uncertain and, as if embarrassed, she dropped her head admitting through her long hair, "Law."

"*You're* studying to be a freakin' *lawyer*!?" Dan backed away, as if Christine were suddenly contagious.

"Yes—do you have a *problem* with that?"

"And here I thought she was such a nice girl, too," sighed Pony.

Christine cocked her hip and let some of her indignation slip as she replied, "Nice girls finish last!"

Pony looked at his watch and said, "Well, I've only known you a little while …"

Dan threw up his hands in exasperation before he started for the bus. "Well, councilor, I say we keep going on … We definitely know there are people out here."

Lisa stepped up to Christine's side. "And where there are people, there's a party!"

Christine considered for a moment and then relented with a sigh. "I still think we should like … totally go home." Christine then looked into Lisa's deep blue eyes and saw something there that made her feel warm inside, and the heat melted her hesitation. "Well, ok … if you insist … *Who* says lawyers can't also have a good time?"

"Not me!" said Lisa as she placed a peck on Chris's cheek tartly.

Christine felt that brief touch as if it were Cupid's dart. Dan opened the bus doors, and announced, "What we need now is some theme music."

"No," said Christine, sliding past Dan and dropping into the driver's seat. "What we need now is to find to find an atlas on this

Wildrahnae, then check if there are any flight restrictions where we are headed and if we should file a flight plan and with whom for that matter … and …" She was ticking the tasks off on her fingers.

Dan stopped her. "Whoa, whoa, what are you talking about now??"

Pony laughed. "She's a pilot, Dan, remember? Maybe she should be flying the bus?"

Lisa turned on the stereo, fished out one of the last of the beers from the 'fridge,' and sat down with her guitar, saying sarcastically, "Oh, yeah, why not make her captain while we are at it!"

Pony reached up and touched the ceiling. "Well, she knows a lot more about flying than any of us, Doc."

Christine started to climb from the seat. "Hey guys, like, I didn't say anything about flying. If we're going on this road trip, I just don't want us to get into any trouble out here before we get to have some fun! I, for one, would like to figure out the legal aspects of our hopping about here in outer space and what laws we have to abide by on a planet-by-planet basis."

Pony groaned, "Suddenly, with the lawyer crap, once she's out of the closet."

Dan put a hand on Christine's shoulder. He knew enough about her to know she was an experienced pilot. He clearly recalled watching her land on a stormy evening just as they were starting to practice in the hangar. When the plane touched down, despite the rough weather, Dan remembered thinking: whoever that pilot is, they're good. When the plane taxied to her hanger, and she emerged—along with a giggling group of girls, all seemingly oblivious to the danger— he had shaken his head in amazement.

"It's ok—you take the controls, Chris. It's almost too easy anyway, and you've been watching me drive all night." Dan pointed to Lisa. "Get your lame ass on the computer and see what the Administrators downloaded. Pony, check out that patch machine thingy. I'm going to make us breakfast. And would someone please turn up the stereo? Let's get this show on the road!"

Christine pulled The Misplaced out into the void amidst the band's music, a song called 'Misfit.'

--

On the Administrator vessel, dozens of sensing devices turned to listen as the bus pulled slowly out of the bay. Deep inside the massive ship, an ancient meter began to rise with the intensity of the music, pushing it from white to grey to black. When the needle hit black, dozens of mysterious machines rumbled to life, and amidst gouts of steam, began powering an antenna dish that slowly unfolded outside the giant ship.

When the bus vanished into its Tension drive, the Administrator vessel released a massive beam of energy through the dish, a beam that was caught and relayed across the galaxy.

--

Christine turned the wheel and pressed on the clutch. Without any more sensation than one would experience in the normal shifting of gears, she dropped out of Tension drive. In the distance, she saw a massive comet and guided the bus toward it.

In the meantime, the band decided to get in a little practice. As Dan began the intro to the song, 'So Much for Lust,' Christine entered the comet's tail. With sparks of light, the tail splashed like icy rain against the viewscreen. She casually activated the windshield wipers, and the scene cleared. With a pilot's instinctive glance to the left and the right, Christine stepped on the accelerator, caught up to the nose of the comet, and rode atop its wake like a surfer.

Leaving the comet's nose, Christine put on her sunglasses and drove around a quasar. As she approached the massive stellar body, one of the six traffic lights shifted from green to yellow and this prompted her to hit the 'high beams' switch which would increase power to the protective field that surrounded them. In response, the traffic light went from yellow to green with a happy mechanical 'ding.'

With a gentle turn from the blinding quasar, Chris decelerated toward an asteroid field, piloting into and around the constantly twisting and turning rocks with the surety of a seasoned truck driver.

Listening to The Misplaced rehearse, she practiced backing, parking, and when the massive asteroids were about to collide, a smooth take off.

Christine eased the bus free of the rocky field and called up the coordinates of Wildrahnae. The planet appeared in the new navigational array, and she verified the long list of coordinates. After a few moments, a small smiley face lit up on the dashboard signaling a lock. Christine shifted once more, and the rainbow road appeared. Through it all, the band never missed a beat.

--

After a few more minutes, Christine looked at the countdown clock for the time to their destination and flashed the cabin lights.

The Misplaced stopped, and Christine announced into the abrupt silence, "Should be pulling into orbit around Wildrahnae in a couple of minutes."

Pony took a drink of water and mopped his brow. "Can you slow down and buy me enough time to take a shower and change?"

Dan echoed the sentiment and added, "Yeah, let's get cleaned up first!"

Christine performed the equivalent of pulling over to the side of the road and got up from the driver's seat, stretched and gasped, "Oh, no! I only have this one outfit. Shit!" She gestured to the comfortable white dress she always wore when flying. It was simple, slightly dressy, but plain.

"Not to worry, hon." Lisa took Christine by the hand and led her to her small cabin, the beginnings of subtle excitement in her stomach. Opening the door, she ushered Christine inside. "We had no idea anyone would be coming with us, so you might have to bunk in my room. I hope that's alright?"

Christine shrugged and admitted, "Better than the couch. Thanks!"

Lisa purred, "Don't mention it, babe, and as for outfits, girlfriend, you are in for a surprise. When we were finalizing the CATIA files that modified the bus, I designed something for just this emergency."

Christine looked at Lisa uncomprehendingly. "What?"

"You'll see." Lisa opened what looked like an empty closet and said, "Take off every thing you're wearing and put it in here." Christine did as she was asked, stopping at her underwear.

Lisa dropped her gaze and asked cryptically, "Are you planning on wearing those forever?"

Christine blushed while she slipped out of the last bits of clothing apologetically.

Lisa tossed in the cute underwear and closed the closet door.

"Now stand here." Lisa positioned Christine in front of the full length mirror, careful to catch the girl's entire reflection. With a glance at the prom queen's figure, she loved the necessity to suppress the urge to touch the beautiful girl … very inappropriately.

Instead, somehow, Lisa's fingers found the mirror, and Chris was surprised to see a computer control panel appear on the glass. Lisa tapped at the controls, and Christine's nude reflection was suddenly clothed.

Lisa smiled with satisfaction. "We can select anything now that the system has your measurements, and I can make it." Lisa began scrolling through a library and outfit after outfit appeared on the reflection. Whenever Christine moved, the clothing moved with her, and they could see how it would look from every angle.

Lisa sighed, "This took me forever to get right."

"Oh, my frickin' god!! You have got to be kidding me?! This is better than shopping!"

Lisa smiled and couldn't resist. With a quick sure-handed blow, she slapped Christine on the rear end playfully, and added, "Cheaper, too."

--

Pony made a doughnut and offered it to Dan, who declined and said, "That drone on the Administrator's ship. That thing was pretty clever. Black and white flashes—had we seen in UV that would have been perfect. Next one was probably a pheromone spray. The cat toy lure—useful for a feline species. The beckoning arm, and then finally, a beer!"

Pony swallowed the pastry in two bites and said, "I was thinking about how blasted anthropological their actions were. Very minimal interference, bro. Very minimal."

"No you weren't—you were thinking about the beer."

Pony shrugged and grabbed a towel. Squeezing water from his dreadlocks, he admitted, "Would have been sweet to taste some really foreign brew. Dude, do you realize that we didn't even have a real encounter."

Dan made a doughnut for himself. "You sound disappointed."

"I am." Pony slapped the couch. "Been waiting for this my

whole life and we meet a robot. Aliens, man, I want to see some real aliens!"

"Dr. McCormick. First it was beer; now it's aliens."

Pony leaned in and smiled, "How about alien beer!?"

They could hear the girls come down the hall long before they could see them. The loud happy clopping was a sound that only came from very big boots. Lisa followed Christine, and the pair stepped out and posed.

Christine was now in a scandalous sapphire blue mini-dress and thigh high fishnets and garters, white corset and matching white platform boots.

Lisa, not to be undone, was in a slinky black vinyl body suit and black platform boots with gold buckles. There was a holster-like purse slung low on her right hip, supported by a golden metal belt, and held to her thigh by a string of what looked like diamonds. Dan saw the wide belt and smiled. Within it he knew was a miniature version of the Coil unit. With it, they could safely rebuild the bus, if pressed. With the IC unit, Lisa's purse was virtually bottomless.

Dan grabbed his backup Coil unit, which was built into his leather jacket, and made sure Pony had his. Dan put on his jacket, pointed to Lisa's belt and then at Christine. Lisa nodded and secretly pointed to Christine's platform boots.

Perfect—they each had a backup IC unit. The party was on.

Chris plopped back into the driver's seat, and in moments, the instant they were back in real space, the new Administrator com system came alive.

"Attention spacecraft designation The Misplaced of Pangaea: your Admin ident is being verified, maintain orbit. Should you be found in violation, your vessel, software, and crew will be detained for the Administrators." The com went dead for a moment. Pony mouthed the word *software?*, and then the voice returned. "Ident verified. You are free to touch down on Wildrahnae with diplomatic clearances. Do you wish an escort? Please reply ..."

Dan made pushing motions and whispered, "Go on, before we get into trouble."

Christine grabbed the old-fashioned CB microphone and held it close to her chest. "What should I say??"

Everyone looked at Dan, who shook his head and put up his hands. "Don't look at me, I just shut up and sing."

Lisa rolled her eyes at his cop-out. If anything, Dan was the unspoken so-called captain of their little crew, but in an attempt to appear humble, he made a point of self-deprecation. Lisa knew Dan was far from humble. She and Pony both had endured some of his only-child-driven adolescent angst and narcissism. At one point, it had nearly torn their little group apart.

The old saying "power corrupts" was especially true if that power was given to the very young. Dan, with his mental tricks, tasted this fact at an early age. The attention, and condescension, awarded to the young so-called genius occurred all too rapidly for his emotions to keep pace.

Puffed up by the adults around him, his dealings with his friends, much closer in age, often degenerated into simple games of subtle manipulation and experiments in dominance.

Lisa glanced at Pony and thought back to when they had realized just what an asshole their friend could be, and it all involved a hamburger.

Barely a week into living on their own in a small three bedroom apartment across from campus, the trio were enjoying the last few days of summer before the start of their first quarter.

The smell of sizzling meat made Lisa's mouth water. Watching Dan lovingly craft the burger, especially his close attention to the shaved pickles, she waited until he turned away for a paper towel and sliced the burger in half. Whisking away with her ill-gotten gain, she offered a quarter to Pony. The two stood smacking their lips in appreciation.

Dan stood on a precipice of sudden rage and indignation, the twin emotions smothered by a haughty indignant expression as he said, "Don't you dare touch my food again!"

The severity of their friend's outburst shattered what Lisa thought was a harmless prank. Pony, veteran of a family of four brothers and sisters, took one look at Dan, reached over, snatched the remaining half and swallowed it in a single massive gulp. His expression, well practiced through countless sibling confrontations, was plain, and it said, *what are you going to do now, Mr. Smarty Pants?*

Dan looked like he was going to cry. His features compressed into a look of such pain that both Lisa and Pony began to laugh.

Lisa reached out to try to soften the sting, but Dan turned away.

With her hands on her hips defiantly and a sisterly glance at

Pony, she said, "Daniel Simon Towne, you are a spoiled rotten brat who has no idea how to share anything with his best friends!"

Her emphasis on the word 'anything' made Dan flush with embarrassment. He started to protest; Lisa stopped him by placing a hand gently on his lips. "No, brother. You've had this coming for a while now. Both of us are sick and tired of your only-child syndrome." Lisa's eyes suddenly lit up. "And I've just thought of a solution."

"What?" Dan's tone was thick with pettiness.

"From now on … until we say otherwise, you are no longer allowed to feed yourself—we have to feed each other."

Dan's dropped-jawed expression was priceless. He took Lisa's statement as literally as if it were a sentence handed down by a judge.

Lisa turned to the refrigerator and began rummaging around for what fruit they had and quickly sliced up an apple. While she did this, Dan looked back and forth between her and Pony in what could only be a state of mild shock.

Lisa fed one of the slices to Dan. Then she opened her mouth like a baby bird expectantly. Dan selected a piece and fed it to her. When Pony leaned in, Dan selected one for him, and so the apple went.

Lisa had many fond memories of their meals for the next few days. It hadn't taken long for him to get the idea. But the change in his behavior had stuck. Maybe somewhere deep inside Dan was still a raging megalomaniac, but in general, he was one hell of a nice guy …

Dan urged Christine to answer the planetary representative with an emphatic gesture that said, *do it, woman, you're the expert*!

Christine nodded professionally before she pressed the key and said as if talking to a control tower, "Negative, no escort necessary, over."

The voice was official and bored. "Acknowledged—welcome to Wildrahnae, Pangaean ambassadors. Travel safely. Note: in some high-density metropolitan areas, flight will be restricted; specific guidance control may contact and redirect. Keep this channel active. You will be informed in any eventuality, in advance. Inocu-p 011-0278. Control out."

"Flight restrictions acknowledged control, Inocu-p 011-0278 confirmed. Misplaced out."

Christine's tone was happy. It was extremely comforting to know that air traffic controllers, with their calm, bored manner essential for such a high stress occupation, were the same anywhere in the galaxy. On impulse, Christine pushed a button that was flashing on the com panel, and an image appeared on the flat screen of an official seal, just signing off.

"Ohhh, I'm sorry guys, we missed them. I messed up—there is a vid link on this new panel … grrr."

"Strike two," said Pony.

Lisa sat at the bar and activated the array of controls set in the countertop. Unlike Dan, she and Pony preferred their graphic interfaces smooth and clean. Dan—a bit of an eclectic—loved the steampunk style of décor, preferring a mechanical gauge over a digital one whenever possible.

Lisa flash-read the planetary data provided by the new nav systems. "Wildrahnae, grav: nominal, whatever that means, atmosphere: ox, nitrogen. We need to wear the 011-0278 patch, no breathers. Average temp … Blah, blah … The Admin database says that the major cities are located on the coast, with the largest near the equator. The city is called Ponroth, main language Noré. It boasts the tallest … yada yada yada, biggest zoo, finest restaurants and … here it is, a prime selection of nightclubs and bars. I say we set down there. I need a drink!"

Lisa's fingers flew, and she whistled.

"There are a lot of bars …" Selecting one at random, she announced, "Ok, let's go to this place called," her eyes scanned the data, "the Last Riots!"

Dan smiled. "Sounds fine to me—like visiting New York."

Chris called back over her shoulder, "Lisa, could you please send me the map?"

"Only because you're the pilot." Lisa pushed the image to Chris, where it appeared within the windshield in a small popup window.

Christine slid the image across the windshield. Stretching it, she covered her view and then faded the brightness until it was a ghostly guide. A small triangle marked their position and direction. "Got it. Thanks, Lisa. Here we go."

Lisa held up her hand for attention and made an announcement as they were entering the thermosphere. "Oh boy, get this everyone: A handshake, while a casual greeting for many cultures, is a request for sex and is considered rape to all Naeians. Eww, and spitting is considered something called 'Tripanna'—searching for a definition …

yikes!—wicked pollution—and is punishable by public flogging, and in some cases, surgical removal of a digit, not to be re-grown, or re-generated, for a period of up to five Wildrahnaen years—however long *they* are?"

Dan grabbed his finger. "Not to be re-grown ...?"

Pony shook his head. "A digit!"

Dan saluted Lisa. "Yes, ma'am. No handshakes, no spitting ... anything else?"

Lisa flash-scanned the database. "Christine would know better than I. So far from what I see, nothing else is out of the ordinary. We just have to behave. Must be why those particular violations were flagged ... Wait a minute ... uh, oh ... all parties involved in disputes will be detained by the administrators for the matter to be arbitrated by the appropriate agency."

Pony groaned and put his hand to his forehead. "The Administrators are the cops!"

Dan rolled his eyes. "I knew it. We got pulled over by the cops on our first drive ... how sad is that?"

Pony's head hung in defeat. "So sad ... I'll get the patches."

Christine chimed in as they broke free of the reentry corona, the windshield wipers clearing the thermal effect like rain. "At least they didn't bust us for the beer."

Lisa still had her eyes on the readout. "I bet the last thing those robots care about is whatever we living creatures ingest. But you never know."

Christine turned off the windshield wipers once the reentry effect diminished. "Makes you wonder what it is they do care about? Unless you guys had a legal library in the files, the Administrators will be hard-pressed to come up with a complete set of our laws without contacting Earth directly ... which they said they won't."

Pony pressed his Inocu-p on his forearm. "The Administrators are probably on autopilot. We don't cross them, and they won't mess with us."

--

The evening's purple skyline was almost normal looking, and yet not. In the distance, the mountain ranges and the shoreline seemed familiar. Beneath them, exactly like the ocean back home, the dark sea sparkled; however, unlike Earth, the color was blue instead of the pearly cast of moonlight. The unusual hue drew their attention upward and their growing disappointment vaporized when they caught sight of the dark rocky moon, encircled by a bright halo of cobalt-colored rings. Eyes to the heavens, they flew along in silence for a moment before Pony was the first to put voice to it.

"Except for the moon, which is very cool, by the way, it looks just like Earth! I've never seen that particular coastline, but it could be anywhere back home!"

Chris hit the brakes and stopped the bus in midair. Before them lay an alien vista, and while the geography of the surrounding area was nearly recognizable, the architecture of the great cityscape definitely was not.

The darkening alien skyline was filled with air traffic. Christine looked at the mass of lights and gasped, "How am I going to fly in that mess?!"

Dan looked out the window and agreed. "Seems pretty tight."

Christine started forward again slowly. "There has to be some type of instrument control system. No way could you fly freestick in that mess at that speed … one mistake and *blam-o*!" Christine pointed at the traffic. "See—no explosions. Like … something is guiding them safely."

Dan shrugged indifferently. "With our shields, we can take any type of physical hit from craft that size. They will slide off us probably undamaged as well."

Christine looked back at the lead singer. "You sure?"

"Absolutely." Dan nodded. "They will suffer little to no damage. Just nose her in and see what happens."

Christine tensed as she approached the traffic. "Oh, this is crazy. They have to have laws …"

The bus moved toward the line of vehicles smoothly when the com began to ring.

Christine snatched up the microphone. "This is The Misplaced. Go ahead Control."

A mechanical voice said, "State destination please."

Chris held up the microphone, and Lisa shouted, "The nightclub, Last Riots."

Christine pulled the microphone back and asked, "Did you get that, over?"

The mechanical voice replied, "Your vessel is not fitted with autonav system. Do not enter air traffic, repeat, do not attempt to enter traffic. Pilot your vehicle to the Alpha port,and set down at bay 9-alpha zzz alpha-23: global positioning coordinates transmitted to your navcom. Signal the porter when you are ready to disembark should you choose to do so, or if you have any other needs after landing. There is a suspension of the 50G docking fees due to your ambassadorial status. Please, enjoy your stay."

A beacon appeared on the ghostly display on the bus windshield. Christine steered toward it, and soon they were setting down in a crowded port.

Dan pressed up his Mohawk and stepped up to the yellow line. "Now … this will be our first contact—we should all be on our best behavior."

Christine opened the bus doors, and Dan Towne was first out onto the wet tarmac of the alien world. The warm night air carried a wide range of scents, most familiar, while others were decidedly alien.

The instant Christine took a breath, she was overwhelmed with an unreasonable panic. Nothing felt right. She kept waiting for the feelings to subside, and they seemed only to increase. Christine glanced at Lisa and the rest of The Misplaced and was struck by a funny thought: the name fit them now more than ever.

Dan flashed Chris an excited smile, and when Lisa took her arm reassuringly, the panic began to subside. Christine squeezed Lisa's hand and visibly relaxed with a deep breath.

"I'm lighter." Pony stretched. "Oh, man, this feels great on my back!" He jumped up and down slightly.

Lisa checked her make-up. Snapping the compact shut, she said, "Don't get used to it, shortstuff. The next place is likely to be just the opposite, and you'll need me to Bedazzle you a walker."

There were dozens of strange spacecraft of all shapes and sizes resting in their designated spaces, small trails of vapor trailing away from a few of the hulls mysteriously. Dan looked overhead at the sky that was filled with vessels landing and taking off and smiled. He had made it.

All it had taken was the idea, and then the work, and now, here he was—with his best friends—exploring a new world, before anybody else from his planet. This was definitely cool.

The so-called parking area on the gigantic tarmac was ringed by a thick yellow and red line of paint. Dan guessed that this was the space into which they were confined until they had probably passed through this planet's version of airport security and/or customs. He stepped up to the line and a set of warning lights went off, a mechanical voice cautioning, "Step away from the border until cleared."

In the distance, a pair of lights appeared to be working its way through the other vessels on a circuitous course that brought them ever closer.

Pony clapped his hands together at the sight. "All right. It's show time. Bring on the aliens."

The diminutive vehicle rolled to the outside of the painted line. Barely reaching Dan's knee, whoever or whatever was driving the thing was very short.

The robot attendant rolled up, and a mechanical voice said, "Please present IDs and remain still for a full scan."

They all held out their new Administrator IDs. Pony could not hide his disappointment.

The robot made a beeping noise. "Your identities have been logged with planetary authority ambassadors. Please present Inocup's."

With deliberate care, the robot inspected each of the patches, and once satisfied, it sprayed a clear adhesive over the entire thing, bonding it to their skin. As it worked, it explained, "Do not remove your patches for any reason, unless directed to do so by a physician licensed to practice on this world. The patches will fall off should you choose to remain on planet for more than five rotations."

When the device was finished with the task of securing the Inocups, it printed out four ID cards and explained, "Return your Administrator IDs to your vessel and retain these while you are on planet. These passes need to be renewed every 500 standard rotations or so. Like the Admin ID, your planetary ID functions as communications and financial transaction units, as well as interface to the planet's information network, Trea. Caution: None of your cargo, other that what you have on your persons currently, has been cleared. Do not attempt to remove anything further from your vessel until it has been scanned by security. Contact control to make arrangements. Violations are subject to Administrative punishment."

"Nice," admired Christine. "Efficient. Nothing in or out without it being cleared."

Lisa took Chris by the hand and looked around. "Uh, Control, could you call us a ..." She stumbled for the word—cab was what she was thinking, but there was no translation coming to her lips.

The robot was patient. "Yes, Ambassador Parks?"

Dan checked the IC in his jacket and interjected, "We need a ride to a place called the Last Riots."

"You wish me to hail you a tran?"

"Yes," replied Lisa.

"All you need do is use your ID. There is a small image of a conveyance on the bottom control strip—activate it with your digit." Lisa touched her ID. "The automated system will be here shortly, providing, of course, you have sufficient funds available."

Dan collected everyone's Administrator IDs and put them in the bus, shut the doors, and locked it from the outside via a keypad. He motioned Christine over and pointed. "Put your thumb, there."

Chris did as she was instructed, and the panel accepted her fingerprint. Then Dan asked her to type in a four-digit code. Once she was finished, Dan showed her how to lock and unlock the bus. Activating the force field, he winked. "If we ever get separated, just meet back at the bus."

As Dan and Chris returned, the robotic porter rolled off, and a driverless 'tran' pulled up in its place. The doors opened automatically, and a voice within said, "Greetings Ambassador Parks, state your destination please."

Lisa slid into the seat and said, "A nightclub called Last Riots."

The vehicle's voice replied, "There is a Last Riots in the area known as the Bridges. Is that the correct place?"

Lisa shrugged her shoulders. "Are there any others?"

"Not within the city limits, Ambassador Parks."

"Then I would say that's the place. Drive on."

As Pony got into the vehicle he said, "Yep, Trea is just like the Internet. See you guys, we are not all that uncivilized!"

The door closed, and the tran's voice said, "The total cost for this trip and all passengers is 12.5 G. If you accept, enter your PIN on your ID and press your photo with the appropriate appendage."

On the face of the ID, over Lisa's picture, appeared the total in red flashing numbers. Dr. Parks did as she was told, and a light scanned across her thumb. In the window, her image was replaced by 'trans action completed' plus a remaining balance, then her face reappeared once more.

Pony rubbed his palms together excitedly. "That's so cool ..."

Christine slapped him lightly. "No, it's not—remember, we only have 100,000 G! And no jobs!"

Dan started laughing as the vehicle pulled away and up into the sky. "Yeah—apiece! If this is the general state of the economy, we should be ok for a while. Besides, outside of travel expenses and entertainment, thanks to the Coil, we don't have to buy anything!"

The automated taxi dove into the traffic without any hesitation. A reasonable distance away from other vehicles, the tran glided along without any collisions or hesitations as if the area were traffic-free. They flew amidst the buildings, and the group could make out vague shapes in the other vehicles, but nothing definitive. In the distance, Pony pointed out a flashing sign. The language, while utterly alien, somehow made sense, though it was still a weird feeling when that happened, and they could make out the words Last Riots.

When they were near the place that resembled a futuristic casino more than a nightclub, the tran dropped out of the traffic like an elevator. Falling downward, the tran followed a wide white beam of light to the main entrance and set down gently. With a quiet electric hum, the doors opened.

Dan said, "Remember everybody: no spitting and no handshakes."

As the tran's doors opened, Dan was forced to shield his eyes from the pillar of light that blazed up out of the landing area floor and into the night. Like a group of shadows, they made their way to the edge of the blinding illumination and onto a thick carpet of continuously shifting colors.

Dan and Christine boldly took the lead. Within two steps, the carpet came alive beneath their feet and proceeded to propel the startled quartet toward a line of beings at the far end only just visible amidst the continuous flashing of photographers.

As they approached, Lisa laughed darkly and said, "Some truths are more self-evident than others. It's kinda comforting to know that, even out here in the wide galaxy, the paparazzi are alive and well. Vicious parasites ..."

"And we totally love them," added Dan.

Lisa grabbed Pony and posed dramatically for the flashing lights. "Yes, we do!"

The animated carpet slowed, and a gigantic figure, obviously the doorman, turned to face them. Standing at least nine feet in height, the being towered over Pony and had the face of a velociraptor and a demeanor to match.

It wore an elaborate suit that was a cross between a toga and a tuxedo, made of a form-fitting Mylar-type material, all shiny and black, that bristled with silver accessories, most of which looked like they were meant to do damage and be stylish.

The being lifted a high-tech clipboard and pointedly looked the group up and down before it asked in an extremely deep and sophisticated voice, "The name on the reservation, please?"

Dan turned to Lisa and Pony and was about to reply when Christine, a veteran of many club entrances, stepped boldly forward and presented her ID, announcing proudly, "We are Ambassadors from Pangaea!"

The doorman casually waved the clipboard at Chris's ID and squinted at the display. "New entries, eh?" The alien's deep voice rumbled in their chests when it spoke. "Let's see here … looking for a night out in the big wide galaxy are we, hmmm?" The raptor took out a set of half glasses to read the display, then turned a practiced eye on the group and started to chuckle as he looked them up and down once again. "And dressed for it, I suspect, if that's what passes for clothing on your planet!"

After a clipboard check of everyone's IDs and Inocu-p's, the doorman continued, "The boss loves this type of stuff. You can go in this once, 20Gs each. You guys are in luck. The Crickets are playing tonight."

When they each crossed the line, the doorman used a special laser marker that left a glowing impression on their skin.

Pony was the last to be stamped, and he stopped. "What type of race are you, if I may be so bold as to ask?" Pony resisted the urge to stick out his hand. "You are the first 'alien' we've actually met."

The doorman raised himself to his full height and replied in a regal manner, "I am an Alvenii." Closing the rope against the next group that was rapidly approaching, he added, "And keep in mind, little Pangaean: from now on, you're the 'alien' out here!"

--

The huge clamshell-like doors slid smoothly apart and strange music flooded from the inside of the club. From their position at the top of the platform, the group watched all faces turn to see who was next to enter the Last Riots.

"Announcing the Ambassadors from Pangaea."

Once the automated introduction faded, the animated carpet carried them down the stairway. Lisa struck her best 'rocker pose' and tried to pretend that they were at a masquerade ball and the sea of strange beings just ordinary people in masks and colorful costumes.

This worked to a point, until she caught sight of several brightly colored gelatinous creatures as they poured liquid into their transparent bodies and started pounding on the table, as if they had just taken shots of whisky. Watching the gel colors swirl around inside of each of them, obviously set in motion by the drink, Lisa couldn't shake the strange feeling that the Jell-O guys were just businessmen at a convention, out for a good time. Maybe the faces were a bit strange, but it was a party nonetheless.

The realization almost made her laugh as Lisa felt herself relax, and she whispered to herself, "I'm the Party Panther."

Pony rubbed the laser image on his skin as they started down the carpet. With a glance over his shoulder at the Alvenii doorman, he sniffed and said, "Little." Lisa posed next to him, and Pony automatically fell into the same manner. Rock and roll was all about cool, and The Misplaced were masters of cool, if nothing else.

His chin up like a god, Pony tried to remain impassive as he took a look at the crowd. And where Lisa saw the gelmen, Pony's eyes found what looked like a scorpion centaur. She was nude from the waist up, with a glistening black lower body. Long red hair flowed down her back and along her lower carapace like a fiery carpet, held in place by beautiful rope ties, each of her insectile legs set in a boot of white material.

Pony watched as she uncapped a wicked tail and stabbed into a large goldfish-type bowl filled with small wiggling balls of fur. He thought he could make out a barely discernable squealing before the furry sphere disappeared into her mouth like a potato chip. Pony caught her eyes, and she leered up at him without any pretense. It made the hair on the back of his neck stand up.

Christine held onto Dan's arm and posed like a prom queen. Concentrating on turning left, then right, and waving elbow-wrist, elbow-wrist, she didn't focus on a single thing. *'Just smile and look pretty for the camera,'* came the mantra, *'turn, smile and wave, turn smile and wave.'*

When the carpet began to propel them down the stairs, Dan took in the entire room with a glance, deliberately ignoring anyone that looked human. This was what he had dreamt of his entire life. He was living his comic books.

Supporting the arched rafters were wide aquarium pillars made of thick transparent material. Within each of the columns, hung gigantic luminescent jellyfish with long flowing tentacles, and like living chandeliers, it was their continuously shifting colors that provided the majority of the subdued illumination for the club.

Dan began cataloguing the various beings, noticing first a group of what looked like miniature redwood trees that were slowly walking toward the stairs as they began the descent.

There were pale vampire-looking beings drinking fire from an elaborate chemistry set through long flexible tubes standing shoulder to shoulder with tall thin green women with plant-like skin, dressed in white and gold togas, chatting with bulbous-headed creatures sitting on flying couches.

In the rafters hung chairs and tables of various shapes and sizes, all filled with every manner of winged beings from what looked like classic fairies to large bee-like creatures sporting metallic vests and strange little fez-like hats.

On a table sat a large vat of liquid the color of a clear blue sky. Within it undulated a mass of pale worms or eels. One of the group's members suddenly pushed its head up out of the bowl. With several delicate appendages, the foot-long worm donned a tiny pair of nerdish glasses and carefully counted out a number of metallic chips from a bag onto the table. It then removed the glasses and dove back into the mass. Above the tank a display panel flashed, 'Service Please.'

Arranged next to the bowl was a large pile of bugs that were similarly clustered into a knotted, ever-shifting mass. While Dan watched, the colony swarmed around the base of the bowl and the display changed from 'Service Please' to "And as we were saying, that wretched Blueknot took all the correct deposits and transferred them into the wrong accounts. Well, you can just imagine what corporate had to say about that ..."

Dan turned his attention from the conversation between the worms and the bugs to the trees that were riding up the escalator carpet. When they were close enough, he spied small furred creatures scampering amongst their branches. One of the squirrely beings took out a miniature camera and snapped a picture of the group as they passed. Dan noted that the little fellow wore clothes.

Dan's excitement jumped up a notch when he realized that the bartender was a large multi-armed machine with a huge glass jar for a head. Within the head buzzed hundreds of firefly-type insects. With every new order that appeared on the screen, a small group separated from the swarm, and a set of arms would extend from the machine to begin working on the order. While Dan watched, the bartender mixed several drinks simultaneously and piled a tray high with bowls filled with what looked like smoldering dirt. Once an order was complete, the serving tray floated up and moved off over the crowd toward the customers.

The floor was brightly carpeted in places, and where it was not ... Dan's eyebrow arched as he noticed that the club extended below them to an aquatic environment just as alive as the one above it. Dan saw octopus mermaids and shark mermen cavorting with other strange and exotic creatures, many of which resembled plants more than anything recognizable.

From halfway down the stairs, Dan took note of what appeared to be an open table, but as he watched, the 'chairs' unfolded themselves, and resembling waddling stumps wearing strange breathing gear, made their way into the dense crowd.

Christine clenched Dan by the arm and said, "This is nice."

"Bit more than I expected," Dan drawled.

Pony pointed to the stage on the far side of the club, the view disappearing as they neared the base of the long stairs. "Look at the band, everybody! They're cricket humanoids."

Standing as tall—or taller—than Dan, they were actively attacking their instruments with the postures of seasoned musicians. One of the band members, his face painted in an elaborate symbol, fluttered his wings, and they caught the stage lights and glistened.

"What type of instruments are those?" Lisa squinted to make out the alien-looking equipment as it passed out of sight.

Pony ignored her and gestured at a glowing concoction, spilling steam on a tray as it hovered above the crowd for a moment before it descended to within reach of the customers. "I want one of those ..."

Lisa agreed and added, "Make that two!"

Christine pointed. "Watch ..." The customer receiving the steaming drink took it, and another customer touched its ID to the tray with its thin blue 'antenna.' This action was replicated by two other patrons, and they saw a third furiously tapping on the keys and touching the ID to the tray at the last moment before the automated server floated up and headed toward the bar.

"You order through your ID. How?" Pony had his in his hand and was inspecting it closely.

Christine looked back over her shoulder at Pony and said simply, "Let's ask."

"I'm on it. You guys grab a table." Dan was about to step off the carpet escalator when a tall robot made from some type of translucent plastic or glass rolled out of the crowd to greet them.

After a very fluid bow, the mechanoid said, "Welcome to the Last Riots, Ambassadors. The owner would be very proud to meet you. Would you come this way, please?"

Hiding their disappointment, the group followed the greeter diligently as it rolled through the crowd. Wherever it moved, the press of patrons cleared a path for their escort as if it were robotic royalty.

Taller than many of the beings around him, with the exception of the Alvenii bouncers, Pony noticed that they were headed toward the stage. Within a few more feet, they passed through some type of invisible curtain bordering the edge of the crowd, and the full force of the band hit them hard. Unlike anything they had every heard, it seemed to be a mixture of sounds deliberately designed to induce nausea.

Dan, who prided himself on loving every type of music, fought to find the beauty in the chaos they heard and failed completely. His face twisted into a reluctant mask of dislike. He pressed his palms to his ears and followed along amidst disappointment. When the one number faded and another began, nearly as unbearable, Dan looked at the 'moshing' crowd and shook his head in disbelief. Once glance at his band-mates confirmed that they, too, felt the same. Astonishment and disbelief mixed with vast disappointment.

Christine was the only one of them who put it to voice and into the din she shouted, "This stuff sucks!"

Pony thought the only thing that these 'crickets' had going for them were the backup dancers. The pair were humanoid aliens, but drastically different from each other. The female had blue skin covered in white tattoos, shimmering silver-blond tentacles for hair and large black wings. She danced with a snow-white man-horse with blood-red zebra stripes and tail, each of its hooves painted midnight black. Together they seemed to find a loose rhythm to the noise The Crickets were making and worked their own brand of magic.

The band, composed of four of the human-sized insects, was dressed in small bits of fur. They were working their hands across strange instruments and appeared to be rubbing their legs together at the same time. There was an obvious break, and one of The Crickets, the one with the painted face, began to make long chirping noises and flutter his wings.

During its 'solo,' their robotic guide reached a square piece of carpet guarded by two Alvenii bouncers. The glass robot rolled smoothly onto the patch and gestured for them to join it. Once they were on, the carpet rose upwards toward a mysterious floating platform high above in the rafters.

When they neared the V.I.P. box, the sound dropped off, and the gang was assaulted by a cloud of strange vapor and odors that was such that it instantly made their heads swim. Positioned near one of the aquarium columns that contained a jellyfish chandelier, the cascade of shifting colors bathed the box's bizarre occupants as they watched the show.

Lisa's hackles began to rise, her physician's instincts unexpectedly coming to the forefront. She could identify a few of the compounds they were inhaling, but most were unfamiliar, and to her that spelled trouble. She fought with herself to maintain this train of thought, but with each breath of the thick smoke, it seemed less and less important.

 The robot rolled into the cloud and announced, "May I present the Ambassadors from Pangaea."

Like a jack-in-the-box, their nearly human host popped up and threw his arms wide and squealed, "Non-con's! Thank you, House!" Dancing around the couch, he hugged each of them. "Welcome to my club, Ambassadors, welcome." His Mylar-looking black and white toga, obviously the style, rustled as he danced toward them on sandals with gold ties. Bald, he wore a circlet of gold material with a long black and white feather in it, and his eyes were pure glossy black.

Around his shoulders was draped a black and white feather boa that sported a pair of eyes on thin stalks that blinked eagerly.

When the host smiled, Lisa noted that he had gills and that his teeth were slightly pointed and set in many rows down his throat, exactly like a shark, indicating a carnivorous diet. The invitation diminished with this realization, and Lisa dredged up a smile as she sadly realized her xenophobia.

"My name is Derlan D'light!" He clapped his hands excitedly, the pale skin striped diagonally by thin black dermal ridges rasping together with the sound of sandpaper. "And it's over-the-top party at Riots tonight!" His singsong voice fit his happy demeanor while clashing with his underlying appearance. It was a cocktail of amusement. Like a comedian shark, he 'floated' around the couches and began introductions.

Ignoring a pair of obvious 'playthings,' Derlan pointedly took the hand of a beautiful human-looking woman with gold and blue eyes and a pair of dainty antennae peeking through her blond hair, and with a scandalous press of his palm, brought it to his lips. She was dressed in a red mini toga that barely managed to conceal anything and a matching pair of high-heeled shoes.

As if displaying a rare trophy, the host proudly announced, "May I present Miss Blixa Altabatt. Of *the* Altabatts." To their uncomprehending expressions he added quickly, "You know, the third largest conglomerate in the galaxy."

Everyone mouthed the word "Oh."

"Miss Altabatt, may I introduce …?" He paused politely and gestured to Christine.

"Hi. Chris Tester." Christine stifled a giggle that came from nowhere. "It's a pleasure to meet you."

Dan took the opportunity and slid to the side.

Blixa cocked her head in an attempt to get a better look at Dan and said, "We are delighted."

Derlan shifted his attention to Pony. "And this is …?"

"Pony McCormick." Pony smiled and gave a curt bow.

Blixa smiled and retuned the nod, her antennae retracting slightly.

Lisa's xenophobia vaporized at the sight of Blixa, and she pushed past Pony. "Hi. You are just gorgeous!" she insisted.

Blixa's antennae practically curled back into her head as she nodded and managed, over obvious embarrassment, to politely reply,

"Why, thank you. You are very pretty as well, Miss ah ...?"

Chris felt a small surge of jealousy over Lisa's unexpected enthusiasm, but simply chalked it up to excitement over meeting another real extraterrestrial.

"Lisa ... Lisa Parks." Lisa tried to maintain eye contact, but Blixa slyly looked around her at Dan and asked, "And this is ...?"

Lisa, Christine and Pony collectively rolled their eyes and groaned. Even out here, lead singers got all the attention.

With a reluctant sigh of surrender, Dan stepped up, thinking, *here we go again*. The girl was pretty, but not what he would call a knock-out. The only thing she had going for her was that she was from 'out of town.' One of his lyrics came to mind: Too many shows; too many places. Too many kisses on long forgotten faces ... Dan smirked inwardly and thought, *I'm such a jaded slut!*

The lead singer extended his hand automatically and then quickly retracted it. Blixa smiled shyly and caught his arm, pointedly putting her strangely soft fingers in his.

Derlan covered a delighted gasp and said, "Oh, isn't she scandalous! And the party's on. Let's make it steam; people, I want to see bubbles!" In response to the host's command, and to the obvious delight of the aquatic patrons, the liquid in the pillar around the jellyfish chandelier began to boil. Simultaneously, the air filled with the same.

Lisa caught the faint scent of cloves as each bubble popped. With a few breaths, the room began to slightly swim. When she shook her head, her thoughts cleared, but when she relaxed, the intoxicant was right there to take the edge off.

Stretching luxuriously, Blixa wrapped herself around Dan's arm. She blushed as the vapors did their work and her antennae re-extended slightly.

Christine looked at Dan and back at Lisa and Pony in amazement.

Pony and Lisa grabbed Christine's shoulders, and Pony whispered into her ear conspiratorially, "We've seen this a thousand times. Chicks, it seems even out here, always fall for Danny boy. He will quietly, and politely, extricate himself from her clutches, as soon as is politically and politely possible." Pony leaned in, whispered into Christine's ear, "You know Dan does not want a girlfriend."

Derlan led the parade to the couches. "Oh, this is The Cricket's biggest hit, the one that started it all!" He made a gesture in the air, and a holographic dial appeared at his fingertips. As he turned it, the 'music' within the VIP booth grew louder.

A mixture of nearly Asian atonalities was accompanied by a nearly rhythmic interlaced off-key chirping. The noise was reminiscent of the natural sounds a desert makes at sunset, but performed as if the insects had absolutely no idea what they were doing.

Dan caught the similarity and blurted out, "Now this one I kinda like!"

Lisa agreed and said, "The other stuff was a bit hard on the ears."

The host slapped his hands together taking mock insult. "Oh, well. And I suppose you can do better?"

Lisa smiled back at the sharkman, matching his predatory expression. "Why, yes, in fact, I believe we can."

"What's this we hear about music?" The words sounded as if a dozen young girls spoke simultaneously.

Their host leaped to his feet and shouted, "Ohhh, how could I have been so rude, rude, rude?" He looked at his boa and shook his head in mock shame. "May I introduce the Hive 812-aa-11 from ... now let me get this right ..." Derlan took a deep breath and said, "Rollmerijixgig'Sharrr'Larrum."

"Perfect." The voices all came from a three-foot-tall egg-shaped device resembling a model spaceship floating a few feet off the floor. The black metal of the egg was banded in places with a clear material. Dan thought he saw movement within as it glided toward them, and they could hear little hissing blasts of its micro thrusters.

Dan turned his head as the thing approached and was shocked to see a crowd of tiny beings waving at him through long windows that ringed the egg. He squinted and made out perhaps a hundred or so very human-looking people, none standing more than a half inch tall at best. The sea of blue faces had one thing in common: they all looked like teenage girls, and like Blixa, they each sported tiny antennae.

Lisa squinted into the craft and pulled back her head in astonishment. "It's filled with little people. Pony, look at this—OMG, how frickin' cute is that!?" She leaned in close and waved at the occupants of the Hive as one would a very small child. "Hello, little people ..."

Blixa interrupted, "Eight here is a bit of a music fan. They have been following The Crickets around for nearly a year? Am I right? I think we first met on Bromfenling at Pleasure Fest, wasn't it?"

The Hive floated around the couches and hovered above a vacant chair as if sitting. "That's what our data reflects." There was a hiss and one of the remaining vapor bubbles, floating near the ceiling, was caught by a tiny tractor beam. A small bay door opened on the face of the craft, and the bubble was carefully pulled within.

Christine followed the Hive and was side by side with Lisa waving at the occupants.

"They all have tiny skirts …"

Lisa grabbed Chris's arm and added, "And cute little socks … just like …"

"Bobbisocks!?" exclaimed Christine.

Almost in unison, the multitude waved back, and the Hive said, "So, you were saying something about music?"

Lisa pulled back and crossed her arms defiantly. "Damn straight. I'm the lead guitar player for The Misplaced. Dan is bass and vocals, and Pony is percussion."

Blixa snuggled closer to Dan and purred, "What's a guitar?"

Derlan pursed his lips. "And I don't think I like the sound of this … concussion."

"Percussion," corrected Pony.

"Who cares?" Derlan waved his arms, nearly dislodging the boa, which struggled to remain on his shoulders like a valiant rodeo cowboy. "Sounds like the same thing, if you ask me!"

"Trust me, it's not," said Pony.

Derlan looked the drummer up and down as if they were about to have a gunfight. His shark-like expression intensifying, he drawled, "Why don't you new entries show us?"

Pony leaned in and threw a glance at the instruments of The Crickets. "No way we can play on those. But I think we can whip something up."

The host clapped his hands excitedly, and then grew serious. "You are good? I mean, I would hate for you to embarrass yourselves." His expression did not reflect the least bit of sincerity.

Politely disengaging himself from Blixa, Dan stood up. His arms felt unnaturally heavy, and his feet felt as if they would rather be taking orders from someone else. Dan ignored the distraction and said over a pointed finger at the stage, "If what we are listening to is any indication, I think we won't disappoint."

"What," began the Hive, "are you going to play? Do you have your gear close?"

Dan smiled at Pony, and they took off their jackets. "We brought this along for just such emergencies." Dan fished out his Coil, and Pony added his to Dan's, the pair now forming a large loop.

Derlan watched intently and called for more vapor bubbles. While Dan took out an iPod, Pony, fighting to retain focus after the wave of vapor bubbles, threw their host a look as they finished assembling the Coil mechanism and set it on a clear place on the carpet. Derlan caught the new entries' expressions and returned it with a gigantic white shark grin of his own.

"I made copies of our instruments and dropped them into the Coil." Dan worked the iPod. "Now I can recreate them, ready to play, and a bunch of other stuff, whenever needed." Dan almost drunkenly hit the selection, and the band's gear magically appeared after a strobe flash. Dan then made another selection, and a generator followed. He looked at the host and smiled. "I figured we would need to bring our own power out here. I saw you had a PA."

Derlan was suddenly aware that his jaw was hanging wide open. This was most unusual for a member of his race, as for the Vulam, a constantly open mouth prevented his gills from functioning and was how one committed suicide. Snapping his jaw shut before he expired, Derlan managed to contain his astonishment by fainting, only to be back on his feet in a moment, clapping his hands excitedly.

"Then the show is on, on, on!" Derlan flipped his boa around his shoulder dramatically and the creature cried out with delight, "As soon as The Crickets are done, we must get you to the stage!"

Blixa shook her head and whispered to Christine, "Did they just make that?"

"I think so," stammered Christine. "Like, I mean that's what that looked like. Unless they teleported them here, and that's just as fantastic!"

*[Readers might need to note that at this point, Derlan, while astonished and overcome by avarice, is in no way a threat to our young heroes for the Vulams are one of the only races in the galaxy utterly incapable of doing any direct harm to someone at one of their parties. For this reason, they are widely known as having the most efficient lost and found division of all races. If you lose it at one of their functions, you will undoubtedly get it back, along with another invitation.]

Dan detached the iPod and quickly stowed the Coil with Pony's help. The host signaled, and one of the Alvenii security men appeared from the shadows to lend a hand with the gear. Together, the group quickly set up the equipment on the floating carpet. Once they were moving toward the stage, Pony looked up at the raptor man and thought his race would make the best roadies.

Christine shook off her awe as she sat next to the Hive and patted her seat in excitement. "Uh, Miss Hive or, uhh ...? Excuse me, but like, can I just call you Bobbisocks?"

The Hive seemed to consider for a moment, and then replied reluctantly, "Yes."

"Well, Bobbisocks, hold on to your skirts 'cause you are in for a treat. Even for bands on my world, these guys are really good."

"Do they have any management?" asked Bobbisocks.

Blixa sounded bored as she added, "The hives make excellent managers and 'Bobbi' here, as you call this one, has been studying the craft for a while, following The Crickets."

"Oh," said Christine excitedly, "back home we had these people who used to follow this band called the Grateful Dead for years. We called them Deadheads. And they virtually lived, and mostly starved, on tour." Christine's eyes watched the band float toward the stage, and for the first time since their road trip began, she felt alone.

--

As they drifted away from the vapor-filled VIP booth and over the crowd, Dan was relieved. He took big gulps of air to clear his head. This was familiar; this was home. Dan quickly located what he assumed were the microphones, but was unable to see the soundboard. He grabbed Lisa's shoulder and could feel her tendons moving beneath the skin as she warmed her arm back up.

Dan took the hint and picked up the bass as he asked, "Lisa, you see a sound guy?"

"Nope." She pointed with her guitar. "I'm worried about the monitors. You go a half-step flat if you can't hear yourself."

Dan nodded his agreement. The bass felt cold in his hands. Dan swung the strap over his shoulder and began absently running though a scale. "I wish we could get some kind of sound check."

Pony dropped down on his stool and asked the bouncer as he began warming up with a pair of drumsticks against his thigh, "Where's the soundboard?" Since they had been rehearsing earlier, his arms and wrists felt perfect. The Alvenii considered for a moment and then rumbled, "Soundboard? Are you referring to the club's audio control system?"

"Very probably," said Pony after a spectacular snap roll. "If that's what runs the sound from the stage to the crowd. Your PA, or the public address system as we call it back home."

"The PA, as you called it, is all automated and run by the house unifiers."

"Unifiers?" Pony stopped drumming. "What's a unifier?"

The Alvenii rolled his eyes. "Unifiers: math-based machines that think!"

"Oh, computers!" laughed Pony resuming the beat.

"If that's what you call them. The 'ears' hook up to the 'PA,' and the house does the rest."

Pony nodded his understanding and was determined to at least try and look like a professional. "We need four ears for my drums, one each for Lisa and Dan's cabinets and one for Dan to vocalize into. Dan's vocal ear needs to be on a stand as tall as his head, and what he sounds like must be played back for him to hear clearly. This is very important! He must hear himself!"

The Alvenii began to speak into his collar, relaying Pony's instructions. He listened for a moment and nodded. "I think we can handle that. Anything else, sir?"

"Yeah, I will need a few bottles of water for everybody." And then on impulse, he clarified, "Clean fresh water, no additives."

The Alvenii relayed the request professionally and grunted, "No problem. You chibs are easy."

The bouncer pointed to The Crickets as the group of insects was carried away from the stage on a similar carpet toward a lone booth. "Those chibs have us running in circles all night for everything from their own private booth to exotic refreshments, some illegal, to specialized heaters and atmospheric-conditioning units. Their music depends a lot upon how warm or cold they are, and their atmosphere is a bit oxygen-rich. And then there is the specific gravity control required for them to even stand under the weight of their equipment, let alone play. And ears, dozens of ears ..." The Alvenii pointed a finger at The Misplaced and said in a jovial tone, "You chibs are a bit of snochbul compared to those clamps on my snout."

Dan piped in, "And I thought having all the brown M&Ms removed was a pain."

"What do you mean?" The Alvenii seemed genuinely interested.

"Back on Pangaea." The name was starting to sound comfortable when he said it. Dan kicked his volume up a notch and virtually shouted, warming up his voice. "We had this famous band that had all sorts of riders in their contract; riders are little requests like specific food and water. In this case, the band chose something really eccentric for the time, like having a bunch of multi-colored candy provided with a specific color removed: brown to be exact, to make sure that the staff was paying attention to details."

"Clamps!"

"Exactly," said Dan.

"So those are the big stars, huh?" Pony double-timed his rhythm.

"No ... those are The Crickets. Not a stellar body in the bunch." The intelligent Alvenii seemed confused. Pony noticed he was slightly nodding his head in rhythm.

Pony stopped drumming. "No, I mean the Top Dogs, the Cool Group."

"The Big Band!" added Dan.

"Ah, slang translation problem again, Ambassadors, my apologies. Out here what you refer to as 'stars' are termed 'pinnacles.' And yes, for the last standard decade, they have been the pinnacles."

Lisa blasted through a solo on her guitar, the strings clicking quietly. "Not for long ... smiles!"

The Alvenii chuckled deeply. "Bold words for a new entry. We shall see."

--

"Blixa is correct." Bobbi floated over to the bar, a tube extended into a glass, and a small bit of liquid was drawn into the Hive's ship. "We have been following The Crickets quite closely. They are represented by the infamous Mr. Tiny Gigantic."

"He runs the biggest management agency in the galaxy." Blixa made a distasteful face. "Some of his artists are notorious for being subversive, violent anarchists."

Bobbi returned to her seat. "We believe there is more to The Crickets than just music. But until we are certain, it is best to remain politically silent."

The tone in the multitude of voices had become conspiratorial, and it set off Christine's attorney's instincts and she pressed. "Sounds like something serious."

Blixa slid to a seated position and interrupted, "Oh, and hives are also prone to gossip!"

--

The last of The Crickets' strange robotic instruments were clearing themselves off the stage as the band gradually approached. The mammoth performance area itself was set in a depression at the end of the club's gigantic room with the audience angling downward toward it. There were two of the liquid-filled pillars, one set on either side of the stage, with a cross-connecting tube running along the ceiling. Within the liquid floated the luminescent jellyfish, not only the very large chandelier kind, but jellyfish of all manner of shape and sizes. For the most part, the smaller variety swimming in the ceiling rack wore large goggles, and when the carpet neared, bright laser-like beams sliced out from their eyes illuminating the band as they settled on the stage.

--

"It's not gossip if it's true …" cried Bobbi defensively.

"What do you know, for sure?" asked Christine, her eyes tracing Dan and the band as they were setting set up.

Bobbi actually seemed to be looking at Blixa and Derlan and then replied quietly, "We can point out one indisputable fact: Several 'one song pinnacles' have mysteriously vanished after playing a show with The Crickets. More than eleven in the past decade. That is a fact."

Blixa considered the Hive's statement and pursed her lips, her delicate antennae curling thoughtfully. Christine fought down a sudden urge to hate the girl. She was so exotic.

"Another fact is that occasionally Mr. Tiny Gigantic signs a group, and they are never heard from again. Even on their own home worlds …"

"Yeah," Blixa admitted cautiously, "that's how Tiny got his reputation. There was some kind of scandal, when I was very young, about a popular group that reputedly committed suicide by flying into a star right after they were signed. But the Administrators didn't take any action, so everyone just assumed there was no foul play."

The host shushed the Hive and said, "Enough of this morbid serious gossip, Eight." Derlan was on his feet and clapping again. "We must introduce the band and get this party started. What do they call themselves anyway?"

Christine smiled proudly and answered, "The Misplaced."

"I think they are almost red, red, ready." Derlan waved to Dan, and Dan looked at Lisa and then Pony, who adjusted his seat, tested the kick drum and high hat. Both threw him the nod. Dan looked back up and gave the thumbs-up.

"What does that mean?" asked the host in sudden panic. "Is there a problem?"

"No, Mr. D'light, that's what we on Pangaea call a 'thumbs-up,' or all is well."

The host's face brightened, and he made a strange gesture in the air. This time instead of a dial to adjust the booth's volume, an 'ear' appeared. The holographic device looked precisely like a microphone.

The host began the introduction into the glowing mic, his voice iconoclastically perfect. "Males and females, amoebaeans, and clones, sentient unifiers and symbiots, the Last Riots is proud to present the ambassadors from a new entry, Pangaea, in the band they call … *The Misplaced*."

The massive audience was a wash of white noise, and the stage was softly bathed is shifting shades of blue. Pony started the intro for their song "Dry." Lisa let the beat build before falling into the music.

As the intro built, Dan stepped up to the ear and said, "I wanna thank you all for being here tonight. I especially wanna thank The Crickets!" The crowd cheered, and his voice returned through unseen monitors perfectly. The clarity almost shocked him. "Can I get just a little reverberation, a little echo?" he said and pointed to the ear. "Let me hear you people. Tell me that you're alive." The last word repeated as if he stood within a small canyon and Dan pumped both thumbs in the air. "I said, let me hear you make some noise!"

The crowd exploded in response, and Dan quieted them down. "That's all right, that's all right! Brilliant beings from around the galaxy, I would like to introduce Dr. Lisa Parks on guitar and Dr. Pony McCormick on percussion, and this first song is called 'Dry.'"

Lisa tore into her opening riffs, astonished that Dan used their standard introduction at a time like this, always omitting himself, and the crowd fell unexpectedly still. Dan plowed hard on his bass line, and the audience seemed to become virtually paralyzed. When he stepped back up to the 'ear,' Dan fully expected their version of a tomato to hit him in the face. It wouldn't be the first time and probably wouldn't be the last.

Into the strange calm, Dan's voice sliced out …

It's a miracle; please stay away, the paint is still not dry.
It's a miracle; please stay away, the paint is still not dry.
Sittin' in the bushes, while the world eats from my hand
Dressing with my towel, it's a fashion in demand.
Curing with a white dove and the ice turns into sand.
A mirror on a stormy beach, where the waves get up and stand.

You see things in a different way as life goes tumbling by.
Like sunset crashing through the trees, from a cloudless azure sky
I skywrite on that big blue canvass so that all the flowers that die
Can know you loved them.

It's a miracle; please stay away, the paint is still not dry.
It's a miracle; please stay away, the paint is still not dry.

Rockets in paradise make no room for us to play.
Tumbleweeds on the water, give,"
and on impulse Dan added, "Pangaea *something to say.*
It's a miracle; now please just stay away! The paint is still not dry."

They played through the rest of the song, and when Lisa bashed into her ending solo, Dan smiled. The girl knew when to milk a single note and when to fly across the fretboard. Sensing the audience's mood, Lisa pushed everything she had into three simple notes over and over, ending the song with a crescendo of epic proportions. As she was playing the final riff, Lisa had a sudden revelation: we need an anthem for our entire planet!

It was as if that simple ending was a fuse that ignited an explosion. The audience went from stoic to overwhelmingly exuberant the moment the song was done. Almost drowned out by the massive applause, The Misplaced smashed through the rest of their set.

--

When the last few notes of Lisa's solo faded away, Christine turned from the V.I.P. booth's window and started to ask, "So what do you—"

Her words were cut off as she saw Blixa, Derlan and Bobbi's combined expression of elated shock.

Once more the Vulam's mouth was dangerously open, and Blixa's antennae, the pink skin stretched tight, now extended almost a foot from her head. The ends, shaped like a thumb-sized five-petaled flower, quivered slightly.

Blixa saved their host's life by shutting his jaw absently, and Derlan collapsed to the floor in a faint. Bobbi seemed to be simply be emitting one long excited scream from hundreds of tiny voices.

Christine bent over and—squinting her green eyes—watched the Hive's tiny girls applaud and jump up and down, some even passing out from joy.

Blixa finally managed to speak. "I have never heard anything like it."

"It's called Rock and Roll," said Christine smugly, "or in some circles, Heavy Metal."

The hive managed to get a portion of its occupants under control, primarily the sleeping shift that hadn't left their communicators on. Unaffected by the sweeping hysteria, these unlucky members of the hive were rousted out of bed and sent to work with these specific tasks:

Legal paperwork must be generated to sign the band.

A galactic publication was to be compiled with pictures of the band.

Commandeer and censor, then re-broadcast all recordings that the Last Riot is making as the sole property of the band.

Double the round-the-clock watch of The Crickets.

--

Starlight reflected from the sensing arrays on the ancient Administrator vessel. Sliding through space, the reflections snapped into and out of sight as they intermixed with the stark shadows when the great vessel's primary array turned towards a distant unseen point of interest, to listen.

--

The Crickets' private V.I.P. booth's temperature elicited a groan of pleasure from Thraxis, his simple eye bathed in a perfect shade of grey, while his over-large cerci took in the hypnotic illumination as if it were a massage. He stretched his long weary jumping legs and preened his prematurely worn carapace by slowly clicking a palp along the rings pierced through his leg ridges. "Jakta, who did that piece of meat say was on after us?"

"Some new entry band; they look like peri-type bipeds." Jakta used a moist, scented cloth and soothed his antenna. The moment the cloth hit his sensitive nose/ear it sent ripples of pleasure up and down his thorax, the powerful sensation making his wings twitch of their own accord, the Macan equivalent of a shudder. "Didn't catch the planet's name, but I think the band is called The Misplaced."

"They note their home world as Pangaea: save it," said the third member of the quartet. "Odd-sounding name, wouldn't you agree, leader?"

The boss only nodded his head as he took a sip from a long plastic tube. The warm bright yellow liquid slid down his throat easily and tasted fresh. Two multifaceted eyes, each circled by white paint, sat beneath a set of powerful antennae, his forehead tattooed with the Macan race's symbol for death.

The leader wore an expression of disinterest in everything around him as easily as someone wore a hat when he replied, "If you say so, Cherrup."

Jakta pushed up from the reclining tree, and the gravity regulator lifted him with only the slightest hesitation. One leap/step, and he was at the tree nearest the window. "Cherrup." The cricket made a beaconing gesture with his hind legs. "Check this out." Jakta magnified the view of the stage.

Cherrup adjusted her skirt over her ovipositor, making sure the tips showed scandalously, and leap/stepped to the window.

The lead scraper stole a glance at her with one cercus and thought, no matter how many times he looked, the girl was still hot.

Cherrup called back over her shoulder to the leader, "Warnik, they are playing what appear to be old-fashioned physically stringed instruments, mid-to-wide acoustic tonals from first observation, how utterly limiting! With a single member devoted to a single tool with the exception of a 'sitter.' Perhaps the primitive is actually going to hit ... yes, I do believe he is! The sitter is intending to strike the tools before him like an animal!"

Cherrup's description was so amusing it snapped the leader from his usual post-show melancholy, and he made his way to the window. "Oh, this is going to crush eggs!"

The leader of the band below, a peri with a fin of hair, perhaps male, took up a position before an ear and spoke. He was confident, and the words were in all ways appropriate. Another pleasant surprise. And like the rest of the audience, The Crickets were shocked into silence within a few moments.

Ever the most responsive of the group, Cherrup, began to sway, her antennae caught up in the vibrations, her cerci closed with delight.

Warnik was able to resist the hypnotic attractiveness of the music until the peri began to vocalize, the translation transforming the music into three dimensions. It was overwhelming.

Warnik hit the mute field, and the sound was suddenly, painfully, cut off.

"Hey chib, you crushing an egg?" chirped Thraxis, his annoyance clearly evident by the lack of motion in his worn antennae. When Thraxis was that still, he was dangerous.

"Yes," began Warnik angrily. "This new sound is unbalancing. It is superior to anything we have encountered or developed ourselves. Our temperature-based acoustic generation is not striated enough to develop that harmonic resonance."

"Less eggs! We cover all the same frequencies but are unable to maintain the cross-concatenation necessary for the total sound," offered Cherrup thoughtfully. "We are limited by the ambient thermal fields and the time required for our biochemistry to adjust. We will be unable to reproduce this music."

"Less eggs!" Thraxis slowly ground his legs together in agitation. "I will sting them."

The leader winced at his friend's eagerness to kill. He himself was weary of all the souls piled on his carapace. They made it hard to jump.

Jakta slid his legs together—it was a death song. "Boss, you know what we gotta do."

Warnik glanced at the crowd. Even through the supposedly soundproof VIP booth, they felt the sudden explosive roar of the audience, the sound forcing his reluctant decision, and he could not, should not, appear weak. "Prep the ship for immediate evacuation, my chibs. We must crush them before they break stellar orbit or suffer the attentions of the Administration."

--

Dan slipped off his bass and stretched his shoulders, waving at the screaming crowd. The amazing reaction, far more than was expected, kept rolling on and on. Dan took a look at his friends and mouthed the word, *encore*. He didn't have to ask twice.

--

Within the Hive, hundreds of its members were hard at work on behalf of the band. And those groups were devoted to items C and D the most. Without formal permission, the Hive put in a Trea block and had the recording done by the nightclub rerouted to the Hive's unifiers. This request was honored by the controllers only because the Hive was one of Derlan's favorites and had been granted a wide range of courtesies.

Bobbi analyzed the data that had managed to slip out and wrote it off as acceptable free advertisement. They had only lost the first quarter of the very first song. And to ensure the validity of the claim, the Hive tagged the band name with itself as representation and rebroadcast the same segment plus a few micro time increments to 'scoop' the slippage. While this was being done, the Hive's 'Cricket watch' was alerted of the band's ship being prepared for emergency take-off.

Midway through the third song, Derlan was back on his feet with tears of joy running down his face. By the end of the set, his hands were sore from clapping, and his boa was firmly wrapped around his jaw to prevent any further chance of death.

Bobbi looked at Christine, and while the human was enjoying the show, she was understandably not as overwhelmed as the rest of the galaxy. "Excuse me, Christine—can we talk?"

"Do you like them?"

"Unequivocally," began the Hive. "We have commandeered the rights to any recording and broadcast and are awaiting the band's approval to arrange galactic legal protection. Does that make any sense to you?"

Christine eyebrow arched, and she replied, "Why, yes … On my world I'm only one test away from being an attorney." The Hive made the translation. Christine heard a group cheer.

"Then you must understand the need to make haste. This product is going to revolutionize the galaxy and you Pangaeans need to control it."

"Right about now it seems that YOU control it, Bobbi." Christine's manner grew terse, and she tried to cross her arms severely across her chest and failed. The vapor seemed to be going to her head.

"What you say is accurate, and we fully intend to use it shamelessly as a negotiation tool in an attempt to get this gig. But in the end, YOU control the rights—we are just keeping them warm."

--

The audience's sound pressure was reduced to a quiet white noise by the acoustic dampening field that surrounded the carpet as The Misplaced returned to the VIP booth. Beneath their feet, the band could feel the crowd's roar, and it felt like thunder.

Lisa smiled and mopped her brow. "Man! That was *fun!*"

"Unbelievable," agreed Dan breathlessly, still waving and 'throwing horns' to the crowd below.

Lisa smiled back at him and rested her head against his shoulder. "We did good, huh?"

Dan shook his head and smiled. "No, I mean it is unbelievable just how much I truly suck!"

Dan turned and laughed. "You guys should really consider firing me and hiring someone who can actually play. All I'm any good for is the odd backflip or occasional handstand!" Dan hugged his friend playfully. "I know this other bass player …"

Pony poked Dan with his stick. "Dude, why don't you ever introduce yourself?"

"For the same reason—I suck!" Dan tried to grab Pony's stick away from him halfheartedly. "When I think I've earned it, I'll introduce myself."

Lisa grabbed Dan in a headlock and rubbed his Mohawk. "Why, I outta smack you …"

Pony leaned back on his stool, grabbed a water bottle, and sighed. "Well, I, for one, like the way we just exited the stage … float in and float out. A guy could get used to this …"

The Alvenii bouncer was resting on his tail, and every tooth in his mouth was visible in a grin that would have frightened the devil himself. "Locutions cannot convey my current emotional state. Suffice it to mention that I am now and forever heartbroken that you have ceased your performance. I stand here contemplating suicide …"

The guitar player pumped her fist up and down at the crowd. "Popped your cherry good, didn't we, Raptorpuss!" blurted Lisa. "As we say on our world, 'long live rock and roll. *Wooo, woo, woo!*'"

Dan marveled at the seething crowd—they showed no signs of stopping their applause. A veteran of a few big shows, to Dan a large audience was nothing new, but this crowd's reaction contained more presence. Dan chalked it up to the fact that these beings had never heard rock. The music was a powerful motivator that found a place within every creature that could understand it, and with the exception of mathematics, music was perhaps the second galactic language. He stressed *perhaps*, remembering the songs The Crickets played. There was little to be universally loved in that alien opera on first hearing. The sad realization that he could not find beauty in The Crickets' work made Dan cautiously reconsider just how close they could have been to bombing. If The Crickets' music showed up on Earth, aside from the fact that it was extraterrestrial, few back home would have cared.

The band was perhaps one hundred feet from the VIP booth when Bobbisocks, utterly unable to contain her excitement, floated out to intercept the carpet.

"That was the most incredible—" The Hive emitted a collective scream beneath the dialogue, and they could see the tiny occupants jumping up and down excitedly within. "You people are unbelievable …" The tiny screams upped their intensity a notch. "Please, let us be your manager …"

Dan looked at Pony and Lisa. They had never needed a manager in the past, but that was back in familiar territory. Out here, they didn't even know where to start. One glance at his friends and they communicated their approval in that special silent way necessary when on stage. Amidst the mental halfhearted insults and various reflexive character slurs, Dan read his friends' decision.

Dan turned back to Bobbi with mock distain and said imperiously, "We are a heavy metal band, which means we have some pretty stiff expectations from a manager." He tried to count on his fingers and failed with a laugh. "First: you must have little to no experience; second: you must be willing to break all the rules; and above all, and this is absolutely crucial: you must know how to party."

--

The bright pillar of light that reached upwards from the landing area of the Last Riots was strangled by the landing craft as it set down. The ship's doors, still hot from reentry, all opened with a soft whir simultaneously. Displaying military precision, beings dressed in black combat armor, faces completely obscured by full face helmets, came pouring out and took up defensive positions outside the carpeted entryway.

Once the landing area was secure, another group exited. This party contained a single figure in very non-military attire. Without a word, they started toward the club. As they marched down the moving carpet, the armored team flowed around them protectively.

The Alvenii doorman caught sight of the procession and alerted security. "House, we've got a serious party inbound."

The sinister entourage came towards him, and the doorman was surprised to hear his ID chirp with a BIG tip. Without any hesitation, the Alvenii opened the way.

--

House rolled up to Derlan and interrupted his conversation with Christine. "Boss, an Altabatt security team has just entered the club. They are certainly here for Miss Blixa."

"Waste!" exclaimed the host. "And it was just turning into a fantastic evening!"

The carpet was approaching, and Derlan turned to Blixa. "It seems your persistent family has finally found us and has arrived to collect you, my pet." Derlan scandalously kissed Blixa's hand. "The party is over for now ..."

Blixa glanced at the band and waited for the carpet to dock before stepping into Dan's arms with a wink. "Maybe not. Dan, honey, I have to go. I just want to tell you how much I enjoyed your show."

Derlan watched as Blixa caressed the new entry with her antennae. The new entry didn't seem to care or take notice—further proof that these were non-con-imple' or galactically naïve. No male would knowingly allow a Canabrean female to touch exposed skin with an antenna without first asking for an antidote to their emotional venom. Without it, he would be unable to resist the Canabrean's requests for several hours. Blixa's venom was especially potent as she was bred to be in the highest ruling caste of the race. In a few heartbeats, the non-conae' would be under her spell for days.

Dan looked like he was about to say something and then shook his head as if bewildered. "Why do you have to rush off, babe?"

Pony and Lisa looked at each other and simultaneously mouthed the word '*babe!?*'"

"Her family has come to 'collect her' as our host put it," volunteered Christine flatly.

"And I'm not about to let them," finished Blixa irritably, with a slight, strange accent to her words. "Now, if you'll excuse me ... House?"

Dan, for some reason he could not define, couldn't let the alien woman go. Instead he tightened his grip on her slender frame. "Do you have to leave right now? We just met."

The robot greeter rolled forward. "The Canabrean security team is at the top of the stairs. They will be here in moments."

Blixa turned back and said, "Yes, I do! Would you like to come with me?"

Without hesitation, Dan reached for Christine and pulled her onto the carpet. "Yes, we would." His response elicited shocked expressions from his friends. "We came here to see the galaxy. So let's rock! Come on Socks."

Blixa casually turned to their host and purred, "Derlan, darling, can I borrow a tran? Just something to any landing port."

Derlan nodded and said to the house robot, "Take them to the garage and hurry." The carpet began to drift away, and he waved. "See you soon!"

Like a smooth shadow, the carpet floated off toward the far side of the club, and Derlan watched the security beings form a wedge at the base of the stairs and slowly make their way toward the bar. Derlan, ever the polite host decided to assist the process. "House, move the booth to the floor."

The moment the booth touched down, the team swept in and made sure it was safe. In their wake, a well-dressed Canabrean male, with Blixa's antennae, pushed past them and made himself comfortable on one of the couches.

Crossing his legs beneath his extremely expensive dark blue toga, the director gave Derlan a level stare, absolutely no trace of warmth evident in the expression. "In case you do not recognize me, my name is Director Cal'dreem Altabatt." The Canabrean rolled the 'r.' "You are the proprietor of this … establishment." He made the achievement of owning the largest nightclub on the planet sound like an insult.

These beings had no sense of style at all, no flash, so utterly unlike his Blixa. He was bored the moment they started.

Derlan glanced at the security men surrounding him and tried to sound calm. "Yes—what seems to be the problem?"

"Where did my daughter run off to?" asked the director, as he carefully peeled each finger from his expensive dolorg skin gloves, his golden eyes on the task only until the last moment and then they locked onto Derlan's. The club owner simply shrugged by way of a nonchalant response. The director gave a tight-lipped smile and continued.

"She was raised to be a galactic director, you know, and we are in short supply of such talent."

Derlan clapped for more vapor bubbles and laughed, "Why don't you just grow another one. That's what you people do, isn't it?" The club owner made a gesture that managed to dismiss Altabatt's entire race. "Everybody bred to do a specific task. Like ants."

Outwardly, Cal'dreem did not appear to take notice of the insult. "That's the empowering thing about breeding beings for a specific purpose," he said, suppressing the urge to slap the insubordinate being. "You tend to have a wide array of highly specialized talent at your disposal. Take for instance, my 'security team.'"

The director gestured, and the armored figures moved in a bit closer, squeezing out any comfort Derlan had managed to gain for himself during the argument.

"As the Administrators do not allow us to transport a military force, we have had to content ourselves with only limited security personnel, and since their numbers are kept to a minimum, we decided to make each and every one count." The Altabatt director's words must have been a prearranged signal.

The security men shifted into an 'L' formation around the owner, but did not draw weapons. "Now take, for instance, these here. Each is equivalent to ten of any normal being, and that includes the best of the Berakean Mercenaries or the Alvenii gladiators. Ten!" He slapped his gloves against his thigh for emphasis. "We know, because we modified both of those races, and were very careful to maintain a superior product."

The director nodded, and a member of his team stepped up to the owner. When the owner's own Alvenii security personnel tried to interfere, they were roughly grabbed and held by the relatively diminutive Canabreans.

Derlan's composure vaporized when his guards were so easily subdued, and he squealed in defeat the instant the guard touched him. Valiantly, Derlan's boa struck repeatedly at the Altabatt, with absolutely no effect.

"I don't have any idea where they are going," cried the manager piteously. "But I do know they are in possession of something of far greater value than your daughter." The sharkman's expression bled avarice when he revealed, "I saw them create matter!" Derlan went on to describe the process.

The Director considered the report. The Vulam could not contain his enthusiasm. Seemingly unashamed of his behavior, he went on in vivid detail about the creation of the instruments and even had one of the 'guitars,' as they were called, brought for his inspection.

The director's hands caressed the wood-grain and strummed the strings delicately; he mused aloud, "With such a device, we Altabatts would be the 'happiest' family in the galaxy, as well as the most prosperous." The Director clenched his fist and said, "We must have that Coil." Cal'dreem smiled sweetly at the owner and had the security team withdraw. "I'm glad we had this little chat."

--

Two vessels flew a twisted path through the last of the asteroid field. The lead ship, smaller and therefore more maneuverable than its adversary, was barely managing to keep any distance. Like hungry teeth, it seemed as if the ever-moving boulders sought to devour any chance of escape. Which, in fact, they were, as they were sick and tired of annoying trespassers who came and went as they pleased without some much as a 'how-do-you-do?'

At every opportunity, the trailing craft hammered its foe with plasma-sheathed projectiles. This, too, was seen as quite rude by the asteroids, who took severe casualties as the smaller vessel continued to be annoyingly successful in its attempts to evade them both.

The interior of the smaller craft shook. "Whoa ..." muttered Christine, seated at the controls as she turned the wheel to avoid the last of the large asteroids. "I'm too wasted for this ..."

Another volley shook the vessel, and Lisa moved to a laptop and said speculatively, "I definitely think that we are being followed ..."

"What was your first clue, Lisa?" laughed Dan.

"Dan, honey ... Are you sure we're safe?" Blixa clutched Dan's arm.

Dan blearily looked at a series of six miniature traffic lights set above the pilot's head. One light was red, one yellow, while the remaining four were green. He pointed at the display and gave her the thumbs-up sign. "As long as we have at least one yellow light up there, we are good to go, Blixa!"

Lisa pointed to her laptop and focused through one eye. "I bet they just want our autographs!" A following blast made the craft shake, and Lisa threw up her hands defensively and added, "... or maybe not."

"Dan." The irritated voice came from Pony. "I told you we should have armed this crate." Despite the shaking, Pony was attempting to pour a cup of tea. Another concussion and the small teacup was lost on the floor. Obviously fighting frustration, he attempted to re-fill the seemingly tiny container.

Dan braced himself. "Completely. Shoulda set the laser printer to stun." After a small hiccup, Dan, in a mock British accent, added carelessly to the pretty woman at his side, "Pony can't 'old 'is tea."

"We are almost free of the star's gravity well," announced Bobbi. "Christine, once clear, it might be prudent to hit it!"

"Just tell me when!" shouted Christine.

Unexpectedly the shuddering ceased for a moment, and with a happy mechanical 'ding,' the yellow streetlight changed to green and the red light to yellow. Pony took the opportunity and quickly finished pouring his tea.

Dan gave a chuckle. "Bet they've run out of ammo—" His words were followed by a severe concussion that threw Pony's tea service to the floor and the cabin into darkness.

Into the scant illumination cast by the traffic lights, Pony said disappointedly. "Aww, man, now I gotta make another pot!"

The lights came back on, and Christine shouted, "First we gotta do something about the bastards following us." Christine swerved and rapidly decelerated before blasting off at an odd angle. "There, that should buy us some time." She glanced at the tiny smiley face that signaled they were clear to engage the Tension drive, willing it to come on. On her view-screen windshield, a tiny mote of light changed course and vectored directly at them with alarming surety. The smiley face mocked her, and Christine tightened her grip on the wheel. "Pony ... they're coming in hot!"

"Alright, alright. Lemme see here ..." Pony flopped down carelessly and flipped opened the armrest on the couch. With delicate taps, the huge drummer worked the controls. "If I re-configure the Coil field to ... there, that should do it! Oh, it's gonna suck to be them, the next time they—"

The attacking ship released another volley. Like a focused mirror, the attack was somewhat amplified and redirected back at the craft. The crew of the bus watched as the vessel began to trail streams of smoke and flame into the void. In a few more moments, the alien transport broke away and vanished from sight.

Bobbi released a collective sigh of relief and indignation. "Serves them right. They have been asking for this for a long time, and it's about time someone gave them a bit of their own work."

"You know who those guys are, or were?" Christine turned from the wheel with a snarl.

"We couldn't be sure until we saw the ship, but it was indeed The Crickets."

"So, like, I guess your assumption was correct, they have been 'eliminating' the competition, so to speak."

"And as far as I know, we are the only ones to have survived."

--

Back on the command ship, the Altabatt director dropped wearily into his elaborate control couch. Like a rolling surf, soothing tones and scents engulfed him in a blanket of serenity. Automated med systems painlessly infiltrated his skin and began purging his body of any unwanted pollutants. There was a cool sensation once the stabilizing euphoric kicked in, and the director was ready to begin the chase anew. A beautiful blank-faced attendant, with both her antennae amputated, checked the equipment quietly. Clad only in the tiniest garments, she was a pleasure to watch move as she faithfully served him.

The drugs did their work well, and in moments, Cal'dreem Altabatt fell into the perfect state of mind in which all of his best decisions were formulated. Shoving aside the irritation of his daughter's escape, he focused on the details of the obsequious Vulam's story. The so-called guitar, now in the hands of his best technicians, was being analyzed down to its basic atomic structure in an effort to divine how it was simply created out of nothing.

In reparations for subjecting himself to the 'visitation' on the planet below, the director allowed his carefully disciplined mind the slight indulgence of fantasy—a fantasy in which he could create anything he wanted at the touch of a button. He drifted along in a pleasant state, the low music punctuated by the quiet sounds of the medical machines.

Eventually his contemplations fell back to his daughter. Her disappearance with these 'Misplaced' complicated matters to no end. The Administration's diplomatic protection of the non-cons made it nearly impossible to track their whereabouts without assistance from the Administrators themselves, something the director was not willing to risk in light of his somewhat larcenous intentions.

"All that girl ever wants to do is party." The director's tone sounded as if he had soaked in exasperation long enough for his cookie to crumble. "It's probably that drink I accidentally spilled into her cloning vat. That would explain everything." Cal'dreem took a deep breath of purified atmosphere from a respirator mask and the clean smell made him feel refreshed and whole.

"But if what that gill-breather said was the truth, we might have a much bigger dra to fry. Now, all we have to do is wait until they make planet-fall … Then it's a race, and sooner or later we'll catch them before they leave."

--

"Crushed ... crushed ..." chirped Warnik. "Can we make it back
to Tiny's station?"

Cherrup's antennae quivered slightly as her forelegs worked over
the controls. "Yes, but lover ... it's going to take a while ..."

"How long is a while?"

"Two dozen sleep cycles," purred Cherrup, a lecherous tone appearing in her voice.

Warnik sighed with exhaustion with the thought of the upcoming
orgy and thought, *at least there are three of us males!*

--

With a happy mechanical 'ding,' the last of the streetlights went to
green. Christine glanced at the smiley face, and it lit up. With a sharp
exhalation of relief, she shifted into Tension drive and asked, "Where
do we want to go, guys?"

"I think we should talk about it for a second," volunteered Lisa as
she helped Pony put the shards of the kettle back in the Coil and make
another pot of tea.

Blixa pulled herself into Dan's shoulder and purred, "Is your
home world like Wildrahnae?"

Dan felt as if he were breaking all his ethical codes when he returned her embrace. It was if he couldn't control himself, like in a
dream, and he no longer cared. The insight steeled him somewhat,
but his instincts were still out of control.

Dan shook his head to try to clear his thoughts and only managed
in giving himself a slight headache. "Yeah, in a lot of ways, now that
you mention it. We thought that was a bit strange. It was the same,
but unfamiliar on so many levels."

Lisa grabbed her guitar and strummed a chord while Pony
poured them each a cup. "At first I was totally freaked out!"

Blixa nodded her understanding. "Most new entries experience
that when they make first planet-fall; that, and in some cases, what we
call instinctive survival paranoia, ISP ..."

While she explained, Blixa casually opened her purse and withdrew a small compressed air device. With a tiny squeeze, she took a
deep breath of green vapor. Blixa closed her eyes as her antennae extended fully and quivered for a moment and then shrank back to

within her hair.

"Ooooh, that's better …" She sighed. "Ah, when a being is unaccustomed to little changes in things like atmospheric content, gravitational and magnetic force lines, it can be a little shocking at first. Eventually, after a few planet-falls, the ISP feelings fade. Once you overcome ISP, you get to the real interesting aspect of the galaxy. And that is: it's the minor cultural details that vary from world to world that make the galaxy an interesting place to live."

Blixa was overcome by sudden excitement that was only enhanced by the vapor. "Take, for instance, your revolutionary music. Most races have music and understandably unique instruments. And 'out here' in the cradle of existence, it's these details that truly have worth." Blixa looked longingly into Dan's eyes.

Dan returned Blixa's expression. Lisa could see a fire lit behind her longtime friend's eyes for the first time in his life, and she was suddenly very jealous.

"And the people?" Dan found himself needing to impress this girl with every ounce of his being. "They provide the details …"

"Life, people, are all that matter."

Bobbi floated up to the couple and interrupted, "Yes, yesss, and that's all very well and good," there was an underlying jealous tone in the Hive's voices directed at the alien woman, "but music also matters, and you guys have a sound unlike anything ever heard in the galaxy! I propose, as your new manager, that we take this opportunity and trap two Calidid's in one pit. I suggest we combine your visit with a tour. We can start making the arrangements immediately."

There was a moment in which the members of the band silently conferred. After a bit, Pony and Lisa shrugged and nodded. Dan took a breath and stood up. "Do it Bobbi. Can't think of a better way to see the galaxy. I only have one 'rider' at this point."

"Yes?"

Dan could envision the Hive's occupants patiently sitting at their tiny terminals waiting for what would come next. "We only perform during a planet's spring-time."

"Any specific reason, Dan?"

"It's always spring break somewhere in the galaxy!" said the crew in unison.

--

Christine dropped the bus out of Tension drive and set the controls to automatic. In the stillness outside and the vast, unimaginably huge expanse, she doubted they would hit anything significant enough to break through their shields.

Unbuckling from the driver's seat, she stretched and made her way back to the couches. "We're drifting for a bit unless someone else wants to drive. I've got to take a break."

Lisa set aside her guitar and patted the couch beside her. Christine flopped down and relaxed against her shoulder. "Wow … like, I don't know about anyone else, but this has been the weirdest day of my life. Oh, shit." Christine bolted up and reflexively pulled out her phone. "I just remembered! I bet they are freaking out back home now!"

"Probably," laughed Lisa, "but there's not a lot we can do about that now. And when we get back …" Lisa let the thought trail off.

"Things are gonna be sooo different!" whispered Christine.

Dan yawned and looked at his watch. "Yikes, it's almost 6 a.m. our time, folks. I'm freaking exhausted."

Pony slapped his legs. "That's it. I'm with Christine on this one. This has been one hell of a day. Good work my friends. I'm crashing." Pony stood up and started for his cabin after a brief hug to everyone with the exception of the Hive. "See you guys in the morning."

Last in line, Blixa couldn't resist, and she caressed Pony with her antennae. As he walked away, she saw the evidence her venom had taken effect when Pony turned back to her with one last smile.

Blixa pitched her voice at the drummer. "Are you sure you won't stay up just a bit longer? You are new entries and have a lot to learn."

Without hesitation, Pony spun on his heel came back and sat down. Lisa took one look at his face and knew something was amiss. She looked suspiciously at Blixa as the girl took a vapor hit, but couldn't see what she could have done to him.

"First things first: the Administrators," began the girl in her soft alien accent. "No one knows where they came from, but they are the reason there is no interplanetary war."

"How do they stop it?" Lisa was still watching Pony closely; he had the appearance of someone under the affect of ambulatory somnambulism. He took deep steady breaths and sat with an unfocused, drugged look in his eyes. She glanced at Dan, and both of them had the same devoted expression directed at this alien woman. Her previous jealousy began to run cold in her veins, and the flat taste of mistrust in her mouth turned to that of intense suspicion.

Lisa glanced once more at Pony.   His deep, regular breathing coupled with a vacant stare was … she searched her head for the right diagnosis and then almost laughed out loud as all sinister thoughts vanished when she realized that she was absolutely blasted on the vapor, and so, undoubtedly, were the rest of them.

Blixa went on. "Basically the galaxy is one big free for all, with a mildly capitalistic bent. As new worlds are inducted, they are incorporated into the galaxy and all continue to grow. Of course, there are small groups of the 'bad sort' that spring up and cause problems, but for the most part, disputes are settled without open interplanetary warfare. The bad sort tend to remain in small groups or else the Administrators find them."

Christine snuggled up to Lisa and asked as she closed her eyes, "What do the Administrators really do when they catch someone?"

Blixa grew sullen as she replied quietly, "They are machines, with no feeling and no compassion. Depending upon the offence: sleep detention or autonomic slavery."

Christine sat up, blinking sleep from her eyes.   "What … Autono … what?"

The Hive floated over and said, "It's where the Admin takes control over the being's central nervous system and then forces the subject to perform menial labor such as janitorial or accounting tasks. Once the subject has served out what time the Admin has required, they are released, typically with a new skill coupled with payment enough to discourage a need to return to previous behavior for quite a while."

Christine was on her feet, unexpected outrage in her voice. "No trial?"

Blixa shrugged. "On planets with legal systems, trial is a method. However, the Administrators seem to have worked it all out when they come for a being. I have never seen them to be wrong."

Dan scoffed, "Never!?"

Blixa shrugged politely. "Never. The Admin machines sift through a sentient being's thoughts and memories as easily as we read text. Isn't that right, Eight? I mean Bobbi?"

The Hive agreed with a subtle flash of a rack of lights and interjected, "This has its advantages when getting to the truth. They are also extremely sophisticated in dealing with living creatures, and the dilemma of attempted temporary existence. They never allow unjust Catch-22's."

Christine pursed her lips. "Telepathic justice ... no lies ... Hey, when we arrived on Wild-whatever, we heard an announcement that mentioned that we would be turned over to the Admin for detention if we did not comply. What was that all about?"

Socks turned slightly, and Christine was beginning to discover that the Hive had a 'face.'

"The Admins enforce a planet's laws within the planet's dominion, if called upon to do so. This enforcement is only related to capture, detention and transportation."

When Pony spoke, it shocked all of them. His deep voice was dull and emotionless as it rumbled from a lack of sleep. "Then they let the local authorities sort it out?"

Blixa exhaled another deep vapor breath and said, "Exactly."

"So." Lisa tried to get Dan's attention surreptitiously but failed. "For the most part, we are relatively safe, 'out here.'"

"Not necessarily." Blixa looked at Dan hungrily, then cast a sneaky wink at Lisa as she was pulling Christine to her feet. "There are other ... dangers."

Dan found his hands on Blixa's shoulders. "Oh, beautiful, these dangers I think I can handle."

Dan's heart began to unexpectedly pound within his chest. When their lips touched, it was as if everything around him exploded. The warmth of her delicious breath and soft mouth, the way her antennae caressed his ears. It was more than perfect.

The unfamiliar excitement made her warm from antennae to toes, and Blixa found herself returning the embrace with more enthusiasm that she expected. There was something about this non-con's biochemistry that seemed to override the Canabrean female's normal distain for the ones enslaved. In this case, rather than being repulsed by her subject, her feelings were somehow growing in the opposite direction the more they were in close contact, and it was strangely ... perfect.

Pony watched Dan and Blixa kiss, as Lisa led Christine away, and felt a slight pang of jealousy well up out of nowhere, the emotion just the impetus he required to override Blixa's envenomed suggestion and go to bed.

Slapping his big hands on the arms of the chair, Pony repeated a sleepy sigh before unsteadily regaining his feet as if balanced on a ball.

"Well, that's about it for me folks. I'm outtie. See ya in the morning." Without waiting for a reply, he carefully made his way aft, following Christine and Lisa, his gigantic arms steadying him on the walls and ceiling.

Dan sat back in the sudden quiet and smiled, the memory of how fantastically silky and soft she was echoing beneath his skin. He slid his nails up her arm and she purred with delight. Tracing his hand lightly back down, he was struck by a sudden itch on his scalp. Snatching his hand away, he hurriedly scratched the offending area.

Before he could return his fingertips to her arm, Blixa sat up and asked, "Is something wrong?"

"No." Dan laughed and started to massage Blixa's hands. "I have to shave my head every few days to keep my hair like this. It's hard to do it and it's just growing out a little and it's … itchy." He repeated the scratch with a bashful smile.

Blixa grabbed his head, and as if inspecting a piece of furniture, turned it this way and that. "What do you use?" She traced her fingers along the scalp where he had scratched, and his skin tingled with delight that ran down his spine.

"An electric razor," he replied in barely a whisper, his eyes closed.

"Can I do it for you?"

"Oh, gods, yes …"

"In return you must do something 'to' me, and then 'for' me." She laughed and pulled his eyes level with hers.

"Anything" and he really meant it. "Anything!"

Blixa looked at the Hive and gave it a smug smile as she blatantly caressed Dan with her antennae. Aloud she said, "For me: you must sing me a song, and to me you must …" She cupped his ear and whispered, her eyes locked on the Hive, dancing with a mischievous glint.

Try as the Hive might, it could not amplify the quiet tones enough to make them out.

Once she was finished, Dan's head snapped back as if he had been bitten, the surprise and delight stretching his features into the broadest smile the Hive had yet seen on the Pangaean as he nearly shouted, "That, I definitely can do!"

--

Lisa's thoughts were vaguely on Dan's odd behavior with the alien girl, but as she led Christine to her cabin and very pointedly locked the door behind them, all other concerns evaporated. Christine managed to giggle before Lisa showed her the shower. That giggle turned into a low moan of relief.

Lisa helped Christine out of her corset and whispered into her ear, "And the hot water never runs out."

--

Christine's skin tingled as Lisa's breath caressed it after the hot water from the shower. When they fell back on the bed, Lisa rolled on top and lightly kissed Christine's lips.

Christine brushed back Lisa's wet hair and smiled warmly. "I just love your eyes!"

"And—" Lisa looked down at Christine's bare chest as she lay on her back. Her breasts were still perfectly round. "I love your boobs!"

Christine tried to cover up, but Lisa stopped her with a deep kiss, and then she whispered, "I'm not kidding, I really do! They're perfect!"

--

The few short steps to the door of Dan's tiny cabin were taken one crushing embrace after another. Wrestling with clothing while trying to keep their mouths locked, they passionately slammed back and forth against the walls of the narrow hallway.

Tumbling onto the bed, Dan kicked the door shut and pressed Blixa into the mattress. She was soft, far softer than any other woman her had ever touched. He grasped her wrists and squeezed eliciting a small groan from her lips before he kissed her.

Pressed beneath Dan's full weight, Blixa felt a brief flash of trepidation. Pangaeans were built a little bigger than Canabrean males, that much was noticeable from the start. Blixa thought about the myriad lovers in her life, all shapes and sizes. Some hideous, perhaps even frightening to look at, yet so divine in the darkness they'd become a painful memory of desire; others so beautiful, and fleeting, to have shattered her conceptions of love-at-first-sight. She wondered how this one would be.

Blixa's hair tumbled around her head like a halo, her antennae gently moving it into an artful arrangement clear from her face. With an indefinable alien grace as she stretched beneath him, an expression of desire in her golden eyes, she unexpectedly whispered, "Release me."

Dan let her go without any hesitation, the venom doing its work, surprised at how quick he was to respond.

She rolled from the bed and removed the last of her clothes seductively. "Get undressed, Pangaean. I want to see what I'm working with."

Like a happy seal, Dan undressed quickly and stretched out on the bed, an expression of admiration on his features as his eyes touched every intimate detail of her body. She was beautiful. Not too thin … just right. Her breasts had blue areole and pert nipples, and were large enough stand out, without grabbing unnecessary attention from the rest of her figure, and she slowly turned around, arms above her head.

Blixa finished her pirouette, putting one knee up on the bed with a dancer's grace, and Dan slid closer. He took in a startled breath when he saw a dainty field of tiny pink antennae between her pale, almost bluish, thighs; as he did so, he noticed how she smelled like warm rain on dry grass, fresh, vegetative and utterly alien.

A sly smile painted across her unusual features as she took his hand and guided it toward her, explaining, "Canabrean women are unique."

--

A pristine image of a world was projected by the Hive. The three dimensional holographic representation looked as real as if they were drifting in orbit. Dan felt that if he put his finger in the ocean it might cause a tsunami. The thought had him clasping his hands firmly in his lap.

Bobbisocks shifted position slightly so Blixa could see clearly, but the image remained rock steady as the Hive said, "Our first stop: Kirjellesque or Kir to the inhabitants." The planet's image morphed, and they plummeted through the atmosphere until a coastline came into view. From there, the scene closed in further until they were looking at a perfect beach, with sparkling sand and glittering sunset.

Bobbi orated as if a tour guide. "Famous for the gold dust sands, the beaches of Kir are known throughout the galaxy as the most luxurious. I made arrangements for you to play a small outdoor venue, starting just at sunset. Promotions and ticket sales have been successful as we have nearly sold out already."

The members of the band looked at each other and blinked.

Then Dan asked, "We've nearly sold out?"

"Already?" interjected Pony.

"We've never sold out a show before," announced Lisa shaking her head in disbelief. "How many seats does this place have—twelve?"

"Hardly," intoned the Hive. "More like twelve thousand."

Dan looked at Blixa as he ran his hand across his freshly trimmed Mohawk and whistled. "That's more than twelve."

"Yep," agreed Pony calmly. "A couple more anyways." He pretended to count on his fingers.

"Bobbi," groaned Lisa. "Dudes, you might'a set up something a little more intimate for our first show!"

"I did," complained the Hive. "I ran the numbers based on the Trea hits downloading your music. Every being was given the opportunity to make a reservation for an upcoming show. The reservations topped fifteen thousand and so … Kir's, Golden Sands."

"How come the numbers are so big, so quick?" asked Dan in mock suspicion. "It's not like we're all … you know … seasoned?"

Lisa sniffed at herself. "I don't think I like the sound of that, Dan. Just what are you implying?"

"Aside from your savory presence, for which I, for one, am very grateful, I'm just wondering why we're so popular all of a sudden is all?"

"The galaxy is a big place, with a lot of folk evidently just starving for rock and roll!" started the Hive. "I broad-beamed your music, and surprise, surprise … it's become a galactic phenomena." Bobbi took on Dan's loose speech mannerisms and added, "Now if you're finished complaining 'bout your overnight success, I suggest we get t' plan'in' the details of your first show."

Christine called from the front of the bus, "Uh, oh … It's starting to sound like a manager."

--

Waves of stars crashed against the enameled hull of the spaceship like the rolling surf. He looked down and found he now stood on a small bare place, amidst the rolling waves that shifted between a rock and a small planet. Every time he tried to take a step forward, the rock or the planet rolled beneath his feet, and he kept slipping back into the surf. Cal'dreem shook his feet as the brilliant starwater ruined yet another pair of perfect handmade five thousand G A'cabba shoes. Outer space was a filthy wilderness, and he didn't like it one bit.

"Sir … sir …" The announcer's voice was excited. "We just got a lock on Blixa's beacon; they have just made planet-fall in the Kirjellesque system."

The director shook himself awake. "It's about time they showed up. And in the future, during the rest of this pursuit, should I be asleep or otherwise incapacitated, feel free to take any appropriate action that may lead to the recovery of my daughter!"

"Understood, sir. Setting course for Kirjellesque!"

The director took a moment until he was fully awake, and then he checked with his staff. The fawning assistants assured him that they were getting closer as they, the Canabrean recovery fleet—the title under which the project was now financed—continued after Blixa.

"Notify me of the least abnormality. I am beginning to grow weary of this pursuit."

"As you order, Director."

The director switched off the communication and dropped back onto his bed as if it were an ordeal to remain conscious. "Busting planets, how do I manage to endure?"

--

Christine had hurried back to the small cabin right after the first performance and had it all decked out in rose petals and candles by the time Lisa made it back. After a soothing shower, Lisa fell onto the bed with a happy sigh.

"Gods," began Lisa, "it always takes me a bit to 'come down' from being on stage. But this was ..." she stared off into her memory, "something else!"

"Not only were the seats filled, but the cluster of ships that hovered over the stadium was amazing." Christine tossed the last of Lisa's dirty clothes into the closet and zapped them into non-existence before collapsing next to her on the bed. "I can tell you, though, Bobbi was furious about them. She said they were freeloaders."

"More like tailgaters," laughed Lisa. "It's gotta be hard to stop someone from parking a few miles away in a spaceship and watching the show through the view monitors."

"Dan sounded great tonight," said Christine changing the subject. "Probably better than I've ever heard him."

Lisa stretched and let the towel fall loose. "Yeah. It must have been something in the atmosphere." Lisa rolled, letting the towel fall open entirely. "Dan said every breath was worth two, and the air felt like silk. Usually his throat dries out when we play outdoors, and he loses his voice after a couple sets."

"Well, not tonight," grunted Christine, as she pulled the towel out from under Lisa. "You guys played what—three or four sets, plus two encores?"

Lisa sighed, "Four. The most we've ever played." She pressed her fingers together and stretched her hands. It felt good and hurt at the same time. The tips of her fingers on her left hand were still buzzing even after the shower. She rubbed them together carefully so as to preserve the calluses and then massaged her wrist. Christine took up her arm and pulled down the forearm muscles, easing the strain.

"You guys were really great." Christine continued to massage her. "For your first live show, I think you set a standard that makes our little mud ball look pretty good."

Christine pressed deeply into Lisa's forearm until she gasped.

"Easy, let's not bruise the tendons." Lisa sighed as Christine lightened the pressure. "Now all we have to do is keep it up."

"Fortunately, as I have assistance, keeping it up won't be a problem on my end." Christine searched beneath the sheets and found what she was looking for. Turning back to Lisa, she asked slyly, "Who's first?"

--

The Falconiean night was awash with bright lights as the fans arrived for the concert. Like meteors, they dropped from the heavens until they reached a particular altitude that best suited them, and then they began to buzz about like hyperactive fireflies, docking with this ship and that as the party began to grow. From the green room's window, the band witnessed the arrival of far more ships than anyone had expected.

"There is no way that all of them have tickets," said Pony.

"Maybe they're here for something else?" speculated Lisa.

Dan scoffed, "Not to be narcissistic, but I don't think so, sis." Dan flash-counted the lights and said, "And there are nearly fifty thousand ships by my reckoning."

Pony whistled through clenched teeth. "Dude, it looks like things could get a might crowded, tonight." Pony felt a strange sensation of panic creeping up his spine. "Maybe we should enact the Riot Protocol, just in case?"

"What's the 'Riot Protocol'?" asked Bobbisocks.

"Could save a few lives," agreed Lisa, as if musing aloud.

"I'm up for it," added Dan. "My voice feels fine."

"What's the 'Riot Protocol'?" asked the Hive, a slightly more urgent tone in its many voices.

Dan ignored the Hive. "We'd have to put the word out. But how to do it so that a second wave doesn't show up before we are ready to start again?"

"I say we wait and make the announcement when there are only fifteen minutes left in the second set," suggested Pony. "Then we change out crowds and plow through. Should be enough to at least let some of the pressure off."

Lisa shrugged halfheartedly. "Twice the exposure. Should work."

The Hive sat in quiet contemplation and then chirped, "Two shows! And you play to those who are sidelining, in the second act?"

"It's better than a riot!" said Dan seriously.

"But, I like riots," admitted Lisa. "Always some good work in the hospital back home after a riot."

When everyone looked at her, she cried, "What!? It's not like I go out in the streets and participate." Dan and Pony glared at her severely. "Not in the actual riot." Then she added halfheartedly, "But nothing says a girl can't defend herself!"

Pony shook his head. "I remember the night we had all that trouble on campus on account of the rival football team winning the homecoming game. As I recall, you not only got in a few fights with the football players, you also were the one who patched up those very same rioters that night in the ER."

"Who better?" Lisa smiled brightly. "I knew what had been done to them."

The Hive floated up to eye level, nearly touching the ceiling, something it seemed to do whenever it wanted their undivided attention.

"We will begin preparations for the second show, simply treating it as if you were extending your set as you did on Kir." The Hive's tone took on a very happy aspect. "This is going to make history!"

--

"This is the Galactic Order Dominion's Voice, your best source for what's happening in the galactic core. Tonight's top story centers around The Misplaced. The Misplaced, a new entry band of ambassadors from a planet called Pangaea, have been tearing up the galaxy by actually playing shows on a different world every night. The Misplaced, peri bipeds, and the music type they call Rock and Roll, are taking the galaxy by stellar storm."

Pony switched off the terminal and turned to Bobbisocks. "How come the big deal about us playing a different world every night?"

The Hive shifted closer with a tiny hiss and whir of its gyros. "Most bands stop and tour a few cities on each planet they visit, minimizing interstellar travel costs and maximizing exposure to a specific market." Bobbi had an internal debate and elected to say this next. "You have generated a highly mobile following that is ready to travel to anyplace you are going to play, at a moment's notice." That statement was said because it just slightly won over *and if we did the same we would make a lot more money,* and it won even more over *Blixa has drugged you and Dan with her antennae!*

"Cool!"

The Hive agreed. "Exceptionally low temperature indeed. And add to it the fact that we are in the heart of the most populated sector in the galaxy. It makes it easy for anyone with a starship to get to a show on very short notice." There was the sound of stardrives.

"Boom, just like that. In fact, some star systems have started limiting 'festival' traffic until one hour before and after show times to minimize unnecessary congestion."

"Speaking of a show!" Blixa flopped down next to Pony. "It's been ages since we've seen Derlan. Is there any way we could drop him tickets to the next performance?"

"Miss Blixa." Pony could hear intense dislike in the chorus of voices that came from the Hive. "Who the band puts on a guest list is entirely up to them."

Blixa looked at the Hive with an accepting expression. It was a most complex being, with a multitude of personalities all tied up into one mind. She knew the Hive had seen her use her venom on Dan and Pony, but instead of embarrassing her, it had elected—no doubt with great internal debate—to remain silent. For this courtesy, she in turn bore any ill will the Hive might display towards her. "I'm sorry, Eight. I did not mean to be presumptuous."

The Hive had a section contemplate Blixa Altabatt. All relevant intelligence indicated that they were still being pursued by the Altabatt Navy, and the Hive's strategy of posting show dates only on Trea had kept them out of the hands of her family. Sooner or later, though, the diligent clones would discover this fact, and they would be met with an unpleasant welcoming committee.

The big problem with this was if Blixa was taken from Dan at this point, and she was unable to administer the antidote to her venom, Dan could very well die of depression, or at the very least, would require special medical treatment only available on Blixa's home world Canabrea.

The Hive scanned Pony and was pleased to note that the single exposure had worn off, but a look at Dan and the addiction could be clearly seen. No doubt reinforced daily. A debate ensued, and the result was to suffer Miss Blixa's presence until the thing ran its course. But they didn't have to be especially nice to the clone.

Bobbi changed its tone of voice marginally. "You were not being presumptuous, Miss Altabatt. We miss Derlan and his magic vapor as well."

Pony noted the Hive's softer voice and chose to keep his previous observation to himself. The relationship between these two aliens was decidedly complex. "So then you want to put him on the guest list for Vlantag?

"It's another outdoor venue." Bobbi turned to Pony. "I'll set him up with backstage passes!"

"Christine?" Blixa jumped up excitedly. "Could we drop out of Tension drive? I want to make a call."

"No problem. I need a break anyway." Christine slowed down, and soon they were adrift in the endless galactic sea of stars.

The blank screen cleared, and the familiar image of the VIP booth appeared with Derlan backlit by the gigantic jellyfish chandelier. Their former host's expression was a mixture of surprise, embarrassment, and unexpectedly, guilt.

Blixa was confused by his reaction. It was most out of character for a member of his race. "You seem surprised to see me, Derlan darling ... Why is that?"

"I assumed your family had caught up to you by now. But I see that isn't the case, you sneaky little thing." The expression of guilt was impossible for the sharkman to conceal.

"There's something you are not telling me, Derlan?" Blixa's demeanor changed abruptly as if she were possessed, her antennae barely visible. In a tone of voice that allowed no refusal, she demanded, "What did you say to my family?"

The host appeared to fight with his hand as it inched toward the com controls. All he wanted to do was cut off the transmission. He needed time to think.

"I will only ask this one more time, and then I will buy your pathetic little planet and have you evicted." Blixa forced all of her presence into her voice. "What did you tell my family?"

Everyone on the bus took in a collective gasp.

A small droplet appeared at the corner of Derlan's mouth. "I told your father about the Coil and how the Pangaeans made their instruments out of thin air!" The admission was followed by two strings of drool that began to drip from both edges of the Vulam's frown, his race's version of tears. "I'm sorry, Blixa, but your father forced me. Those security beasts of yours are horrible! They frightened me!" Derlan's ever-present boa nodded agreement emphatically in its master's defense.

Blixa's smile was understanding, yet, her eyes remained as hard as starship hull plating when she announced, "Your race's reputation for hospitality is famous galaxy-wide. I was sure it would be as impenetrable a shield as it had always been in the past. That impeccable reputation is forever besmirched by your conduct, and I will make sure it is known. Derlan, darling, I disrespect you for what you have done. In time, I shall punish you. I counted you among my few friends. It saddens me to discover it is not so." Blixa didn't wait for his stammered apology as she angrily shut off the communication and slid back into her seat, her antennae extending slightly.

Dan looked at his friends and then back to the suddenly alien girl. She was smiling inwardly at some secret joke, and with a sigh, returned to her old bouncy self. The change was amazing, and he couldn't resist kissing her cheek.

Pony glanced at Dan, his eyes wide. "Buy his planet?"

Blixa tried to laugh it off. "Not really. Well, maybe ..." She shrugged her shoulders. "Looks like the Zlip is out of the envelope." Her expression returned to a semblance of its former intensity. "My people won't stop until you negotiate some sort of licensing agreement. Like it or not, we Altabatts have enough legal clout to force you to make a deal."

"No they don't!" Christine cleared her throat. "I've been studying up on your, er ... our trans-galactic law in my spare time."

Blixa leveled her stare at Christine, and the young legal student glared right back at her and recited, "According to your trans-galactic intellectual property guidelines, all we need do is file a protection request with the Administrators, and we are covered."

Blixa agreed, but added cryptically, "Have you ever tried to file with the Administrators?"

Christine shook her head, surprised at how she had to suppress a familiar flash of attorney assertiveness, even in this unfamiliar territory. "Like, this just came up, so now would be a good time to address the issue, wouldn't you guys agree?"

Lisa massaged Christine's shoulders and nodded her agreement with the rest of the crew.

Admiring the hidden strength the diminutive girl had previously displayed, Dan patted Blixa on the leg and said, "Bobbi, could you please have legal conjure up the proper documents, and we will file them now!"

"Yes sir," fawned the chorus of voices.

"It won't do any good," said Blixa with a singsong manner as she slipped back into a fraction of her former aristocratic demeanor. "The Administrators get requests of this type in such a constant stream as to make a gas giant collapse into a black hole." She hated the way they looked at her, but was resolved to press forward the seriousness of the situation. "You can file, but chances are they will never act on it. The galaxy is a big place, and a lot of people need their assistance, whereas you only want it."

Christine considered Blixa's statement, and it rang with truth, especially the word need. She looked into the golden pools and saw the alien girl's conviction deep in her eyes. So far on this trip Blixa had been quiet, conscientious, and kind, in an aloof sort of way, the perfect groupie girlfriend. This new aspect of the alien woman was suddenly intriguing. Here was someone sharp, serious and powerful.

Christine caught Lisa's eye and felt that sharp thrill of excitement shoot through her every time she looked at the woman. Unexpectedly, Lisa's expression was one of jealousy, and Christine couldn't help but notice how she glanced at Blixa and then back to her very pointedly.

"So I guess it's on to Vlantag?" Pony stood up and stretched his frame. "Let's rock and roll and keep this show on the road. We get in and out quick before Blixa's fam' even knows we were there."

Christine shook off Lisa's intent stare and made her way to the driver's seat. "So then it's on to Vlantag?"

Dan looked at Pony and Lisa, and they both nodded. "Hit it!"

--

The Vlantagiean evening was clear and serene as her twin suns worked their way towards the great Sentular Ocean. Dan checked his ID, and exactly one hour before show time, the sky was suddenly filled by a solid wave of ships, the closely packed mass entirely obscuring the suns-set almost simultaneously. Immediately, everything on the planet's surface felt their combined presence with a distant sense of inescapable claustrophobia.

The stage was set in a wide bowl. Lit from every angle, the simple rectangle of stone was transformed into a buoy of illumination amidst a sea of undulating shadows. The Misplaced stepped into that glowing arena and filled the ship-packed night with ear-blistering music. And when they were done melting faces, the mass in orbit departed as quickly as it arrived, the pristine starlit sky seeming to breathe a sigh of relief.

--

An Administration vessel moved its vast listening array away from the Vlantagiean system and powered up the transmitter. Carefully repositioning, it fired a beam into the galactic core.

--

A crowd of strange beings met the Misplaced when they arrived on Nalhalafath. With a few hours before the show, Bobbi directed Christine to put the bus down in the facility's parking lot. The local Nal police were present, standing roughly human height, a red-skinned centaur-like race with very reptilian faces, captivating blue/black eyes and crowns of multicolored feathers for hair. With padded batons, the severe-faced guards held the crowd back, but just barely.

A feeling of concern struck Dan, and he said under his breath, "Big crowd."

"I thought there was a time limit on arrivals," said Lisa as she polished her guitar.

"That's just for those coming from off-world," said Bobbi. "These are the fans that made reservations for places to stay."

"Looks like it will be one hell of a show!" said Dan. The increasing size of their audience seemed to press down some of his enthusiasm. They had only played a few shows, and the crowds were increasing exponentially. They were the new galactic fad, and the responsibility was growing.

Dan gazed at the press worriedly and watched the guards fight to keep the crowd back. He saw some of the beings at the front of the line go down only to be nearly trampled. The sight caused him to wince and take in a sharp breath along with everybody else. It was one of the sad facts about becoming a success. For some reason, people always get hurt.

All of this was a distraction. They had not come out into the galaxy to 'go on tour.' Yet, here they were, thrust into a galactic maelstrom of fame, without paying any dues. It was almost disappointing.

Pony took the lead. "Let's get out of here and into the venue before anyone really gets injured."

The crowd exploded when the group exited the bus, and before the news could filter back and cause a deadly press forward, the band made their way into the Nalhalafathian concert hall at close to a run.

As they approached, Pony noted that the structure looked as if it were a gargantuan clamshell facing the sea. And when they passed through the doors, Pony realized he was right.

"This thing is huge!" exclaimed Pony.

"Just imagine the amount of butter it would have taken ..." Christine gazed around and whistled appreciatively. Just thinking about it made her hungry.

"I would not under any circumstances repeat that, Christine," said Bobbi. "From what I can tell, the Nal used to worship these things in their primitive past and now culturally have a taboo against eating shellfish."

"Good to know!" replied Christine clutching Lisa's hand. "Good to know."

"Speaking of which, are there any other 'taboos' we should avoid?" Pony remembered the first world and its laws against spitting and handshakes.

The Hive was silent for a moment. "Aside from the normal, and the shellfish worship, everyone on this world drinks with their left hand. Apparently to use the right is to salute their most evil deity."

Dan raised eyebrows and said, "Oh really?" With his right hand, he threw the rock and roll symbol for the 'devil horns' made famous on Earth by a dark rocker by the name of Ronny James Dio—one of the greatest. Dan felt a chill go through his soul. Dio had passed away only a short time ago. He had specialized in entertaining the alternative crowd with his devil worship act.

"Bobbi, we will all need mugs with water," said Dan. "This is not a 'please' situation."

"Done," replied Bobbisocks.

"Bobbi?"

"Yes, Dan?"

"Does this 'evil deity' have a name?"

There was just the slightest hesitation as if Bobbi did not want to divulge the information and then the Hive said, "Pagek."

Lisa watched Dan and knew exactly what he was contemplating, and it made her smile. It would be interesting to find out just how much the young were rebelling throughout the galaxy. If nature willed out, as it had on so many worlds so far, she was sure that adolescent angst would be present in abundance. Dan was about to ignite the fuse. In the '60s, it started a revolution and changed the world. Counterculture found its greatest strength through the unifying force of music. And she could tell by his expression that Dan was going to stir the pot.

Dan glanced at his ID, and it showed that they still had a few hours before the show. "Bobbi, would you please ask them if they are ready for us to do a sound check and have the gear unloaded."

"Yes, Dan," replied the Hive with a slightly giggling tone to its voices. "We are way ahead of you. The stage will be ready in a few minutes, and the gear should be—" The doors opened, and instead of the expected equipment, a crowd came crashing in.

Caught completely off guard, the band was mobbed. The last thing Pony remembered was three beings—each with a handful of his dreadlocks—fighting over him as if he were a Coach purse at a secondhand store.

--

The light lifted him from the dark and then faded into shadow as a cool moist cloth was placed back over his eyes. Pony felt like he had actually been chewed up by a gigantic mouth full of fangs. Tiny pinpoints of pain flared all across his body as if he had nearly been pulled apart. He reached up to his head and almost cried out from how much his scalp hurt.

"Don't touch," came a silky deep feminine voice. "Let the stitchers do their work. They're almost done."

As his senses began to return, Pony could feel tickling all along his scalp as if insects infested his head. Wherever the strange sensation rolled on his head, the pain diminished only to be replaced by a severe itch that faded soon after.

By the time the compress on his face began to become warm once more, the voice said, "There, they have sealed the flesh and melded with it." Pony felt a tender inspection with gentle fingertips and smelled a strange perfume. "Looks like that was the worst of it: aside from the aftereffects of being drugged, how do you feel now?"

Pony found his voice was a faraway thing for a moment and then, "Drugged! What the hell happened? Who the hell are you, and where's everybody else?" Pony started to rise and pulled the compress from his eyes.

My name is Ta'relli—I'm a Danlean. And I rescued you from that mob, particularly the Kovian who used her soporific breath on you." There was concern in her voice as she continued, "I don't know about the others, although the Hive was doing its best to protect them." She folded the cloth and dipped it once, bringing it up to a severe scratch on the side of her head. "It wasn't an easy fight, but it was worth it."

Pony made it to his feet with her assistance, steadied himself, and took a closer look at his rescuer.

Obviously of Peri descent, the rail-thin Danlean stood almost at his eye level and had soft green skin and snow white and black rope-like growths for hair, the alien dreadlocks bound just like his with rings of silver and gold. She wore a short, nearly transparent black toga, ripped in places, like it was armor and a pair of scuffed-up white sandals. Her extremely narrow face was thin, blessed with oversized pouty lips, her high cheekbones resting beneath a set of multifaceted green eyes twice the size of any human's.

When she moved her thin arms, Pony noticed one graceful wrist was weighted down by a mass of silver bracelets, the other by an arm holder for her ID, and over her shoulder was a plain white purse on a long silver chain.

Pony looked around. They were in a smallish room that appeared to be someone's office. The usual resident was not in attendance, but evidently by the fishbowl seat and waterproof terminal keyboard, it was a safe bet that the being was aquatic.

"How did you manage to rescue me?" asked Pony. "You don't look like you can lift more than your purse."

The Danlean smiled and hoisted Pony off of the floor with one arm very easily. "We Danleans are quite strong, though we may not look it."

She set him down gently with a nearly demure smile beneath which was a fierce heart.

Pony took a step back to compose himself and then formally extended his hand. "Thanks …"

The Danlean looked at it as if it was an insult. Pony snatched it back, suddenly afraid that he had broken yet another social taboo.

Ta'relli laughed at his stiff formality.

Pony thought his heart flashed to life as if he had been shocked when he heard her laugh. The translator did not bother to color the tones, and they came out as if a dozen macaque monkeys screamed in unison. It was loud, joyous, and utterly alien.

As the sound faded, Pony felt his ID vibrate. With relief, he saw it was Dan. "Dude, are you ok?" they both asked simultaneously.

Pony laughed and managed, "As well as can be expected. How about everyone else?"

"We're alright, but when we lost you, we were a little worried. Where are you?"

Pony looked at Ta'relli, and she said, "I carried you to one of the open offices. We're still inside the stadium, if that's what you mean."

"I'm still in the venue, someplace, hiding in an office," repeated Pony. "Is everything contained?"

"Pretty much. The centaurs cleared the backstage. See if you can make your way to us. We've still got a sound check. That is … if you're feeling up to it." Dan's tone conveyed real concern. Pony knew they would cancel the show if he so much as hesitated.

"Hell no, this is rock and roll!"

Pony checked the door cautiously and saw it opened to a hallway blessedly free of anyone. "Which way back to where you 'rescued' me?"

Ta'relli led the way, her sandals making quiet noises. She moved with a strange gait, more like a deer than human. With deliberate grace, she snapped her knee as she set her heel down firmly, followed by a rolling motion of her entire foot. Pony admired her exotic nature and was happy it was someone like her who had rescued him rather than some unspeakable being with whom he could have little in common, save music.

Pony was about to start into 'twenty questions' when they reached the end of the hall and emerged directly into the backstage area.

Lisa ran toward him and threw herself in his arms crying, "Dude, that was so insane! I'm so glad you're ok. Wow! Yeah!"

"Seems like you enjoyed it," said Pony.

"Hell yeah!" cried Lisa. "Now that was rock and roll! It's especially cool that no one got injured."

"That might a put a crimp in the show," said Dan, obviously not as enthused with the events as Lisa.

Lisa's exuberance faded somewhat, and she looked at Dan soberly. "Dude! Don't say that! You know I don't give a damn about the show. If either of you got hurt ..." She looked at Dan and noted his anger, and felt a slight wave of unfamiliar embarrassment in front of Blixa and Christine.

Dan made his feelings plain. "This business is getting out of control," he said with an unmistakable edge to his voice. "It's all fun and games until someone loses an eye, and then the party really starts: is that how it is to you?"

"Pretty much, yeah," admitted Lisa, suddenly on the defensive. "I can fix eyes." Lisa repeated her favorite saying under the circumstances, "To be a great doctor, you have to also know how to inflict harm."

"Well, it's not for me," admitted Dan hotly. "This has turned serious suddenly, and I, for one, am starting to grow a mite concerned."

Christine saw the tension build and started to laugh. Both Lisa and Dan turned to her with severe expressions, and it further fueled her giggling.

"What the hell's so funny?" asked Dan.

"And you were about to start a galactic revolution," laughed Christine. "Seriously—drinking from the right hand and all!" Christine hugged Lisa. "The big bad dark rocker is suddenly what? Whining about a little mob of adoring fans? Like, come on, Dan ... think about it!"

Dan contained a sudden urge to push Christine and knew she was right from his emotional response. He searched his feelings and realized the reason he was truly angry was because he had lost control of the situation, aside from the fact that his friends had been in danger. Dan relaxed and smiled at Christine.

"Next time you go being right, little lady," said Dan, as he ran his hand through his Mohawk, letting the tension fade, "make sure you're a bit less civil about it. It's a bit unsettling the way you say things sometimes."

"No promises," replied Christine happily.

"I didn't expect any," said Dan with a sigh as he turned toward the stage. "Come on, people, we've got a show to do."

Pony noted Ta'relli crossing her hands in front of her as if she was trying to hide, obviously embarrassed at being overlooked.

"Whoa, wait a minute everybody: I want to introduce my rescuer." Pony took up the Danlean's hand and said, "Ta'relli, this is

Dan, Lisa, Christine, Blixa, and Bobbisocks."

Blixa was the first to extend a greeting with a hug, the diminutive Canabrean barely reaching the bottom of Ta'relli's small breasts. The Danlean's arms seemed to completely enfold her in the embrace.

After Blixa, Christine made to hug her, and she was surprised when Lisa held her back by gripping her arm tightly. Christine looked at Lisa and saw a subtle flare of jealousy in her eyes before she let go.

With a tight feeling of worry in her chest that bordered on paranoia, Christine followed Lisa's lead and simply waved and said, "Hi."

When Lisa took Christine's hand and squeezed it, as if to say 'thank you,' Christine felt her heart melt.

Dan stepped up to the Danlean, straining his neck to look her in her strange eyes, and said, "Thank you, Ta'relli."

"You are welcome." Ta'relli bowed her head with polite dignity. The action seemed exaggerated by the length of her neck. "Not to sound trite, but just like most of the galaxy, you guys are my favorite band. I swear on my ropes!" she added, shaking her alien hair.

Pony brightened, "Doesn't sound trite at all, does it, gang?"

"No," mumbled everybody in complete agreement.

Pony turned to the Hive. "Socks, see to it Ta'relli here is treated in style. She pretty much saved my carcass tonight, and I would like to show some appreciation. Cool?"

"Yes, Pony," replied the Hive.

"Alright then." Pony turned to Ta'relli and took up her hands. "With your permission, we have a show to do. When we are done, I'll see to thanking you properly for my rescue."

Ta'relli's face turned white and then back to her normal shade of green with an obvious uncomfortable expression. Lisa noted the reaction and said to herself, *what an interesting blush response.*

--

Pony sat at his kit and felt tiny aches all over his body when he tested the kick drum. Through the sound check, it was apparent that Dan and Lisa were likewise playing through the pain. Pony pounded his way through a speed roll on the snare and could also tell that the planet's gravity was not on his side. His hands felt slow, and his sticks somewhat heavy.

Dan and Lisa started to fuss like an old married couple with minor details about sound, and he was struck by the old joke: *What's the difference between a drummer and a proctologist? A proctologist only has to deal with one ass at a time.*

Pony stretched his shoulders and worked on warming up his wrists and ankles on the high hat and the kick drum. Eventually Lisa and Dan came to an arrangement, as was always the case, and they managed to push through three songs and set the levels for the show.

During the second song of the sound check, they fell into the groove, and Pony felt their friendship bolster him along as he played out the kinks in his battered body. When both Dan and Lisa turned to him to catch the perfect accents, it was as if they were a single mind, all in the service of the music. By the end of the sound check, Pony felt as good as new, and later, when the lights came up at the start of the performance, Pony owned the stage. During his typically understated drum solo, he spent no less than ten minutes on the kit pounding himself into a sweaty mess.

Once Pony's solo was done, Dan waited until the crowd's applause subsided to manageable levels before he pointed to the mugs.

Hot and sweaty, Pony was the first to snatch his up with the left hand as did Lisa and Dan.

Dan stepped up to the 'ear,' and made a point to switch the mug between hands. Following his example, Lisa and Pony did the same, and the crowd fell silent.

Dan stood on a precipice. Running through his mind were stories of dove heads, puppies under lawnmowers, and everything counterculture that epitomized rock and roll. The frenzied clash of the youth against the establishment, and all that came with it.

The bright stage lights made it impossible to pick out any one being in the audience. Nevertheless, Dan could see the youthful faces in his mind's eye. They were craving something to shake them out of their boring lives, but was it this? When the Beatles exploded, their message was not one of counterculture disappointment and discord, it was all about love. And the sixties rocked.

From what he had seen so far, the galaxy did seem a bit squeaky clean, but consider the alternative. Dan had the sudden comparison of ice cream parlors that gave way to biker bars, record stores that were replaced by porn stores. Revulsion shook him, and he looked at Lisa and Pony and very dramatically changed hands. With a deep pull from the mug, he toasted the crowd and said, "We are the Misplaced, from Pangaea." Dan caught Blixa's eyes. "And if there is any one thing we want to say to the galaxy it's this: We love you all! Thank you!"

Lisa and Pony followed suit and Pony felt a warm flush from the crowd's approval. Together they drained their mugs and tossed them to the side.

--

Instead of leaving the building directly after the show, as was customary, Pony had insisted they remain and party with his rescuer.

Dan followed along for a few minutes before he pointed to Blixa and then into space. The realization snapped Pony out of his romantic intent, and although he was reluctant to leave, he made his excuses, and they departed.

The comfortable familiarity of the bus lulled the weary group into a pleasant sense of relaxation.

Blixa stood by a Coil and was casually dolling out refreshments when Christine returned from the rear of the bus on her way to the driver's seat. As she brushed by, Blixa turned and gave her a spontaneous hug of affection.

The gesture was obviously nothing more than genuine friendship. However, Lisa's eyes lingered on Christine, and Lisa had to fight to keep a conversational tone to her voice.

"Looks like we're going to have to start stepping up security," she said. "Maybe it's time to introduce all the rock band subterfuge."

"The what?" Bobbi's synchronized chorus of voices dripped with eager anticipation.

Lisa could just see dozens of the tiny beings within Bobbi leaning over keyboards, waiting for what she was going to say next.

"Where I come from, big bands have had to do a lot of crazy things to make it to the show, on time and in one piece."

Blixa shifted in her seat. "So you do have trouble where you're from. How often do your pinnacles get killed?"

Dan laughed. "No, it's nothing like that!"

Pony tenderly touched his scalp and groaned, "No, it's worse."

Lisa slapped Pony on the arm with an expression that said 'poor baby' and continued, "Anyway … as I was saying. Bands have had to

do a lot of crazy stuff back on Pangaea. Secret identities, doubles, duplicate travel routes—all planned with corporate/military precision."

"The only problem is," said Bobbi, "in this case, our travel itiner-
ary is posted well in advance. The only protection we have is that
your presence in a system will not be publicly broadcast as you're
non-cons. Just letting anyone find out who you are and trace it back
to your home world before your planet has had a chance to acclimate
is discouraged by the Administrators."

"Sorta like protecting the country kids from the big city," said
Dan.

"Precisely," agreed the Hive.

Lisa waved it away. "That's the game." Her smile climbed high
enough to make the Hive's mood lighten. "The fans always know
when and where you are going to perform. It's the movement and
accommodations that are kept secret."

"Since we have a comfortable place to stay," Dan indicated the
bus with a grandiose wave, "all we have to do is cover our tracks."

Lisa smiled and crossed her hands behind her head. "As Bobbi
just said, precisely."

--

*Within the very heart of the Galaxy, a compressed mass of stars whose
combined energies are bright enough to shine through over a thousand miles
of solid concrete as if it were a shiny new plate glass window, was the Administration headquarters, a station almost a light year across.*

*Located deep in the heart of the ancient facility, a series of esoteric meters
pushed their needles into the black for the first time in a record that stretched
back into history. Far back.*

*Somewhere within the vast vessel, relays clicked into place, and a new
protocol was implemented with thousands of ships fanning out across the
galaxy to gather the energy created by this new music.*

--

The Mestathieans are one of the oldest races in the inhabited dominion. Famous not only for their sense-altering Mesta sauce, they
are perhaps best known as the only race in the entire galaxy to have
eight rectums. Accordingly, they also discovered plumbing before fire

and have perfected the technology into an art.

Waves of white noise flowed up from the crowd and bathed Dan in its soothing embrace. The sheer pressure of the thousands of fans cheers was louder than any audience they had performed for yet.

Bobbi informed him that special audio equipment had been brought in to suppress the planet-smashing crowd's ambient sound pressure to nominal levels, else they would not be able to hear themselves play, even through the massive monitor system.

The planet's stage crew worked in the sides, at the boards, and in the rigging set up for the lights. Dan and Lisa kept their gear to a minimum and relied on the venue's systems to augment the small trio's minor amplifiers.

The reason for the diminutive gear was simply so that Dan did not have to sing too loudly, something that not only made for poor performances, but would ensure that his career would be very short.

It's easy to turn up an amplifier, yet impossible to turn up the vocals past a certain point without feedback. Dan witnessed many bands that made this mistake on a regular basis: the instrumental equipment so loud that the soundboard couldn't compensate.

Any instrumentalist who did not understand this had no business in a band with vocals. Dan had repeatedly tested his theory with sound meters. The loudest the drums ever reached naturally was around 115 decibels. Repeatedly, whenever he checked most others bands against that number, the instruments were running at 119 to 120 plus, the spurious argument being the instruments have to be louder than the drums. This is never the case, unless one is playing a show with only the gear on stage; the PA should be used to balance the sound. The amps should be set at the minimum volume required to achieve the proper sustain and that's that.

In Dan's mind, the most heinous crime an instrumentalist can perpetrate is turning up their amp once the levels have been set. It's the most disrespectful thing that can be done to a vocalist and the rest of the band. If the amp is set to its minimum, the stage monitors can always adjust. And all a band member need do is ask for the level of their instrument to be brought up in the onstage mix. If the amp is set too loud, the monitors don't have a chance to compensate. It takes a professional to recognize these facts and work accordingly, and it's one of the things that separate the wannabes from the real players. Well that, and talent, work ethic, and most importantly a sense of just how ridiculous the whole rock star mentality is.

As they were faced with a massive audience, they would have their gear set at its maximum and, as Dan had just mulled over, that in itself was a problem. For, in many instances, as ironic as it might seem, the sound would be so loud that he could not hear a thing.

To remedy this, Bobbi supplied Dan with what were essentially in-ear monitors: ear plugs, with tiny speakers and counter frequency defenses to eliminate any sound other than his own voice and the instruments.

When Dan turned them on, he felt a slight sucking sensation as everything went absolutely silent. He fingered his guitar and heard it squeak; just a minor click with his tongue into the microphone and he heard the sound clearly.

Dan glanced at Lisa and Pony, and Pony hit his sticks together and said, "One, two, three, four …"

The mix was perfect, and Dan blasted into the first song. However, half way through, he knew something was going terribly wrong.

One of the cardinal rules about singing is that one breathed in through the nose and sang out through the mouth. This prevented drying out the vocal cords. Dan, trained from an early age, did this habitually. However, for some reason, this did not seem to be enough. Maybe it was the lack of moisture in the air or just the composition of the planet's atmosphere. Regardless, by the end of the first song, Dan could hardly carry a tune.

Lisa, listening closely in her own in-ear monitors, heard Dan's voice squeak and squawk like a demented saxophone with delusions of grandeur. She could see by the expression on Dan's face that he was battling with his voice. She glanced at Pony and silently communicated that she was going to repeat, replaying the end riff long enough for Dan to down some water before the supposedly seamless start of the following song. A deep dread began to clench at her heart. If he was losing his voice on the first number, they were going to have a rough show.

One of the grand personality traits of any performer is their willingness to place themselves in a situation that could result in severe humiliation. This masochistic aspect of most entertainers is often balanced by the deep-seated need to well … entertain.

The desire for attention, coupled with the selfish need to share their art, outweighed the risks of the occasional 'bad performance.'

Dan took a moment and swallowed carefully. After gargling with another sip, he followed Lisa and Pony into the next song. Careful to not take a full breath, Dan approached the 'ear,' intent on using perfect vocal technique on the first line.

"Little rain drops they fall with rhythm
splattering on the streets.
Dropping down their life-filled burden
to wash away the sleet."

Lisa heard Dan's voice, and she nearly started laughing. He now sounded like one of the Chipmunks from the Christmas records rather than his usual clear tenor. Dan's expression was classic. Through obvious mortification, he finished the song with a sham of dignity, three octaves higher than normal, as if it were nothing out of the ordinary.

There must be a rich helium content in the atmosphere, reasoned Lisa, or another mixture of gasses that would have the same effect on the larynx.

When they started into the only serious love ballad they performed, a song called simply 'You,' and Dan's silly voice squeaked out like a joke, Lisa couldn't help herself, and she started laughing so hard tears ran down her face while Dan crooned to the ladies across the galaxy like a cartoon character.

Bobbisocks, a section of the Hive having been incarcerated for hysterical laughter, had a fresh team contact the venue's engineer.

Experienced with off-world requirements, the technician used the pressure from the sound dampening field to enclose the front of the stage. While he made the adjustments to the field and the atmo, he activated the doorway airlocks, subsequently transforming the performance area into a contained environment for the venue's comprehensive life support system to make the proper adjustments based on Bobbi's specifications. By the end of the third song, Dan sounded like his old self again.

Once his normal voice returned, Dan could sense that the audience was slightly disappointed. It made him smile inwardly, the feeling erasing all of his previous mortification. Closing his eyes, he focused on his voice and worked through the rest of the set.

--

Dan smacked Pony on the shoulder and laughed. Pony smiled and shook his head in wonder and said, "It's been a great couple of weeks. Man, Kirjellesque and Vlantag rocked almost as much as Falconiea!"

"Dude, the crowds just keep getting bigger." Dan tweaked the controller in his hand, and the miniature suit of Force Five Power-Amor punched Pony's duplicate micromech in the jaw.

As the miniature armored combatant fell over, Pony laughed. "Ohhh, good one, Dude!"

With a quick set of movements, Pony had the micromech back on its feet and circling like a wary predator. He feinted left and then fired his laser to the right. Dan's robot fell over, only to quickly scramble back to its feet, and the battle continued.

"How did you solve the armor's joint friction problem?"

Pony took aim once more. "Thermal sinks and grav manipulation. I put micro-Coils as inertia redirectors as well, wired them into the kinesthetic model for adaptive response and voilà: almost human agility, and flight, in any gravity."

Dan laughed and added, "And since the Coils tap into fulcra, they just take what power they need, only when they need it. No batteries required."

Pony worked the controller in his hand, using the armor's boot thrusters to fly upward over Dan's block to deliver a devastating blow to the top of its opponent's head with a miniature warhammer. "I'm going to make one of these that we can ride in!"

As the only experienced martial artist of the bunch, Lisa sat like a referee and watched the bout, happily commenting on their combat technique. "Don't you dare color mine pink, you bastard!"

Blixa, bored of the endless battle, stretched on the couch and then sat up. "I'm fixing dinner everyone. Any ideas?"

Dan looked at Pony, and they exchanged a conspiratorial look. Dan suggested hopefully, "Hamburgers?"

"Oh, for your planet's sake." Blixa cocked her hip in exasperation. "You two have been hopping around the galaxy, sampling every type of food we come across, and all you want is a hamburger?"

Lisa called up to Christine and asked, "How about it, hon? You want anything special?"

"A Kirjellesque Verm salad with those freaking big brownberries, a slice of hot baked A'cabba's Snow-root quiche, and a bowl of that Falconian Boxie soup, add extra Mesta sauce." To the windshield she added, "I don't think I could go on living without extra Mesta sauce …"

Blixa agreed. "Oh. Very galactic choices, Christine! That's three planets' specialties in a single meal. I like, I like …"

Pony looked up at Dan sheepishly. "You gotta admit, bro, Mesta sauce is mighty tasty. And it makes your whole mouth tingle."

Lisa redirected another flash of jealousy at the alien girl and pushed Pony, causing him to lose control over his robot. "That's gotta be neurotoxins, dumbass."

"Whatever," laughed Pony. "It's good."

Dan capitalized on the opening Lisa provided and pinned Pony's micromech to the floor and had his Gladiatron begin hammering Pony's with both tiny robotic fists. "I suppose I could take some Mesta, on a hamburger …"

Bobbi floated across and said, "Blixa, how come you always do the cooking? We took you for the spoiled, manipulative type."

The beautiful woman ignored another in the Hive's continuous halfhearted insults, shrugged and admitted, "Back home I don't get to do anything like this. To even attempt it gets people punished for not stopping me. Something as mindless as cooking and cleaning frees what you would call my spirit. Plus it makes me useful in a small way." She turned to the Coil. "And so I clean and I cook." She tapped at the controls, and lunch was done with a ding. "And it's so difficult with this new Coil oven." She feigned exhaustion as she took out the food.

Blixa called to the front of the bus, "Christine, you should eat."

Christine shook her head.

"Are you sure?" Blixa replaced the food in the Coil with Pony's mangled robot. "You've been pushing yourself awfully hard on this tour."

Once the toy was remade, Pony snagged a brownberry and set his mechanical gladiator back down ready to fight anew.

Christine nodded her head. "It's only about ten hours to our final destination on this tour. I can handle it."

Lisa interjected, unable to keep the irritation out of her voice, "Leave her alone, Blixa."

"Lisa!" Christine hit the clutch, shifted, and the road appeared before her. "I'm ok, Blixa. We gotta long haul ahead of us. Let's get started, and I'll pull over in a while and treat myself to some soup then."

--

"We should talk." Bobbi fought down a segment of the Hive population that wanted to reveal Blixa's poisoning. Instead, the Hive said, "As you have been noticing, your music's popularity is growing at an unprecedented rate with every passing day." Bobbi projected a screen with a segmented diagram. "We have offers for you to play with the very best talent in the galaxy, at the very best venues. And your final 'Spring Break' show is completely sold out! Incidentally, the pirated recording of your performance, the one on Fednirallas at Crystal Shores, made the illicit publisher almost a million Gs."

"Speaking of money, Socks." Pony's robot managed to toss Dan's micromech to the floor. "How are we doing in that department?"

"You have sold millions upon millions of copies of that very same recording virtually overnight." Bobbi floated toward the ceiling. "This is no longer about making money. You need never worry about that again. This is about fame. As you would say, this is about heavy metal ruling the galaxy and melting faces!"

The Hive devoted a section to research and investigation into the phenomena of music groups and had them crunch numbers on the chances of the band's continued future. That segment of the Hive took into account race and gender, but more importantly, it factored in age.

In moments, the group returned with this interesting trend: adolescent musical artists tend to remain in cohesive groups for longer periods of time than musical artists past this point of age. The research cited instances such as the Susstan, a race of intelligent shades of the color blue, whose most famous adolescent group, Chiaroscuro, managed to create over fifty records before they melded into a single pool of psychopathic azure and lost all ability to create anything original.

The second most famous were members of the Isod group, Lava, a silicone-based race whose adolescence, which for the cactus-like creatures, was measured in scores of decades, managed to record for centuries. And their music has endured for millennia since, even though it took the Isod months to play songs that, when compressed, were rendered down to minutes as unfortunately otherwise their live shows often resulted in beings perishing of old age before the concert ended.

The rest of the research indicated that groups that were formed by young beings had a better chance of surviving. The Hive was relieved by the data and comforted by the report. They had a future together, perhaps. The thought of the final show was both a bit of a relief but also worrying, profoundly sad, extremely happy, vexing, and to a small section of renegades, pleasant.

"So, we have our last show in about twenty hours from now?" Dan managed to extricate his robot with a clever judo maneuver. "Ten to get there and then ten to rest."

"At Bluestone," finished Socks, "on one of the oldest planets in the Dominion. A place simply called 'Soil.'" Bobbi projected an image of a great stage resting within the bowl of a tall semi-crater. The surrounding volcanic walls, composed entirely of a translucent crystal, created a natural amphitheater. When viewed from a distance, the color of the ocean turned the extinct volcano blue.

Even Lisa, somewhat surprised at how jaded she had become in such a short time, was impressed. "Wow!"

Bobbi snapped the projection off and said happily, "This is one of the largest venues within your 'riders,' and as anticipated, the residents are eagerly awaiting your arrival. It might interest you to know that the Galactic Stocks and investment firms have priced the black market sales of pre-owned tickets greater than the entire lifetime income of most galactic inhabitants—as much as three hundred thousand Gs for the worst of the seats. There are fortunes being made on your performance, perhaps even changes in local economies for some members of the galaxy. Just to watch you perform live."

Bobbisocks faced the members of the band, and there was a low tearful sobbing in the Hive's undertones. "So, you have a few hours to get there, catch up on sleep, and get ready for your final show."

Pony tossed his controller and let Dan dramatically finish his micromech. "Socks, why so sad? This is only the end of the beginning. Cheer up. We have a long way to go and a short time to get there. It's about time we popped back home, let them know we're alive and break the news."

Christine turned around and laughed. "We have been gone long enough for them to almost declare us legally dead!" Christine pounded the wheel as she realized, "Oh, shit … Like, I missed the Bar exam!"

Pony was on his feet excitedly. "That's the least of it. Imagine what the announcement is going to be like? Uhhh. Hello, we've been to another planet, uh, we would like you to meet, Miss Blixa Altabatt, and our manager, the Hive mind, Bobbisocks!"

"And the crowd goes wild …" Lisa let her hand trail the thought off.

"And the blood begins to flow …" Dan's statement caught all of their attention. He raised his hands apologetically. "What, did I miss something? Did human nature change in the past few weeks we've been out here?"

"He's right …" Christine took a sip of Pony's latest batch of Earl Grey. "This will have to be handled very delicately and very quietly."

--

The Tension drive's rainbow road twisted on into infinity. Christine shielded her smarting eyes against the glare as they flashed through another star and steadied her grip on the wheel. She glanced at the countdown timer. A little less than an hour to go, she thought, and then I can get some sleep. In the distance, another star was rapidly approaching. Christine took note that this system had no 'Open' Worlds.

Open worlds were planets that were part of the Galactic Order Dominion and safe to make contact. Apparently there were many habitable worlds in these systems they passed, but they could only legally stop at a few, relatively speaking that is. She squinted as if she were passing a driver with the high beams on as they flashed past its star.

The road gently curved upwards. Chris kept the bus in the center of the tube, and inevitably, another star became visible in the distance. This time the navigational array read that the system had a single 'Silent' planet. Christine closed her tired eyes for a moment as they approached to shield them from the expected painful flash.

"Wake up, Christine … wake up!" Bobbi's voice preceded a violent wrench that threw Christine against her seatbelts and the Hive against the ceiling. As the bus slid off through the rainbow wall of the road, all the streetlights went from green to red.

Then, with a happy 'ding,' a single traffic light switched to yellow, and Christine hit the high beams reflexively as mysteriously the Inocu-p unit began to print patches.

The windshield came to life in time for her to catch a glimpse of the planet they were falling toward. She had a brief glance before they hit the atmosphere and the view was covered by a sheet of flame. In the display, she read a single source of power on the planet and tried to angle toward it. Encased in a ball of flame, with her foot on the brakes, Chris pulled back on the control yoke and tried to keep the nose up.

Christine fought with the sluggish controls, coaxing every bit of altitude correction manageable. Despite all her best efforts, they were flying like a bus.

The altimeter neared zero, and she felt a tremendous crash. The single yellow traffic light switched to red, and then there was another impact, followed by skidding for a very long time. When they finally stopped, it was a surprise they were still alive. With a sigh of relief, Christine managed to say before she passed out, "Any landing you can walk away from …"

--

Using his wings in the low gravity, Warnik traveled the miles of twisting transit tunnels to the core of Mr. Tiny Gigantic's fortress. He glided along the pheromone trail directly into the presence of the most powerful media emperor in the galaxy.

Mr. Gigantic was a largish Gelfelregin. Typically, the Gel are ten-foot-tall massive amphibian creatures that resemble squatting mushrooms with frog-like mouths. Tiny stood just a fraction over eleven feet, with a head almost ten feet across.

With sixteen manipulators, each tipped with eight fingers, Tiny worked the stream of information that played across his unifier monitors. Warnik could not help but notice that The Misplaced were featured on the big screen and that one of their songs played on the chamber's audio system previously dedicated for his band alone.

Tiny's prehensile appendages dropped from beneath his toadstool-like head. They were strong enough to lift the weighty Gel and still delicate enough to be used for microsurgery. Sixteen cerci eyes, similar to those Warnik possessed, encircled the cap and each followed an arm. But set within the fleshy head, directly above the expansive mouth and surrounded by many articulating eyebrows, rested a pair of malignant portals some would call eyes. It was in these gateways that the Macan read bad news was forthcoming.

Warnik fluttered to his couch and was only partially relieved to find his usual plate of refreshments and warm, scented towels. The wary cricket looked about and couldn't see any Berakean Mercenaries standing in the vestibules that ringed the media master's inner sanctum. Not that Tiny needed any—the massive Gel could crush him easily. The absence of the four armed giants, comforting as it was, could not erase the disquieted spike growing in his heart.

Light from the multitude of monitors illuminated the slick surface of the Gel's head. Beneath the shiny exterior, Warnik saw the circles, and dark black spots, that only the oldest of the race ever developed.

"Rest de thorax Cric'leader, Warnik," groaned the nearly subsonic tones. The deep voice issued from the mushroom's mouth in an accent that even the translators found difficult to relay.

"Yoo de best ender. Why de feeling trepidation?" Tiny did not wait for an answer and went on. "De find me after de burrow in de busted up liner. Twa took de net a month of a slowcrawl through de cold, cold void. Why de do-it? All de need do is chirp!"

Warnik refrained from offering excuses. "Took a crush."

Tiny adjusted the monitors to display the biped band. "Twa lem de do-it?"

The cricket nodded his antennae.

"I want lem."

"As usual ..." Warnik drew a soothing towel across his forehead. "I will delete them—"

Tiny interrupted, "Twa de been so crushed de don't see it, not even wit six eye!"

"*Data,*" sighed Warnik wearily. "Just give me the data ..."

"Twa peri tones, dey have real galactic grocery potential. I want lem to work."

"Now I comp ...   No deletion, instead insert them into your mechanizations."

"Perfect roots! Lem de mine!"

--

Pony couldn't remember if he had been dreaming when the automatic airbag restraint system kicked in with the first severe jolt. He wrestled himself from his bunk and grabbed his jacket, thinking, *"If the hull is compromised ..."* He let any further thoughts trail off. Now was the time for action, by the book. His engineer's mind locked around the protocols they had developed. With the portable Coil unit in his jacket, Pony quickly made a pressure suit, and fighting the air-bags, managed to slip it on. Careful to seal the helmet and check the suit's integrity under pressure, he was about to open the door when he heard a muffled knock.

"Pon ... You alright!?" It was Dan's unmistakable gravely voice.

Pony snapped opened the helmet. "Yeah. Do we have pressure?"

"Totally, and from what I can tell, now that you're accounted for, everyone is relatively ok."

Pony opened the door and was relieved to see everyone else in the tight hall was also wearing pressure suits, although Christine's was a bright pink and Blixa's a nonconformist fuchsia.

"How's Socks?"

The Hive's voice was almost cheerful as it replied, "We suffered only minor casualties. Replacements are hatching as we speak. We're good to go."

"And the bus?" Pony looked at Christine and she dropped her head and reported apologetically, "We have a single yellow light. Will that be enough?"

Pony glanced at Dan, and he gave a slight shrug. "Only way to find out is to take a look."

Christine moved out of the hall and flopped down on one of the couches. Everyone could see she was crying. "I'm so sorry. I should have taken a break—what was I thinking? I almost got us all killed."

"You," Lisa sat next to Christine and took her helmet in her hands and banged hers against it, locking eyes, "just like the rest of us, were swept up in this road-trip and didn't think anything could go wrong!"

"Well it has, and it's my fault!" Christine tried to turn away, and Lisa held her firm.

"We are ok. That is all that really matters at this point." Christine tried to pull away once more. Lisa held her fast and said, "Hey, listen to me—we are O.K.!" Lisa would not let go of Christine's helmet until the young woman nodded acceptance. "And once we get going again, you can bet your life we will never let you forget this. We have ammunition to hack on you forever."

Dan's voice took on a German accent. "You vill grow veary of the apologies, my dear ... I promise you."

Blixa dropped next to Christine on the long couch and looked pointedly at the bass player. "Dan, honey, you should really see just how bad it is ..." She held Chris's hand and motioned with her head. "Things like this can turn dangerous quickly, if one delays. Space is never concerned about life."

She spoke with the voice of experience, and it sent Dan's hackles up.

"Well, we've got basic power to every system, and the pressure force-fields are intact, so we are safe. Good idea, Pony, making the hull a single piece of tri-phased titanium aluminide and carbon fiber composite. That freakin' crap probably saved our collective hides."

"It was the hardest stuff I could imagine." Pony patted the wall. "I knew our baby was tough!"

"The fact that you have discovered one of the greatest breakthroughs in science is what saved our collective hides," argued Bobbi. "Your planet's fantastic music aside, this Coil technology of yours is nothing short of revolutionary."

Dan's smile rolled into a laugh. "And it's that same tech that's going to get us back on the road again. Looks like it's time to go change the equivalent of a cosmic tire."

"Let's see what we can see ..." Lisa reluctantly left Christine in Blixa's care and moved to her terminal. In the low light, the reflection of the monitor nearly blotted out her features inside the helmet. "Looks like we have atmosphere and the Inocu-p unit made us a few patches. Bobbi, what the heck does a 'Silent' world mean?"

"It's a category of worlds that, while part of the Order, do not actively engage in contact. Typically worlds of this type are religious centers, spiritual retreats, and places of self-imposed isolation for cultural reasons."

"And," Blixa shuddered, "what Bobbi isn't telling you is that these places are always fantastic getaways. Too fantastic."

Bobbi suddenly sounded very worried. "Blixa is right. Occasionally pinnacles of singular talent have stumbled upon such colonies, never to be heard from again. We call it 'lost to the spirit.'"

"Sounds like a commune." Lisa absently pressed her patch on a forearm. "We had a similar thing happen on our world—the so-called 'enlightenment' altered that group forever."

"For better or for worse?" The Hive's serious tone conveyed such a concern that Lisa took a moment to face the collective being.

"The jury is still out on that one."

Dan removed his helmet. "So I gather it's safe to go outside without a suit and take a look?"

Lisa nodded, and Bobbisocks floated in front of Dan, blocking him. "Did the crash damage your brain? We are the best choice for such a task."

"Sorry … sorry." Dan shook his head and laughed, "I sometimes forget that you're a miniature space-ship, Socks."

"Unfortunately, while we are a self-contained highly mobile colony, we are running low on fuel. And while we are more than up to this task, we are somewhat limited in our capabilities at the present." Embarrassment painted the multitude of voices as the Hive added, "We were going to fill up at the next show."

--

The doors opened, and Bobbisocks drifted clear of the bus and into a paradise. The deep blue afternoon sky contained a few stray clouds dusting three golden moons, just above the horizon. Surprise was registered within pockets of the Hive as Bobbi discovered the exterior of the bus was almost entirely covered in flowers.

The quiet line of peri bipeds stretched from the shore of the lake and into the surrounding garden of a forest. With a collective gasp, the procession dropped their offerings and fled into the woods the moment Bobbi appeared.

The Hive floated around the bus, brushing away the massive bouquet with its manipulators. "It never ceases to amaze us how even the most gentle of beings are so willing to sacrifice defenseless plants for virtually every occasion—poor flowers."

On the lake floated a magnificent temple. When Bobbi saw a line of boats detach and begin angling in their direction, the Hive quickly finished its scan and reentered the bus.

"The natives are restless," announced Bobbi. "And from what we can see, the ship is intact."

"We only have one yellow light." Dan tapped the metal cases hopefully. "If we have the time, we might as well as wrap the Coil around and remake her. Can't do any harm."

"It's not that simple, Dan." Pony's gut tightened like a rock around the realization. "The Administrators made modifications after we Coiled the bus. Didn't think about copying it, after those mods." Pony fought off a wave of self loathing at the error. "We rebuild now and we fly without nav systems, comms, Inocu-ps and so on …"

Christine winced. "I had just gotten used to those little luxuries." She tried to be lighthearted and nearly succeeded. Lisa slid back over to Christine and wrapped her arm around her shoulder.

Blixa removed her helmet with a flourish. "When The Crickets were attacking, you said as long as we had one yellow light we were good to go." After dropping her gloves in her helmet, Blixa shook her hair and tousled it free of her antennae. "So why don't we just go?"

"We could." Pony fought down the strong urge to touch Blixa's antennae. "If we wanted to take a chance of dying. Those little street-lights each represent a redundant ship-wide system designed to make the bus pretty much idiot proof." Pony's smile grew across his face, and its warmth was contagious as he added, "We like to party some-times."

Dan dropped into the driver's seat and started flipping switches. "With only a single ship-wide system marginally operational, any-thing fails, and we suck void."

"Don't they repair themselves?" Blixa's statement was followed by a happy mechanical 'ding' as the yellow light switched to green and a red light switched to yellow.

Dan laughed at the timing and answered, "That would be a yes."

"So how long do we have to wait?" Bobbi floated around Dan as he jumped up from the seat.

"Depends upon how much we want to chance it," Dan shrugged, "and how fast the systems repair themselves. I say once we have three green lights, we are at least good enough to get off-world. If it's smooth sailing, the rest of the systems will come online as we go."

Bobbi flashed a countdown timer. "We don't have a lot of time before Bluestone—if we aren't in flight within ten hours, we will be late!"

"I bet they won't start without us," laughed Pony.

Christine rested her head in Lisa's lap wearily. "We were only an hour away ..."

"Knock it off, Chris." Dan squatted down, gripped Blixa's knee and smoothed Christine's hair. "Lemme tell you about the band Red Axe: they rolled their truck on their way to a show and still kicked ass."

"Really?" Christine looked up hopefully, snuggling warmly into Lisa's lap. "I've heard of them."

"Yeah." Dan flashed a smile and brushed his hands through his Mohawk. "They totally crashed and burned, but still managed to play a killer set. And I'm not lying when I say one of the members even played with severe road rash and another with a minor concussion. I swear!"

"We were most likely saved serious injury by the airbags." Pony nodded in the direction of their cabins. "If we had been sitting on the couches, things might have turned out differently."

Dan used Blixa's leg and regained his feet with a sigh. "Socks, what's the weather like out there?"

"Clear skies with a one hundred percent chance of religious zealots, we're afraid."

--

"It may not seem like much to you, babe, but the sight of three golden moons ... incredible!" Dan took a picture and turned to Blixa. "Just one more, hon, please ..."

Blixa released a sigh of mock exasperation as she joyfully struck a very provocative pose. "Dan. I have to tell you something."

Dan framed the shot, careful to capture the moons over the floating temple and the boats. Dan snapped another picture of just the temple and the boats. So far, they remained offshore, apparently content to simply observe, and the 'flower children' Bobbi had described were nowhere to be seen.

"What is it, baby?"

Blixa smile fell as quickly as it appeared. Dan failed to notice as he looked thoughtfully at the image on his camera. Blixa took his hand and said quietly, "There is no easy way to explain—the only way it can be done is to show you."

"Show me what?" Dan's eyes came up and were filled with adoration as he stepped close. Blixa knew that was about to end. She savored his expression and drank in one last loving look before roughly biting him on the shoulder.

"Ouch! Oh, I see how you like it! You've never done that before …" Dan grabbed her playfully and started to wrestle when his smile fluttered and then fell. He put his hand to his arm and caught the small trickle of blood. "I feel dizzy …" He turned and staggered to the sand, barely conscious, his expression transforming to fear. "Honey? What did you do …?"

"It's more like what I have been doing." Blixa extended and then retracted her antennae. "This is just the withdrawal. Believe me, it gets much worse."

--

The shore of the lake was rugged in places and well overgrown by alien trees. Drifting in the dappled shadows, Christine saw hundreds of unfamiliar insects going about their daily lives. Satisfied they had a good measure of privacy, Lisa threw down the blanket and gently set a basket aside.

Christine relaxed down onto the blanket and stretched herself into a tremendous yawn.

"You should really be sleeping." Lisa took out a handful of grapes and dangled them above Christine's nose.

Christine took a bite. "We haven't had a chance to relax like this anyplace. It's all been like … shows and the road … and then more shows and the road." Christine took another grape.

Lisa sighed. "That's life on the road, babe. You live in hotels and only go out to go to work. That's why real rock stars kill themselves when they're off-tour. They're making up for lost time!"

"What do you mean 'real rock stars'?"

"You know real rock stars, like the ones back home. Duhh?"

"Duhh, yourself!" Christine took a grape and threw it at Lisa playfully. "You know—for a doctor—you're pretty slow. You guys are like what? The biggest friggin' rockstars in the, oh, I don't know … the GALAXY!"

"That's just until they hear someone good!"

Christine got to her knees and crawled close. "You guys are good!"

"Not as good as … as …"

This time it was Chris's hands on Lisa's face holding her and denying Lisa any chance of escape. "Shut up woman. Just shut up!"

Christine's lips made sure that Lisa put forth no further arguments.

--

Warily, as if expecting violence, Blixa moved out of arm's reach when Dan sat up. Dan sadly stared out at the boats on the water and tears began to build in his eyes. He raised his chin and swallowed against the mounting tide of emotions.

"Why do you do it?"

"I had to get away from my family!"

"No, I mean …" He took a deep breath. "Take it away …?" Dan tried, but the tears overflowed. "For me, it has always been music and school." He gripped his Mohawk as if trying to wring sense out of his emotions. "I had never been in love before!"

"Never …?" Blixa looked incredulous. "But you've …"

Dan waved away her implications. "Oh, sure, I've had girls, but never a girlfriend, and never any real emotional commitments." He leaned back up and exhaled deeply. "I've never loved … and what you showed me was … was …"

"A lie!" Blixa's voice held an edge Dan had never heard. "What I did to you was a lie. Had you not been a new entry, you would never have let me do it. The Canabrean touch is so well known, it's almost a cliché."

"But it felt so real …"

Blixa softened her voice. "Chemically, it is."

"Heartbreak is a small word compared to what I'm feeling right now, Blixa. It's like every breath I take is freakin' misery. *Oh* …!" Dan swallowed his tears and sniffed with a bit of unexpected laughter. "Oh, I've got to write about this!"

Blixa looked bewildered as Dan stood up and hugged her. "Blixa baby, you have given me a great many gifts. I don't think I need any chemical assistance when I honestly say that I still love you."

Blixa's smile took a moment, but gradually, hesitantly it began to grow.

"So you said you were doing it to get away from your family, but you've had ample chances to slip away at every show." Dan swayed back and forth with Blixa in his arms.

"Although the exact number is highly debated amongst the upper echelons, my race is made up of clones from roughly five hundred originals. We are all grown, modified and educated in vats to be of a particular 'use' as we call it." Blixa pulled away and a familiar dignity surrounded her as if she was wearing a business suit. "I am a Director of the Altabatt conglomerate."

The illusion vanished, and a new aura replaced the old, and this one said *Hey there, sailor!* Blixa cocked her hip and laughed sensuously. "But as you can see ... I am not! I would rather make a living as a host for Yelamite larva."

"Ewww!" And when she started to eagerly explain, Dan raised his hands, "Don't even tell me."

"Anyway ... Then you came along, and I've been kinda happy ever since. You new entries have such a fresh perspective and way of reacting to everything you see, it's infectious. Who wouldn't want to tag along? And besides all that, you are cute!"

--

Pony finished the galactic equivalent of a text and hit the send button on his ID. An alert told him that his message would be transmitted at the first available opportunity. "Socks, what's this mean?"

"We are on a Silent world, Pony, incommunicado, as you have said." Bobbi floated over to Lisa's terminal. "There are no gravcom repeaters in this solar system."

"No way to call for assistance?"

The Hive closed the laptop delicately. "That's the idea—isolation for isolation's sake. Makes our collective skins crawl. I bet those people out there have never heard of you."

"I was sending a message to Ta'relli! She was going to meet us at the next gig."

"We have her on the guest list for Bluestone." The Hive had perfect records regarding venues. "She must be wealthy to have been able to follow us since Nalhalafath."

"It's never come up. Now that you mention it, I suppose you're right, Socks."

"She is a beautiful, tall Danlean." Inside Bobbi, dozens of residents were crying their eyes out in jealousy. However, the Hive's tone remained professional. "Other than the guest list, do you wish to add any 'riders' for your rescuer acquaintance?"

Pony pursed his lips thoughtfully. "In this case, I guess we should make sure she has escorted access to the green room before we get there."

"As soon as we are off-world, and within range of a repeater, we will make the arrangements."

"Bobbi, you rock my socks off!"

Ding!

"That's two …" Bobbi let slip the colony's collective applause.

--

The gentle waves stirred up by a warm breeze made the boats rock slightly. The motion caught Dan's attention briefly, and he waved. "I wonder why they won't come any closer?"

"I'm always suspicious of these spiritual types," said Blixa seriously, her exotic accent coating her words with distaste. "Their motivations can be arbitrary, punitive, and absurd at times. You should hope they keep their distance until we can get off-world."

"You wouldn't like to take a closer look at that temple?" Dan absently snapped another picture.

"Most likely it's off limits to such as ourselves, perpetuating the elitism to maintain the fantasy-based theocracy."

"Wow." Dan turned and caught Blixa's eye. "That sounded impressive."

Blixa gave an indifferent shrug. "I have my moments. I'm not a *total* vapor head."

"Speaking of that, I noticed you stopped awhile ago."

"Oh, I've still got it." Blixa pulled out the small aspirator and put it back in her suit. "I've just cut down between shows." With a bright smile, she added, "How much longer do you think we will have to wait?"

"Let's get back and find out."

The ground beneath Dan's feet seemed to shift, and he staggered for a moment, bumping into Blixa. He laughed sheepishly, tried to take another step, and felt sudden heartburn grip his chest with all the subtle grace of a milkmaid's handshake.

"Oh, boy ..." were Dan's last words before he collapsed into the alien grass.

Blixa put her hand to her face as she dropped to her knees beside him and screamed.

--

Lisa heard Blixa's cry, and its urgent pitch sent a chill through her, alerting her doctor's senses. That tone was universal: anguish brought upon by unexpected injury or danger. Gathering what she had to have of her clothing, most importantly her Coil unit, she dashed off in the direction of the cry before it could fade.

"Let's go!" She called back to Christine, who having finally fallen asleep, was painfully dragging herself awake.

"You go—I'll catch up. I just need a second," called Christine.

"Go!"

The alien landscape flowed beneath her feet, and it only took Lisa a few moments to find them.

Dan lay facedown on the ground, and Blixa was kneeling next to him, trying to wake him. When she saw Lisa, she screamed, "Help him!"

"What happened?"

A host of expressions flowed across the alien girl's face, from guilt to resignation, and finally she said, "He was fine, we were talking and ..." She let the sentence trail off and looked away, embarrassed to say more and make Lisa hate her.

Lisa misread the girl's guilt and thought she was hinting that they had been having sex, and that the strain had caused some sort of episode. But Dan was far too young, and in far too good of condition. Anything that would put him unconscious was serious, unexpected, and severe.

Lisa checked his vitals and located an arrhythmia as well as the bleeding bite mark. Unlike a full-blown heart attack, he was in overdrive. Dan's body rocked back and forth slightly with each beat of his heart, so severe was the condition.

Lisa looked around and sighed. This was hardly the place to work, but under the circumstances, it would have to do, if she were to save her friend.

Gently turning Dan over with Blixa's assistance, Lisa was happy that she had spent the time 'dropping' every piece of equipment and drug she could borrow from the hospital. And in the case of some of the larger, more complex gear, she had snuck in a Coil and made copies. She practically had an entire hospital's resources at her fingertips.

Dan's color was acceptable, his pupils responsive, and his breathing regular. Certain he was not instantly going to go into arrest, Lisa found her Coil and opted to take a blood sample and analyze it first. In a few touches, she had all the equipment necessary as well as a portable power source. After some quick instructions to Blixa and Christine, the makeshift lab was up and running.

Blood: the only tissue in the body that is easy to transplant or transfuse. The sanguine liquid transports oxygen, nutrients, hormonal signals, and carries waste to the liver, kidneys and lungs for disposal. Part of the immune system, and critical to maintaining temperature via oxidation, it was also the body's hydraulic fluid.

Mental recitation pushed all emotion aside. Dan ceased being her 'friend' and was now a complex combination of processes that had to be put back into homeostasis. Shutting down any emotion, Lisa locked her mind into its medical mode and went to work.

She pulled back from the microscope and considered for a moment. There was an alien multi-potent stem cell loose in Dan's blood. Lisa glanced up at Blixa and to the bite mark and guessed at its origin. The alien stem cell transmitted chemical signals to red blood cells and these, instead of nourishing Dan's heart, were sending it into arrhythmia. The multi-potent was also killing another enzyme that was completely unfamiliar to her, and upon first glance, appeared to be a unique psychotropic compound.

While Lisa watched, her mind flicking through possible treatments, she was surprised to see the alien cells begin to erupt and die. In a few more moments, Dan's blood was clear. Lisa looked at her friend and watched him take a deep breath and saw his eyes flutter.

Dan groaned and tried to sit up. Lisa put her hand on his chest and said, "Don't move."

Dan nodded his acceptance, relaxed, and asked, "What happened?" He felt weak and exhausted.

"I think Blixa may have inadvertently poisoned you while you guys were having sex." She pointed to the bite mark. "How do you feel?

"Like my whole body's asleep—I can't make a fist." Dan loosely clenched his hand and then let it fall to the alien turf.

Lisa took another set of vitals and drew more blood. A quick glance under the microscope at the new sample and she grunted her approval; his system was clear. "Well, whatever it was, it's gone now."

"I'm sorry, Fenee!" cried Blixa softly into her hands. "I had no way of knowing that would happen ... I'm so sorry." She smoothed Dan's thin line of hair and rubbed his shaved scalp affectionately.

"Fenee?" asked Lisa.

"Yeah, you know, sweet—grows on trees—fenee," sniffed the young Canabrean woman.

Dan felt his strength return in a heated flush and sat up unceremoniously. "Wow, that was freaking amazing! What a rush!"

His friends helped him to his feet. Dan took a breath and swung his arms. "The aftereffects of Blixa's antidote made me almost euphoric."

Blixa caught Dan's eye, and he read her embarrassment and discomfiture in her delicate smile. For the first time in his life, Dan decided it might be best— just this once—to not tell his best friend everything. If there was one thing he knew about Lisa, she was protective of him like a sister. If she ever suspected that Blixa had drugged him, and that the antidote was responsible for this episode, there was no telling what she would do to the alien girl, regardless of her Hippocratic Oath.

"Do you feel well enough to walk?" asked Lisa.

Dan gave an enthusiastic nod and a bright smile. "Sis, I feel good enough to run!"

--

The systems check showed everything was in the green. The bus was ready to roll. Christine flipped her hair back behind her ear.

"You sure you want to do this?" Dan stood just behind the yellow line, concern in his voice.

"I've got to get back on the horse." Her eyes caught Lisa's in the review mirror, and she blew her a kiss. "Besides I've had a nap, and I feel great." Christine rechecked the coordinates for Bluestone. "And if I can't fly, I'm no good to you."

Lisa practically leaped to her feet and shouted, "Just get us in the air, bitch! Dan, sit-the-heck-down!"

"Right! Grab a hold of something that doesn't mind!" Christine hit the clutch.

--

"This is G.O.D.'s voice, your galactic information network head-quarters. We are here, live at the Bluestone amphitheater, and our top story tonight: the safe arrival of The Misplaced in the Soil star system only a few hours before they are scheduled to play one of the most eagerly awaited concerts in memory. But before that, here's a short interview with one of the leading authorities on music today, the crea-tor of the Slybright Tran-Site, none other than Mr. Tiny Gigantic."

"Mr. Gigantic, you are perhaps best known for your management firm Tinytalent. You've handled some of the greatest, and perhaps *the* greatest, The Crickets. Just what do you think about this musical revolution?"

"Lem that can do … do. Lem that cannot do … squwak. We like this rock and roll!"

"Quite a few dominions have silenced themselves against what some say is a corrupting influence, especially to the larvae."

"If tis make lem happy! But soon all will come to the call and have lem faces melted."

"And there you have it, Mr. Tiny Gigantic's take on the whole situation. You can bet it's safe to say that this rock and roll is here to stay."

--

Isolation was a balm to Cal'dreem's senses. Altabatt directors were notoriously sensitive to subtleties and this manufactured autism often made ordinary life tedious and uncomfortable. Bred specifically to be the leaders of a multi-galactic trans-corporation, they—the clones—were intelligent and perspicacious to the point of appearing clairvoyant. The same cannot be said for the subordinates whose en-forced inferiorities were a constant source of distress to one with such gifts.

For this reason, they had been one step behind the roving rock band for quite some time. In fact, it wasn't until the GOD report had described Blixa as one the band's mysterious followers that they had been able find them at all. Once the report had been brought to the director's attention, it had been a simple matter to select a place along the tour route to stage the ambush.

With the Altabatt influence, and vast amounts of bribe money, the stage was set. The Canabrean fleet was now secretly in orbit around the planet called Soil, in readiness to 'rescue' his daughter—and her new friends' mysterious 'coil' technology.

He stepped up to the command podium and smiled down at the team. The costumes were exact—dressed as service personnel and security staff for the venue, they looked perfect and would have no difficulty infiltrating the highly guarded concert.

The director cleared his throat and used his best command voice to address the clones. Conditioned to respond to his instructions as nearly a post hypnotic suggestion, they stood at attention, eagerly awaiting orders.

"When the Pangaeans and my daughter are in the so-called 'green room,' you will use the gas and rescue them unharmed." The Director rocked back and forth on his heels contentedly and added, "And sadly, the show will not go on …"

--

The decoy escort, complete with police vehicles and a ridiculously long limousine-like tran, pulled ahead. Dan had Bobbi drop back out of the pack and take the side streets to the venue.

"What's the protocol this time, Socks?" asked Pony.

The Hive's voice was a happy chorus. Its scans of the band showed that Blixa had administered the antidote, and Dan seemed none the worse for wear. If anything, the absence of the venom only made Dan's attraction to the Altabatt stronger. "After a scenic circle of the Volcano, we dock at side access door six. From there we have a short meet-and-greet with special ticket holders at the side stage bar, and then you hit the green room to warm up, relax, and get ready."

"Sounds like a plan!" Lisa slapped Christine's leg and smiled. "We're all dressed up with someplace to go!"

"This is one of the greatest natural wonders in the galaxy." Bobbi maneuvered the transport to give the passengers the best possible view. "We thought you might like to see it."

Light from the sunset fought its way through millions of facets within the quartz of the volcano to explode victoriously in every possible combination of color. With only a small ring of sparsely developed shoreline, the natural amphitheater seemed to be a tsunami set afire by the sun.

After one complete circuit of the isle, they noted that the side access door was clear, a good sign that their decoys had done their job. Bobbi set the tran down, and they exited quickly into the subterranean complex.

The Hive floated ahead of the band. "Most of the resort is underground, carved out of the quartz and geothermically powered."

The quiet tunnel ended, and Bobbi paused at the doors, signaling they had arrived. The doors opened after a moment into a party.

Applause flowed as they made their way past the line of fans. The band took a moment and signed the expected autographs and posed for pictures.

Warnik mingled and remained unseen within the crowded bar area. The Cricket only managed to gain access due to his fame and the fact that Tiny had spent a lot of Gs.

The band stood for one final round of AV recordings, and amidst a flood of mock apologies, they made their way towards the green room.

A pair of helmeted guards stood watch and checked the members' identification formally. Blixa thought there was something familiar in their mannerisms, but she let it slide.

"Here we are," announced the Hive. "Christine, could you please accompany us? We need to refuel. It's a delicate process that leaves us indisposed for a few minutes. It's nice to have someone we can trust watching out."

Chris shrugged and threw a smile at Lisa. "Sure … Do you mind, hon? Say hello to Ta'relli for me and tell her we'll watch the show together, please?"

Lisa made a pffft noise and waved her hand dismissively. "No problem, take the little dearie and get something to eat. We will be right here."

Bobbi floated off with Chris in tow. Without a word, the security detail closed the doors and took up guard positions.

--

The green room was a lavish affair, yet despite all the elaborate preparations, including unique dishes from around the galaxy, Pony only noticed a single thing when they entered.

"Ta'relli!"

The Danlean wore a sheer white mini-dress that left just the perfect amount for the imagination as she trotted toward him on a pair of silver high heels. Her perfectly pouty lips sparkled with silver lipstick, her high cheekbones rested beneath a set of gigantic multifaceted green eyes highlighted by silver eye-shadow. With a squeal of delight, she jumped into Pony's arms and shamelessly wrapped her long legs around the drummer's torso.

"I was so worried." Ta'relli spoke between kisses. "When they said you were delayed, I was afraid something awful happened like last time." She pulled away and inspected Pony's scalp in a very motherly fashion.

"Nothing serious, honey—here we are …" Pony was laughing. "Ok, ok, we're alright … Chill, woman …" Ta'relli seemed content to keep up with the affections for a few more seconds before she disengaged herself and slid to her feet. With a flurry of smiles and swirling of hair, Ta'relli hugged, greeted the rest of the band. When she came his way, Dan noted that she had the strong scent of cherries.

"So, what happened? Why the delay?" The Danlean's eyes were wide with curiosity and looked like pools of sparkling green water.

Lisa took the galactic equivalent of a potato chip and scooped a hefty mouthful of Mesta sauce. "We had a 'flat tire' so-to-speak, nothing serious. Oh, and Christine says, 'hi.'" The chip vanished.

Ta'relli looked around. "Where is she anyway?"

"Getting some fuel for Bobbi at the bar."

"Well, I tell you what." Ta'relli swung her braids around behind her back dramatically. "Just a little thing like your suspected delay was seen as the biggest news in the galaxy! I was mobbed by interviewers on my way here. It was a good thing you had me escorted. I might never have made it."

Blixa frowned at the too-familiar security guards and snuggled close to Dan, her head dropping strangely. Dan thought it suddenly very odd how her words were taking a long time to reach his brain, and he felt like he was leaking something from somewhere indefinable.

"Well, we all did. So let's just focus … on having a …" It was as if each painstakingly selected syllable had to be specially packed and then sent on a flight, its baggage lost, then found. And when they reluctantly arrived through airport security to his tongue, Dan finally managed to almost finish clearly as he dropped to the floor. "…a … good … time."

The security guards started to move the unconscious figures. "What should we do about this one? We've got no orders, and she's not on the list …"

Ta'relli heard the last words before the dark claimed her. "Leave her, take the others and get to the trans."

--

Warnik had to look twice to be sure he was seeing the security beings quickly exit the green room with mysterious large bags slung over their shoulders. He counted four, the same number as had just gone in. Warnik's sensitive antennae tasted Mesta sauce mixed with A'cabban soporific gas.

"Crush!" The Macan grabbed for his ID. "The targets have been abducted, and they are exiting via side access door six."

Cherrup's voice was right there. She and a fleet posing as floating fans were locked in a flight pattern around the island.

The female Macan chirped, "We have them: the targets are being loaded on a Canabrean security liner."

"Catch that ship before it gets out of the atmosphere!" Warnik pushed his way through the crowd. "I want the targets secured."

--

The panorama was only slightly distorted in the gigantic viewscreen. Filling the entire wall from floor to ceiling, it seemed to be more a window than a colossal monitor.

The island was visible on the surface of the ocean, small and unspoiled; it was the last in a chain that stretched from a nearby mainland. There was a readout that displayed the status of their transport. The pilot informed them that they had secured the cargo and were en route, and the display detected the launch. Strange numeric lists flashed, displaying velocity, system stability, and fuel as the craft lifted toward them.

The director sat comfortably on a well-padded chair. The soothing medical apparatus that surrounded him stabilized his physiological responses to the stress of command, and it was with pristine clarity of mind that he watched the operation.

He mused, with minor drug-dulled irritation, over the fact that he could not make the port authorities give him unrestricted access to their vessel. The band has become too high profile for that it seemed, and he would have to be content with his guests.

A movement on the monitor caught the director's attention. Below, tiny motes closed in and surrounded his security liner, like a swarm of gnats.

"What on Canab!?" The director pitched his voice, "All security units launch and defend, repeat: all security units launch and defend!"

With a quick mental estimation, he knew that the fastest of the security craft would be unable to reach them in time to be of any assistance.

"Patch me into the ship—I want to speak to the commander!"

There was a moment of dead air, and then the speakers exploded with sound. They could hear the professional crew as they fought against the mysterious fleet. Orders and flat-toned acknowledgments were given and received with professional calm that rapidly evaporated into panic. From the onset, it was apparent the Canabreans did not have a chance against the Macan ambush.

"Sir, we are outgunned almost a hundred to one." There was a severe crashing sound. "Sir, they have boarded. We—" There was the sound of blasters discharging and then silence.

On the screen, they saw the fleet disengage, scatter, and arc toward space.

The director pitched his voice and called, "Have the entire Altabatt navy engage and disable those ships. Do not destroy, repeat, do not destroy. We are looking for family onboard one of those tiny craft. Use extreme caution. Out!"

The director looked at the screen and beamed as he picked up a drink and dropped back into his chair laughing. "Would have been too easy …" He took a deep sip. "Almost got you!"

The director thought about the stifling confines of the office, and how much he was going to miss this chance to stretch his abilities to the fullest now that this chase had become interesting. And in this case the rewards. If he succeeded, the office would be a place of far more interest.

"Director Altabatt?" The voice flowed from nowhere and everywhere. "We have a possible trace on the craft that destroyed our liner. Unfortunately, the attack group split up and made the jump to FTL."

"Tell me what you've got!"

"The design and makers of the identical craft have been traced through three shipyards, and two refits. Whoever uses this type of vessel did not want the fact to be traced back to them."

"Then you're telling me it's a dead end!?"

"No, Director, we managed to capture one of the ships; unfortunately, the crew—entirely Macan—perished in the attempt. We were, however, able to decode their nav log and trace the vessel back to its last point of origin. We also discovered this as well."

The speakers filled with a strange noise that resembled a desert at sunset in which the insects were making noise like a junior high orchestra on drugs.

"The Crickets!"

"Yes, Director, we are positive that this particular ship originated from Mr. Tiny Gigantic's media station located in the Suterine system."

"Recall the security detail and set a course for Tiny's headquarters. Have the entire family fleet slave to this command ship and rendezvous with us at the destination. I'm authorizing an Advanced Project Change Notice. Reason for change: Repossession. Have the proper documents sent to me for verification immediately." The Director got to his feet and rubbed his hands together. "I do believe we have some business to discuss with Mr. Gigantic."

--

Bobbi floated over to the bar, took the canister of fuel, and returned to Christine. The Hive settled down on the table and used its manipulators to attach the large cylinder to the side of the ship via a flexible tube.

"Once fueling begins we deactivate all primary systems and do a diagnostic restart of every Hive unifier. This takes about five minutes. And like we said, during this time, we are incommunicado."

"No problem, Socks. Looks like the crowd has thinned out. I'll just order something to eat, and by the time it gets here, you should be good to go."

"See you in five."

The lights on the Hive went dead. A steady steam of LEDs on the canister showed that the fueling was in progress. And for the first time since Christine could remember, the Hive was completely still.

Christine had the menu in hand and was about to order when she heard the commotion.

A Danlean who looked a lot like Pony's new girlfriend Ta'relli came running toward her, shouting, "They've been kidnapped!"

"What!?"

Ta'relli was sobbing. "I heard them say 'leave her, take the others and get to the trans,' and when I woke up they were gone!"

Christine glanced at Socks. "This couldn't come at a worse time." She fished out her ID and flagged the converging security personnel. "We have a situation."

--

The Administration vessel monitored the events following the announcement of The Misplaced's abduction as the late arrival of the band had already caused serious concern. The resulting economic instability and public outcry succeeded in drawing the attention of even the massively distracted Administration. Newly established protocols from the galactic core made the band's survival somewhat of a minor concern.

Parts of the Administration's massive decision-making matrix were not overjoyed at this prospect, and they wished they could get back to the nice job of punishing the living. It was so much more rewarding than trying to sort out their constantly shifting affairs and make them 'happy.' But for the most part, the Administration was becoming partial to rock and roll and was listening.

--

A breeze flowed across the silky alien cloth and gave Lisa goose bumps. Lisa fought the aftereffects of the anesthesia and shook herself awake. Twisting her head painfully against the restraints, she noted that, like her, the others were strapped to gurneys.

They were each carried by four of the Macan, the buzzing of their wings echoing off the walls of the tunnel as they made their way along. A single Macan led the procession, a bundle dangling by a thin chord from his harness.

"Where in the hell are we?"

One of the Macan bearers struck her savagely on the leg. "No sound."

"Ouch! Sonofa—you filthy bug!" Lisa struggled to free herself from the gurney. "Do that again and I will kill you!"

The Macan contemplated her words and then very deliberately hit her once more. Laughing for emphasis, he was joined by the other bearers, the sound echoing off the tunnel walls as they flew along.

Lisa took careful note of this one, his clothing, painted markings, and jewelry, and thought, *Just let me down. A slap on your antennae and a punch on the center carapace above the thorax, and you are dead, insect!*

"Lisa, chill out!" Pony's voice barely reached her over the Macan's laughter.

She managed to turn her head enough to catch sight of the drummer. One glance told her he had suffered a lot more than she had. Sight of the severe black eye made her hold her tongue.

Warm currents occasionally brushed Lisa's bare skin as they flew through the maze. She tried to memorize their path, but gave up after a few dozen twists and turns. Head pounding from the gas, her thoughts drifted to more mundane matters like desperately needing a simple glass of water.

Drifting along, she was caught off-guard when the tunnel abruptly expanded into a large room. Almost delicately, they were lowered to the floor. The lead Macan dropped his bundle on a table and took a seat as they were set nearly upright before one of the strangest creatures they had ever seen.

It resembled a gigantic mushroom, with over a dozen octopus arms and two very large eyes. Behind it was an elaborate media setup, complete with monitors showing various feeds. Featured on the center screen was their newly released live video from the band's last performance.

The monstrosity itself was guarded by several four-armed bipeds sporting ferocious horns from their crab-like faces. Each of the things stood as tall as Pony, and all bore large rifles. With the sure balance of fighters, they stood dressed in sophisticated body armor that glistened as if cast from crystal. Lisa searched those truly alien faces and could

not make out anything that she recognized as an expression in the
black beady eyes.

Now you would be fun to fight, she thought.

The mushroom creature spoke with a mouth large enough to
swallow a horse. "Welcome! De thanks for de rescue na needed."
The being gestured. "Free lem!"

The Macan hurried over and released the restraints. Lisa and
Blixa smiled quaintly at each other and posed in little more than a bra
and panties. Dan and Pony stepped free, and the boys looked like
they were ready to fight.

The Macan that had struck Lisa had apparently forgotten about
her threat. When it strayed close, she made good her promise, and the
creature fell dead to the floor. Unexpectedly in response, the four-
armed aliens guarding Tiny looked at each other and started laughing.

"Good ender!" The mushroom stopped the other Macan from re-
taliating with a gesture. "Leave lem!"

The mushroom reached out, picked up the dead figure and
started carefully removing its clothing and jewelry, as one would a
peel a piece of fruit, before it unceremoniously popped the entire body
into its mouth. Chewing thoughtfully, it looked at Lisa.

"Good one. But tha all de get! No more the ending. Twa good
now?"

Lisa said nothing, but gave a slow nod and crossed her arms.

"I rescued de from de clones." He pointed at Blixa with several
arms. "They came for de, using the gasses of A'cabba. Good gas from
A'cabba," he added almost absently.

"Thank you for that, Mr. Gigantic." Blixa slapped her hands together and started looking for a way out. "Now how much will this
rescue cost?"

"Lem!" The Gel pointed with eight arms directly at The Misplaced. With the other eight, he pointed at the main screen where
they played.

"I beg your pardon …" Dan touched his chest. "What do you
mean, *us*?"

"De working for I now …" The Gel spit a portion of the Macan to
the floor. "Making I fat with de new music tones a'rock and roll."

Dan looked humorously at the Gel and said, "We already have a
manager."

"Twa de that make de contract!" shouted Tiny, pointing absently to his computer with a pair of arms. "Twa de can break it!"

Dan took the opportunity and began flash-reading and memorizing all of the information that scrolled down Tiny's monitors.

"We like our current arrangement." Pony started for the bundle he hoped was their clothes, but the Macan sitting at the table drew some sort of weapon and motioned him away.

Lisa sighed, "May we at least get dressed?"

"Nae. De clothing is part of the negotiations."

"This is some first class bullshit, man!" Pony pointed at the Macan with the weapon. "Is this how you operate, muscling talent to work for you? Wait till the Administrators hear about this!"

The Gel began to laugh. "So good, so far … that's why de here in secret, biped. The Suterine very hostile, some say notorious for their warlike tendencies. While de within this star system, de can do no wrong harm. De are out of Admin jurisdiction, here."

Lisa smeared her foot across the remains of the Macan defiantly. "Well, no matter what you do, I think it is safe to say that you can go right to Hell!"

"Some bold words." The Gel leaned in menacingly. "De see how de feels after a few days of privation." Tiny slapped two 'hands' together. "Negotiations concluded for today. Let the record reflect de came to no agreement." Then he added with an underlying tone of amused menace, "Take lem to de green room."

The Macan guards kept a respectful distance with their weapons carefully trained as they escorted the bipeds to their nearby holding cell. Exhausted from their ordeal, the group went quietly.

Dan continued to flash-read and memorize all of the screens around Tiny until the very last moment they were escorted out. He currently had a wealth of information. Now for the chance to put it to use.

When the peri were out of sight, Warnik said confidently, "They will come around."

"Lem better, as I'm canceling your contract, now."

"What the crush?!" Warnik's eyes suddenly began to perspire.

The Gel blanked the terminals, and the room fell silent. "You are reluctant and tired as an ender, and as a music maker. I see it in de eyes, all six of lem." The Gel's bulk shifted, and he said almost affectionately, "De had a long flight. Longer than ever anyone b'fore. De tones played across the stars and make all much grocery. Now at de peak, de retires with honor and reputation intact! A pinnacle forever!"

After almost twenty years working for the callous manager, Warnik knew enough to take the offer or else risk ending up as another snack. There might not be any further negotiations. When the Macan considered the rest of the band, he ignored his own personal outrage and thought it best to accept. His was not the only life Tiny threatened. Warnik fought down the unexpected wash of pity and guilt he suddenly felt for the peri band.

"I agree." The Macan rose from his seat with a fluttering of wings. "Retirement plays soothingly across my heart. It will give me a chance to finally raise a clutch and brood them beneath my wings." Warnik was careful to keep his weapon free when he said, "It has been a pleasure working with you, Tiny."

"And de ..." The Gel reawakened the monitors and appeared to turn his back, which the Macan knew was basically impossible. Warnik, without another word, fluttered away.

--

The 'green room' was a spacious cell charmingly designed to make almost any warm-blooded carbon-based being uncomfortable. Every single inch of the walls, floors, even the tall ceiling had a spike texture, not quite sharp enough to break the skin, but close. Every step in their bare feet was agony, and there was no place to rest without constant pain. To top it off, it was chilly, and a steady mist continually sprayed.

The cold water made them shiver after only a few moments. "Nice ..." Lisa edged closer to Blixa, Dan, and Pony. "Ouch, uh, come on guys, let's huddle up."

Pony shook his dreads free of accumulating moisture and wrapped his arms around both his friends. "More than a couple of days in here will kill us." The chill fell on him like a leaden cloak.

"Less, if you want my medical opinion." Lisa's flat tone left no room for argument.

"Goddamn it, if I only had a Coil!" Dan dropped his head in resignation. "We would be outta here!"

Blixa snuggled into Dan's chest and kissed him. "Calm down, honey. Conserve your energy."

"Maybe we should rethink our position?" Pony's statement silenced everyone's shivering for a moment. He touched his eye gingerly. "I don't know about you, but I'm starting to get cramps in my feet and legs. I think it's getting colder."

They all stared at each other in silence, only Pony's occasional stubborn grunts of pain passing between them.

Dan winced. "I'm sorry about this, guys."

"It's not your fault!" Pony gave him a slight squeeze for emphasis.

"No, I'm talking about this." They heard a long squeaking noise, and Dan started to laugh.

"Really?" Lisa pulled back, and the slight draft cut through all of them. "Oh, really!? This is worse than a Dutch-oven!"

Pony smacked his lips and grimaced. "You sick bastard—what in the galaxy did you eat?"

Blixa answered for him, a look of disbelief on her delicate features. "Extra Mesta sauce."

--

"Crushed!" Cherrup shouted loud enough to hurt even Warnik's antennae, desensitized from years of loud concerts. "All our eggs, crushed! After all this time! And all that talent we dispatched to keep him on top!"

The spacious cabin of the Macan liner became suddenly cramped as Cherrup leaped about in agitation.

"We are free." Warnik could only repeat the phrase by way of an apology. "You can go back there and try and chirp him out of it, if you want."

Thraxis was dangerously motionless. "But we've done everything he has ever asked us to. How could he just throw us away like that? Where's the respect?"

"He has bigger shelt to fry." Jakta's wings fluttered in annoyance as he avoided another of Cherrup's agitated leaps. "And we gave them to him."

"Now we have again consigned others to torture." Guilt made Warnik's forelegs twitch in agitation. "He has them in the green room until they agree or die."

"Crush them!" said Cherrup alighting for a moment. "I don't care about the peri. What smashes my eggs is that he will profit from all of this!"

"The peri have yet to sign a contract." Warnik was careful to keep his tone level.

"Then we should arrange that they never do!" Thraxis was so still he almost looked petrified.

"I agree." Warnik's smile at crossing Tiny made his palps ache.

--

Over a hundred massive starships hurtled through the endless void, each sleek hull barely light-seconds apart from the others in the fleet. Carefully arranged into attack groups, the Altabatt Navy—or security force as they called it for Administration reasons—dropped out of FTL and converged around Tiny Gigantic's headquarters.

Cal'dreem Altabatt did not waste any time with formalities. "Mr. Gigantic, this is the Director of the Altabatt Conglomerate, and you are hereby notified that we will engage your space-station if you do not immediately hand over my daughter and her companions, unharmed. You have one minute to respond and five minutes to comply. Thank you for your cooperation."

The response was swift and decisive. "Director, we have multiple vessel launches and missiles in-bound."

The director was on his feet, eyes flashing across the monitor at the battle. "All attack groups: maintain formation and initiate random evasion orbits—captains: fire at will. I want all fire directed at communications and engines. Let's shut him down people. Boarding parties prepare for departure."

The sides of the gigantic monitor streamed data as the battle unfolded. For the most part, the director was content to watch the conflict without any micromanagement, although occasionally he would order an attack group to retire and another into its place. Soon, regardless of his losses, his boarding parties would make their way into the heavily guarded fortress.

--

Jakta's antennae twitched. "Did you feel that?"

"Patch me into the station's com." Warnik's new harness

squeaked as he loaded it with weapons.

Cherrup's manipulators moved slightly, and the speakers came alive with battle chatter.

"We've got multiples in sector twelve over the AK4 thrusters, target and dispatch, over."

"This is the AK battery, targeting ..." There was a moment of silence and then, "Confirmed hit."

"All stations, this is control. The situation is stable ... Repeat, the situation is stable. All weapons batteries at maximum efficiency. Maintain positions."

"Fire details to com sector nine, fire details to com sector nine. Repair crews to follow."

"We have unconfirmed reports of boarding parties in sectors eight and seventy four. Send heavy response forces to repel or destroy, repeat: repel or destroy ..."

And on and on ... Warnik and Thraxis looked at each other for a moment in utter astonishment; neither had any belief in divine intervention. In fact, the concept of a deity had long ago been thrown in the psychological trash heap along with 'karma.' To the Macan, existence was very simple: there were the way things were, and the way one would like them to be, the deciding factor being a willingness to go several steps further than the other poor bastard would even consider.

Cherrup pulled up the station's log and replayed the director's initial communiqué and chirped, "It seems that The Misplaced have been found."

"I'm not one to turn down a diversion." Jakta hefted a large sack of grenades. "Let's see if this commotion will make things easier or more difficult."

--

"Dan, honey?" Blixa sounded exhausted and defeated. "I don't think I can keep standing much longer."

"Me either." Dan took a bit more of her weight. Waves of pain sliced up from his bare feet. He kept rolling over what he had learned in his mind, but could find no way out of the so-called 'green room.'

Lisa tried to huddle next to Blixa, but the moment she touched the alien girl's strangely soft skin she was overcome by a mixture of anger and guilt. The twin emotions forced her to pull away from the much-needed warmth.

"I'm going to try to sit cross-legged on the floor." Lisa extricated herself and stepped painfully a few paces away. "Ouch, ouch—it can't be as bad as a bed of nails."

"Yeah, that's cold, woman!" chattered Pony.

Lisa began slowly working herself down when the doors opened. Adrenaline hit her, and she was quickly up on her feet.

The giant crab-faced guard pointed a weapon into the room and ordered Blixa to accompany him. "Mr. Gigantic would like a word, Miss Altabatt."

"No—I won't go without my friends."

The Berakean's reply was to simply pull her from the group, easily managing to extricate her with its four powerful arms. It casually tossed her over an armored shoulder.

Blixa pounded furiously on the mercenary's back, her expression apologetic. She shouted through the closing doors as she was carried away, "I promise I will work something out!"

Lisa stood quickly and huddled back together with her friends. "Ugg. That bitch! Dan, I can't explain it, but for some reason, I've started hating Blixa lately."

"Why?" Dan's teeth were beginning to chatter slightly. "What's she done?"

"Aside from banging you, whom I consider to be like … my brother and an ex-boyfriend all wrapped up into one, she looked at Christine once, and I've been pissed ever since."

Pony's deep voice vibrated her chest as he said, "But, has she actually done anything?"

"No …" Lisa struggled to put her feelings into words. "I mean, I can almost stand her being your girlfriend, Dan. That irritates me, but not as much as just the thought of her paying the slightest bit of attention to Christine! Even bullshit casual conversation freaks me out!" Lisa shook her head. "Why is it that I'm comparatively ok about you, but absolutely frickin' outraged about Christine?"

"It's because you girls are way too complex." Pony painfully adjusted his feet and shook out some of the water accumulating in his dreadlocks. "And more importantly, you're way too sensitive about every little remark." Pony hugged Lisa. "You know we both love you like a sister, but there is always way more drama when you are with a girl than when you're with a guy. But you're happier when you're with a girl than when you're with a guy." Pony looked down. "Guys bore you—girls don't."

"That's 'cause guys are so easy." Lisa hated this admission. "All you think about is getting laid. And once you're getting laid regularly, you stop really trying to get laid." Lisa shrugged. "With girls it's always constantly changing, and you have to be so careful, and this for some reason is always interesting. So, when Blixa even looks at Christine, all bets are off."

Dan was silent through all of this, and he knew if he revealed Blixa's drugging him that Lisa would go ballistic and might never forgive the girl.

"I'm sorry to bitch about your first real girlfriend at a time like this ..." Lisa glanced at Dan with an apologetic expression. "I know how important she is to you, but it's been bothering me for a while."

"Now is as good a time, as any ... But, keep in mind that I love her, Lisa." The admission made Dan's chest grow tight with unexpected emotion. Dan tried to laugh, but the shivering made it come out as a sputter. "Aside from that, I'm just thinking about how messed up things are all of a sudden. I mean, first we almost crash, and now we've been locked up here. And then it suddenly hits me: we're in frickin' outer space! I keep reverting to the mindset that we are still at home. When I remember that we are actually in outer space, I start to kinda freak out!"

"Welcome to my world all the time, man," sighed Pony. "I keep doing the same thing. It's giving me nightmares. I go over technical details all the time looking for somewhere we've messed up and reassuring myself that everything's all right."

Lisa snuggled closer to her best friends and tried to relax in their warmth. "You guys are so sweet. You've been experiencing your cute little cosmic agoraphobic trauma while I've been fixated on murdering Blixa."

"You should be ashamed of yourself, Lisa," chattered Dan through clenched teeth. "Blixa hasn't done anything to deserve that," he lied.

"I know, I know ..." Lisa shook her head in agreement apologetically. "Like I said, with other girls it's ... complicated."

Only a few minutes after Blixa was gone, there was a muffled explosion, and the doors opened once again. It was a Macan, the leader who had guided them into Tiny's presence. Pony never considered himself a racist and had been amazed at how, wherever they went in the galaxy, beings of all types were introduced by their names—and sometimes planets of origin—but never by their races, although after suffering a beating from the hands of one of these insects, xenophobia made him feel all warm and fuzzy inside.

"Would you consider exiting the green room?" Warnik waved his gun towards the hallway.

Painfully, amongst much ouch-ing and complaining, the group made their way to the blessedly smooth floor of the hall without any hesitation, too glad to be out of there to worry about anything else.

"Did Tiny give in?" Dan tried to make his joke sound light-hearted and failed.

"The situation has changed somewhat."

Dan noticed that the other members of the Macan were pointing their weapons away from them, as if on guard, except for Thraxis who still had them in his sights. He asked worriedly, "How so?"

"Tiny must not be allowed to profit from you."

Warily, Dan eyed the crickets' guns.

"He won't. Get us out of here, though, and we'll find a way that he can't profit from anyone any more." Dan slowly extended his hand. "You have my word on it."

Warnik cocked his head, thought about it for a moment, then glanced at the other crickets who reluctantly nodded. He cautiously put a foreleg into Dan's grip.

"Then you are not in any danger from us. With the exception of Thraxis, most of us are tired of killing for that greedy chib mush-room."

"Yeah, I still like the killing." Thraxis simply shrugged. "Sorry."

"We should get them off-station expediently." Cherrup gestured with her weapon. "Even the well-timed distraction won't keep Tiny occupied for long."

"What well-timed distraction?" Pony crouched down to relieve some of the pain in his legs.

Warnik's palps clicked. "The Altabatt Navy is attacking the sta-tion. They have demanded your unconditional release. Needless to say, the hostile negotiations are still in progress."

Lisa groaned. "From one green room to another … That's why they took her! She's a hostage!" Lisa's instinct to preserve life unexpectedly reared its head, and she found herself worried for the alien girl.

"We need to find Blixa and our gear," said Dan emphatically. "Help us get to our stuff, and we can get us off this station, I promise."

All of the Macan turned to look at him, their constantly moving antennae now absolutely still in astonishment.

Warnik shook his head. "You have got to be crushing us?"

"We cannot leave our friend or equipment in his hands." Dan paused. "If he discovers what he has—you have no idea how much more of a monster he would become."

"I can understand your mate, but what is so important about that small bundle? I carried it myself."

"It's a secret technology from my planet, and trust me, my insectile friend, it's way more revolutionary than our music." Then Dan added confidently, "Follow me. I know a way to the 'stage entrance' in one of the vestibules in his control room. I've got the code to open the doors."

"How?" gasped Warnik. "I've been working for that toadstool for a long time and even I didn't know there was a backdoor to his control room, let alone the door code!"

Dan shrugged. "I read it on his terminals."

"You weren't even in there for a minute! That's impossible!" The Macan took a step back in astonishment and looked him up and down. "What kind of beings are you?"

Dan simply shrugged and replied, "Clever."

--

Tiny scanned the report and grunted a signal for his elite group of Berakean Mercenaries to act as personal defense. The clone boarding parties had somehow managed to get close enough to be a threat to his person, and to the manipulative Gel, this was most disconcerting. The very thought that he was in personal danger was … embarrassing.

Sweat began to form on his head, making every breeze cling nauseatingly as the Berakean charged into the room amidst much boot crashing and tooth grinding.

Following the guards, the mercenary arrived with the clone in tow.

Tiny focused his attention on the Canabrean female.   She was such a small thing, little more than a mouthful of flesh. Her legendary antennae were close to her head, a sign she was afraid. He liked to see that—everyone negotiated better when there was a mutual 'respect.'

"De family has arrived and demanded de release. Get dressed." The Gel pointed to the bundle on the table.

"It's about time you showed some manners, you old toadstool!"

"De will see I manners, from the inside of I mouth, clone. Yoo are I hostage!"

"Have you lost your mind?" Blixa winced when she stomped her bare and still sore foot. "Oh, this has really gone too far!"

"I thinking the same thoughts, why not just re-grow de? Twa be cheaper, would it not? Why de big fleet!?"

As she got dressed, Blixa looked at the data she could see scrolling across Tiny's monitors, and at first glance, tended to agree with the infamous manager's assessment. If this was a rescue operation, it was way over budget.

"I think you made a mistake believing you would be safe hiding in this star system. It's a double-bladed razor." Blixa stood and fastened her boots. "Our Navy hasn't had a chance to conduct a full scale operation like this in memory. That alone could be the reason for their persistence, my own ego aside."

"De na thinks it could be about de band?"

"What in the galaxy gave you that idea?" Blixa sat back down at the table and gathered the bundle protectively in her lap. "You're the music mogul, not the Altabatts. We don't even have a music subsidiary."

"Too much grocery being spent for just a clone!" Tiny slapped the floor and moved the distance to Blixa in only a few 'strides.' Pushing past the Berakean mercenary guards, he said, "Maybe too much even for this rock 'n' roll …"

Under the Gel's direct scrutiny Blixa suddenly regretted her decision to grab the gear. She should have just left it alone as if it were nothing.   Fighting every instinct in her heart, Blixa set the bundle aside and sought to run. "Keep away from me, you spore!"

Tiny's reach was far greater than she expected, and soon she was dangling helplessly over the table. "Now, Miss Altabatt, de remains hostage until I decide." She tried to touch his arm with her antennae, and Tiny delicately shifted her away as if they were poisonous when he gently set her down. "There is more to this twa meets I eyes."

With a gesture, the Gel had two of the Berakean beside her table, weapons drawn.

Blixa did not move, nor in any way did she make an indication that the clothing was important. She found the ability rather simple, as if the strict discipline were a part of her basic nature. The realization prompted other ideas as well.

"Tiny, you do understand that should you succeed in obtaining an agreement with the band, you still have to deal with former management's claims."

The Gel pointed to the monitors. "I legal will deal with de Hive. I have paid for de already, clone. They have not the grocery to buy de back from I and pay de cost on this negotiation. No matter what happens, de be mine. Now I want to know what is de real grocery value of I clone?"

Blixa shrugged and held onto her poker face. It was a mask of perfect indifference when she said, "I am a Director of the Altabatt Conglomerate. Isn't that enough?"

"Cha! Give I no résumé." Tiny was not convinced. "De know something, chib. And I think pain be the key to unlock de secret. Hmmm?"

One of the Berakean standing at the table growled in agreement and drew a wicked-looking knife.

Before the mercenary could use it, an Altabatt security guard took careful aim, dropping the Berakean before the rest of the squad spilled into the room amidst a blaze of stun blasts.

"Come to I," said the Gel.

Blixa shrieked and ducked beneath the table before Tiny managed to grab her.

Wincing from the Altabatt stun blasts, the Gel backed away in frustration. Too large a target to hide, he suffered as the clones concentrated their fire on his toadstool-like head.

Tiny managed to make it to his control chair before they could cause him to black out. With a slap on the controls, he raised a personal shield and screamed, "End lem!" The Gel shouted in frustration, "End lem all!"

Blixa grabbed the bundle and hid beneath the table. She saw her family's guards gesturing for her between bursts of covering fire. Blixa ignored them and crouched low. Tiny's Berakean were using weapons that were designed to stun and had the entire group pinned down at one of the chamber's entrances. The Altabatts were good and managed to make perfect use of the cover. The problem was, for the most part, there wasn't any. And Tiny's guards kept arriving.

Blixa searched for a way out. The inner sanctum was constructed in the round concert-style with his control chair set in the center on a raised stage. The room had four entrances, all equally spaced apart, and bordering the large chamber were small alcove-like rooms. Each appeared to be a dead end.

Her eyes caught movement, and in one of the vestibules, she saw Dan frantically trying to get her attention without being noticed. Blixa fought down her surprise and started to quickly crawl in his direction. As soon as she moved, some of the Berakean opened fire, forcing her back beneath the table.

"They've got her pinned down!" shouted Dan.

Lisa felt ashamed of herself when she began to secretly hope Blixa would be hit.

Warnik leaped to the top of the vestibule and crawled to have a look upside down from the lip of the doorway.

In an extraordinarily nonchalant manner he said, "Thraxis, old boy, would you be so kind as to play that song you call 'grenades' for those bothersome mercenaries?"

Thraxis smiled as he tossed several in their general direction and shouted, "Get crushed!"

Swallowing her fear, Blixa followed the explosion. Trailing gunfire, she ran for the vestibule. Unfortunately, one of the four-armed Berakean mercenaries appeared out of nowhere and caught her. Blixa barely managed to toss the bundle to Dan. The girl's self-sacrificing expression, filled with love and farewells, sent an unexpected wave of anguish through Lisa.

The mercenary held Blixa with two arms and fired blindly into the vestibule. Braving the random gunfire with the rest of the crickets, Dan and Lisa managed to close the doors unharmed.

"So much for a rescue," said Lisa, inwardly nauseated at the surge of excitement she had felt at the thought of Blixa being killed. The girl's martyred expression echoed in her mind, and it made her feel horrible at her previous thoughts, the jealousy she had felt burning away. Blixa fully expected to die so that they would have a chance.

"We can still make our way around maybe?" As Warnik pointed, gunfire shattered the open back door, and Jakta fell to the floor.

Cherrup palmed the stage door's control switch, sealing their only exit and screamed. "Jakta!"

The cricket managed to cough and smile. "I'm alright; it just grazed me, crush my eggs!"

Cherrup caressed his antennae with hers. "Can you stand?"

Dan shook his leather jacket free of the bundle and tossed Pony his. "He doesn't have to."

--

Sweat ran down the Gel's shiny cap as he fought to maintain concentration. The Altabatts had managed to land not one, but two of their boarding parties, and try as they might, not even the expensive Berakean mercenaries could stop them. His security forces outnumbered the clones a hundred to one, and still the Altabatts gained ground.

The com buzzed. "Boss, The Crickets are *aiding* the hostages. We have them pinned down in the stage entrance vestibule. We believe the band is with them."

Tiny switched the monitor to another view and confirmed the green room was vacant. He looked at the vestibule, and its doors were closed.

"Keep lem there. I deal with lem after I finish this negotiation." The Gel called for more reinforcements and gestured to the Berakean pinned down by the Altabatt's gunfire. "Bring I clone."

The merc made a dash for Tiny's podium, and the Altabatt security men stunned him. Blixa landed roughly, but managed to make it to her feet.

Tiny switched off his ever-present force field and reached for the girl.

The Gel's grip was firmly on Blixa's arm when the vestibule door opened, and there was a flash of bright pink as The Misplaced stepped out in three giant suits of power-armor.

"Get away from her, you bastard!"

Lisa groaned. "Dan, you promised me you weren't going to say that!"

"But," Dan pointed toward Blixa defensively, "he's grabbed her, jeeze!"

Pony dropped to one knee and took aim with his focused coherent discharge weapon. When designing the real-sized armor, he had had Dan make three weapons—aside from the sheer physical strength of the armor and its blades, they also had the hailstorm as he called it, which was basically a 'Vulcan cannon,' a plasma-sheathed particle beam (stunner) and a focusable coherent discharge (laser.)

The Coil fields around the armor's wrists created a tight laser beam and Pony carefully drew a blazing line between Blixa and the monster. The Gel lost an arm in the process, but managed to pull back into his force field before Pony fired again, ensuring that he remained there.

Immediately the combined force of the Altabatts and the station's security personnel became focused on the trio. Unfortunately for all those on the opposing forces, the trio retaliated.

Blixa scrambled to her feet and ran for the vestibule while The Misplaced managed to keep both groups at bay.

Lisa concentrated her fire on the mercenaries, extravagantly protecting Blixa's dash for cover by swinging her hailstorm back and forth. Dan picked off the Altabatts with bursts from his particle beam, while Pony continued to see just how much damage Mr. Gigantic's force field could withstand.

His shield close to fading, Tiny activated his emergency escape system, wondering, *How did lem find I back door?* With a metallic clang, a dome shield snapped into place, and the Gel's control platform dropped out of sight.

Blixa cupped her hands and shouted so hard her throat felt raw. "We have got to get off this station!"

Dan gave her the thumbs-up of acknowledgment and waded out into the battle to press down hard on the clones with his stunners. Amazingly enough, the human-sized Altabatts evaded blast after blast. Try as he might, Dan could not stop a pair of the agile clones, and they managed to leap onto his armor.

"Alright, you little shits, I was trying to be nice!" He slapped one of the clones away, and the man rebounded off the floor and back at him like a monkey. At the same time, the other remaining rider drew a weapon and fired directly at Dan through the windshield— fortunately, to no effect.

Dan looked at the clone and gave a menacing smile as he shrugged and said, "You asked for it."

Crushing the man like one would a bug, Dan turned and caught the other in mid-flight, tearing him in two with a single savage wrench. Throwing the bodies into the Altabatts, he roared, "Get out of my way!"

When Dan opened fire with his hailstorm, not even the Altabatts had a chance as a deadly wind of lead pellets choked the hallway.

Covered by Lisa and Pony, Blixa—grunting with effort—sprinted for the exit surrounded by the Macan.

Deck plating screamed as Pony wrenched up a section to shield them from the RPGs. The explosions reverberated, and Lisa followed it with hailstorm blazing. "How much further to your ship?"

Warnik crouched behind her leg and fired down the hall. "Not much. I would never have thought we could have made it this far."

Lisa caught another grenade and tossed it back in the direction it came from. The satisfying thump was followed by screams as the hallway filled with smoke. "We're not out of the woods yet."

Pony pulled up another piece of plating, the metal screaming out its protests, and used it to cover their backs as they pressed forward. Dan kept up a steady stream of fire from his cannons and pushed past Lisa.

Further on down the hall Dan saw the shadow of a large piece of machinery being moved into place. "Trouble ahead." Dan fired his thrusters and roared forward. When he cleared the smoke, Dan caught clear sight of the massive alien gun.

It was a very big gun, thought Dan. Much bigger than it should be, given the circumstances of that he would rather continue among the living. Unfortunately for Dan, the gun had no such preconceptions, but instead it rather liked the current situation, especially given the fact that it was aimed directly at its target.

"Oh, shit!"

The weapon discharged and hit his armor directly in the chest, stopping Dan dead in his tracks. He felt the concussion as if it were a hammer. His armor's systems dropping in and out, he managed to fall to the side to evade a second shot. From the floor, Dan opened up the laser and pushed the Coil for as much as it would produce before the suit completely failed.

"Eat this, crusher!"

There was a blinding flash, and the offending artillery weapon exploded.

Dan tried to stand, but the armor would not respond. Twitching and stuttering, the servomotors fluttered as if they were gigantic muscles suffering cramps.

"I'm down, dudes," called Dan, "I'm down!"

"No matter, we are almost there." Cherrup pointed and chirped, "The gun was in the hangar, where our ship is."

Before crawling from the acrid smoke-filled cabin of his armor, sparks illuminated Dan's hands as he activated the self-destruct while Lisa and Pony cleared the way forward. With a bright strobe flash, the armor transformed to energy behind them.

Warnik helped Dan to his feet as he coughed the foul-tasting smoke from his lungs. During a deep breath, Dan felt his ID buzz. "Who? Whoa! It's Bobbi!"

The Hive's questions all ran together. "Where are you—are you safe— what happened—is everyone all right?"

"We're on Tiny's station and are now fighting our way to the hangar, and The Crickets' ship, so we can get the hell outta of here!"

There was suspicion in Bobbi's voice. "The Crickets?! But you were captured by the clones!?"

"I know, I know, and yes, The Crickets!" Dan grabbed Blixa's hand; it was smooth. Just that simple touch sent a wave of reassurance through him, and he said, "Look, there is too much to explain right now. Once we are off this station, I'll fill you in. Where are you?"

"We followed the Altabatt Navy because we thought they were the ones who abducted you."

"They were," interrupted Warnik. "We were sent by Tiny to abduct your friends from the clones."

"Ohhhh." The sound of wonder in Bobbi's combined voices was almost comical. "Well, Christine has us orbiting behind the navy, but we're relatively close."

"Hang out and wait for us," said Dan. "We may need you to run interference if things get dicey once we hit space."

"You got it."

Using the remains of the alien gun as cover, Lisa peeked out into the large hangar. Spacious enough for several football fields, it was dotted with ships—and using those spacecraft for cover was Tiny's veritable army of security guards. Lisa caught sight of the Macan craft at the far end of the hangar, and surprisingly, it was not one of the vessels being used as an attack position.

Wading out into the open, Lisa drew fire away from her companions. "*Go Go GO!*" she shouted.

Pony followed her lead and began picking off anything he could kill. Together they tried to keep the entire attention of the mercenaries.

The Macan led Dan and Blixa from spacecraft to spacecraft, working their way ever closer.

Halfway to their destination, they crouched out of sight for a moment, and Thraxis chanced a look. A burst of fire drove him back.

"Crush, we've been spotted."

"How many?"

Thraxis rubbed an antenna. "Couldn't tell—at least three."

Dan fished out his ID and called Pony.

"Hello?" Dan could hear the muffled sounds of the battle over the connection.

"Pon, we're totally pinned down!"

Pony grunted with some Herculean effort required by the fight and replied, "I can't see you!" His vision, obscured by another of the big guns, only came in brief glances of the hanger floor around the weapon.

"We're about half way." Dan glanced at the liner they were using as cover and added, "We're by a big red ship with the blue stripe on its rudder."

"Lisa," shouted Pony over the suit's com, "Dan's pinned down! I'm going to try and draw their fire." Pony evaded another of the large alien artillery attacks by sliding beneath a space-liner. With a thunderous concussion, the vehicle exploded above him and pinwheeled away, trailing flame. Rolling forward, he landed in a football crouch, using his boot thrusters to leap upwards and evade several of the fire teams' attacks simultaneously. From his momentarily elevated position, he saw the ship Dan described. Thrusting in a controlled fall, Pony angled in its direction and landed on the small craft the guards used as cover and mowed the surprised mercenaries down with his stunners.

Lisa elected against using her range weapons and satisfied herself with throwing pieces of wreckage at anything that moved. Wielding the tailfin off some alien craft like a battleaxe, the guitarist sliced through a liner and tossed the two sections at the large artillery weapons shifting into place.

Flowing along with the battle, Lisa edged toward one of the large guns before it could bring itself to bear.

"I hope these things are expensive." She grunted with effort and slammed a perfect chop down on the barrel. Pulling back slightly, she reversed the motion of the arm and brought up the elbow on the same point, and the barrel shattered.

With her left arm, she used the Coil field to keep the fire crews at bay, alternating between hailstorm and laser.

Several more of the big guns emerged, and she could see reinforcements pouring in from around the hangar. Lisa swirled the suit's arms in a fluid motion, ending the movement in two solid fists.

"Oh, you poor bastards, I have waited for something like this my entire life." Her smile made her face ache. "Momma's gonna get some …"

Lisa fell on the alien forces like the Wheel of Karma. Throwing all caution to the wind, she sought out and destroyed anything that moved.

On the heels of the distraction, Pony cleared the way for the group. "Let's get while the getting is good."

Dan pulled Blixa along, and the Macan took to their wings. Jakta pushed into the lead and chirped, "Nearly there, nearly there."

--

The escape shaft took him directly to his auxiliary control room fitted into a special liner. Small and highly overpowered, the ship was designed to act as a temporary command center until he could reach another of his media control stations. Two questions filled his mind as he rode downward, the sinking feeling in his core mirrored by the rapid descent. Where had the band obtained those weapons? And once more, how did they know about the backdoor, let alone the codes to open it!

Within a few more moments, the time marked by systematic appearances of a red bar of light that served only to illuminate Tiny's anger, the trip ended. Grunting aloud, the frustrated Gel swung from the supports like a cross between an octopus and a monkey, transferring his bulk to the voluminously upholstered command couch on the liner. Behind him, the hull sealed with soft hiss.

As the ship's systems came to life around him, the sweat on his head quickly evaporated along with his anxiety. Safe in his control room, far from any chance of danger, the Gelfelregin could focus his faculties. Pain and itching dominated his lost arm, but the sensations took a backseat to the relief he felt about his narrow escape.

Having to content himself with only three cameras, the Gel did his best to take control of the situation from his auxiliary command post. Cursing the lack of 'eyes' throughout the hangar, Tiny watched the progress of the battle and orchestrated his forces with a meticulous aim toward capture.

When he saw one of the band members easily destroy a piece of A'cabban military equipment, he mumbled out loud, "Who are these Pangaeans?"

Tiny paused and considered simply venting the atmosphere. Almost unconsciously, a 'hand' selected the proper menu, and his 'fingers' hovered over the controls. He watched the scene on his smaller main monitor unfold, and another thought crossed his mind; this one stopped his 'hand.' *It's hard to question dead bodies.*

Instead, he opened a channel and ordered, "Slide all remaining A'cabba guns to I hanger. All remaining mercenaries twa I hangar. Put down those weapons, but save de hostages. I want lem alive."

The being, presumably the lone female of the group judging from the unusual color of her weapon, seemed unstoppable. Exhibiting nearly perfect biped Berakean form, she avoided every attempt to stop her. The A'cabba guns seemed unable to compensate for her nearly acrobatic movement and score a direct hit like the one that had incapacitated the first of the weapons.

The fact that the treacherous crickets were aiding The Misplaced galled the manager, and at the same time seemed appropriate business behavior after their termination.

They could not be allowed the chance to escape. "Target de Macan liner and destroy."

--

Concussive waves from the explosion stopped them all in their tracks. Dan barely pulled Blixa to safety behind a leg of Pony's armor in time to avoid the shrapnel and flaming wreckage rolling toward them in the slightly lower gravity.

Jakta, slowed by his injuries was not so fortunate, and was swept away by the blast, the Macan screaming, "Crush me!" as he vanished from sight.

The explosion drew Pony's attention momentarily, and the A'cabba gun began firing. Blast after blast slammed into the armor as every cannon found their target. Pony's suit staggered under the combined assaults, forcing Dan and Blixa to run for safety with the remaining crickets.

Lisa targeted the closest of the big guns and did her best to dismantle it. "Oh, no, you do not mess with my boy!" Flying from the wreckage, she crossed to the next gun. Always moving, always changing direction, she made it impossible for the tanks to pin her down.

When Pony's armor finally crashed to the ground, Dan spun around and sprinted toward it, shouting, "Pony, set the self-destruct, and get out!"

The armor was silent. Warnik waved Dan to follow while Thraxis and Cherrup laid down a steady stream of covering fire so precise that not even the mercenaries dared retaliate.

"Pony?!" Dan pounded on the chest piece. "Pony!?"

--

The refreshing coldness of deep space caressed the Administrator vessel as it moved in a deep orbit outside the Suterine solar system. Directives indicate that the Suterine allow any and all conflict within their dominion and Administration was only to intervene if called upon.

The vessel rechecked with primary control. The directive was still in effect and there were no requests for assistance. Ancient protocols held the vessel in place.

--

"Pony!?" Dan pounded on the power-armor futilely. "Dude!? Can you hear me?"

Blixa was at Dan's side, pulling him away. "They're coming!"

"We are not leaving here without Pony!"

There was a whirring sound as the armor opened. Pony was covered in thick hydraulic cables that resembled snakes. He shook his head and said sheepishly, "Sorry it took me so long. I got some hydraulic fluid in my mouth, and I was remembering our fight with that anaconda …"

"You frickin' douche-bag …" shouted Dan happily. "Set the self-destruct and get your lame ass out here—we gotta go!"

Pony climbed from the armor, just as it began to transform into energy.

"But where are we going, honey? They got the ship." The sound of Lisa's hailstorm, the crickets' weapons, and the roar of the remaining big gun nearly drowned out Blixa's voice.

Dan fished out his ID, and as they ran for the cover of another liner, he shouted, "Socks, we have a change of plans: we need the limo to come pick us up!"

"Just give us directions." Bobbi responded as if they had been waiting by the phone, which Dan was fairly sure a small portion of the Hive was. He was suddenly at a loss. He had no memory of this place.

Dan looked at Warnik and asked, "Where are we?"

"Hangar 42." He chirped, "We're in hangar 42!"

Dan covered the phone and looked at the Macan incredulously. "You've got to be kidding me."

The cricket just gave a shrug and nod of his antennae for confirmation.

"Hangar 42, guys!" laughed Dan. "Hey and hurry the hell up. We're under a lot of pressure here!"

"We're on our way!"

--

"Where is hangar 42?"

"We're checking now …" There was a moment of silence. "Ah, near the bottom, where all those ships are massing …!" The sudden panic in the Hive's voice intensified Christine's fears. The Hive tied into the bus' computers and highlighted the target area. Christine tried to focus her thoughts, but she kept returning to a massive black hole of worry over Lisa and her friends.

"Socks, I'm pushing the shields to maximum." Christine hit the high beams. "I gonna try and use the drive tube and cruise through the hangar door!"

"If you miscalculate, it will get very bumpy, and then we will die."

"Well, I don't have a chance of fighting through that bunch of ships—so, unless you have any better suggestions ...?"

The Hive was silent, and Christine took a breath, but before she could hit the clutch Bobbi interrupted her.

"Christine, if this does not work?"

"I know ... I know ..." Christine eyeballed the door. "But, how else can we get through those ships, the stations defenses, and the hangar door? Under minor Tension drive we can virtually teleport through!"

"You don't know what the inside of the hangar looks like." There was a sense of resolution in the Hive's tone as if it had already determined the outcome of this conversation. "What if we break out, and you're too close to a wall to slow down. We will go splat, at best!"

"This is all my freakin' fault," argued Christine. "If we would have arrived on time, we might have spotted the Altabatts. Well, you would have like ... totally."

"You won't do anybody any good if you get us killed!"

"I can't." She felt a familiar wave of confidence return from nowhere.

"Why not?" snapped the Hive.

Christine locked her hands on the steering wheel, Lisa's smile cemented in her mind's eye, and replied, "'Cause I'm in 'The Zone' ..."

--

Recoil washed up Thraxis' arm, and it felt wonderful. Since his carapace had hardened, he had always wanted to serve as a security guard or soldier. Just the smell of the weapons, leather, and steel was an aphrodisiac to the Macan.

For the first time in his life, Thraxis let loose with a wild abandon. Moving from position to covered position, he sought to be three targets ahead of where he was firing. Suddenly the battle fell into a combat-time, where his memory aimed the weapon, while his mind soared free to locate threats. It was like being in a dream as mercenary after mercenary fell to the song of his guns.

Suddenly, Thraxis felt a dull pain in his side, and as he turned, everything went white. "Ahh, crushed!" swore the Macan.

"Thraxis!" screamed Cherrup. "Crushing crushers!" She was suddenly in the air, raining death down on the mercenary and his two companions. She managed to hit all of them, but only two of the Berakeans fell to lethal wounds; the third calmly shot her in the forehead.

Warnik watched his two friends fall to the mercenary's stunners. Relief that his friends were not dead washed away some of the anger he felt about the situation. Shocked at the necessity to contain his emotions after so long a period of apathy, the Macan focused his attention on keeping them out of Tiny's oh-so-many hands. He pondered the implications of hijacking the liner they used as cover, when a massive pressure wave silenced everything.

Rainbow-colored light exploded into existence for only an instant, its presence burned into the visual organs of every being in the hangar. Silhouetted against the sheet of blinding illumination, the bus hit the deck of the hangar and skidded to a stop amidst a great cloud of white steam and smoke.

Christine opened the doors, and Bobbisocks flashed out and above the fray, every cannon on the Hive's ship raining down fierce pulses of plasma. Within the Hive, the little members manned guns with a vicious efficiency.

"Looks like the cavalry has arrived!" shouted Lisa, clearing a path to the bus with her hailstorm and laser.

Like professional medics, under the barrage of covering fire provided by his friends, Dan, Blixa, and Pony helped Warnik carry the stunned Macan on board.

Lisa waited until everyone else was aboard before she set the self-destruct on her armor and was followed by Bobbi into the bus. Once the door was closed, Christine wasted no time and hit the clutch.

--

The gigantic wall monitor on the Altabatt command ship was focused on the boarding parties as they fought to breach the space-station. The operatives looked like tiny ants moving in a very intelligent manner on the hull of the fortress. Little sparks of light could be seen, created by their cutting devices, as they worked at various airlocks around the hull.

Encircling the boarding parties, their ships provided the necessary protection for the fragile teams to do their dangerous job. As a result, the landing platforms were suffering a continuous assault that, even though it came from underpowered weapons, was having a cumulative affect.

"Group seven has reached condition yellow," warned the communications officer, her tone especially flat.

"Have group seven withdraw and provide cover from a safe distance," ordered the director. "Group fifteen to replace group seven; have them close in a single file, repeat: single file vector. Each liner to be no more that ten beats apart until they reach defilade, then emergency stop, scatter and assemble on position one for breach."

There was a flicker on the screen, a tracing of light.

"Intelligence, give me a report on the nature of that flicker. Was it a screen glitch?"

"Investigating ... running diagnostics ..."

The director watched the progress of group fifteen. One by one the expensive craft and its crew of family members were vaporized until the last two ships in the line managed to make it safely onto the hull of the station. Both ships activated their magnetic landing gear and dropped heavily onto the outer plating in a defensive 'V' formation around the remaining members of the initial breach team.

He zoomed in and saw tiny figures emerging from the spacecraft. Clad in black tight-fitting pressure suits, some provided covering fire with the absolute professionalism that had made the family a power throughout the galaxy, the rest pushing the mobile docking ring into place around the already compromised airlock. Once the structure was secure, the remains of the crew would begin blasting and cutting their way through the door.

The com voice relayed, "We have detected the FTL signature of The Misplaced ship." There was a pause. "They are currently in the hangar. They have somehow managed to bypass the door."

"That's not possible!" cried the director, a moment before the screen flicker occurred once more.

The dry voice announced, "The Misplaced vehicle has just exited the hangar; hold—their vehicle is now on a trajectory that will take them out of the system."

"After them!"

--

Tiny watched the armada surrounding his headquarters vanish after The Misplaced and stifled his outrage. For a few moments, he stared at the empty screens and pondered the mystery surrounding the band. There was much to contemplate and investigate concerning this group of peri bipeds who called themselves Pangaeans.

For a bunch of new entries, they had cost him a great deal of resources. The greedy Gel considered the itching stump of his lost arm and thought sourly, *a great deal of resources indeed.*

--

Light from the stardrive road illuminated Christine's face as she cheered, "Hell, *yeah*! Is everybody alright?"

"With the exception of our Macan friends, we're ok," shouted Dan.

"The who?" Christine kept her eyes on the road.

"The Crickets," said Lisa. "Like Dan said, they sorta rescued us from that nasty fungus."

Bobbisocks hovered defensively over the unconscious Macan, weapons trained. "But I thought they were trying to kill you?"

"We were," admitted Warnik flatly from across the room, no trace of an apology in his tone. "But the arrangement has changed."

"Warnik and his pals broke us out of our cell." Pony remembered the green room and Tiny's negotiations with a shiver. "Tiny fired them and tried to get us to sign a contract making him our manager."

"That sneaky chib," gasped Bobbi.

"That's not the worst of it." Warnik pointed to the side viewscreens through the Tension field—they saw the Altabatt Navy. "I believe your fam' are a bit annoyed at your escape."

"Oh dear," said Bobbi.

"Chris," Dan shouted, "once we're free of the star's influence, give her all she's got! See if we can out-distance these chibs."

The little smiley face blinked on sooner than she anticipated. Christine pressed the clutch and pushed the drive into third gear. After a few moments of her foot flat on the floor, the navy began to drop behind.

"So what do we do now?" asked Christine. "We're clamped!

We've totally blown the show, and from what we have been able to tell, pretty much thrown the known galaxy into chaos."

"Maybe we can kill two chibs with one stone," offered Dan.

"What are you suggesting?"

"That we have a free make-up show at a new venue, and Bobbi can vid and broadcast it. All we need to do is advertise and see if we can draw a crowd."

"How are we going to broadcast anything? If we slow down, the navy will be all over us!" Bobbi's multitude of voices sounded on the edge of frustrated tears. "And that is an awful lot of ships!"

"We don't have to slow down. I know how we can get a signal out!" The solution came to Pony in a flash of memory. "We use the Administrators' Einstein-Rosenberg Bridge, the one they first used to contact us: open a wormhole in the Tension field, and voilà! Piece of snochbul!'"

"Dude, you're a frickin' genius!" said Dan proudly.

Pony shrugged. "Naw, just clever, that's all. The hard part is gonna be removing the 'space' within the EM freq, to squeeze it through a hole no bigger than a neutron!"

"Leave that to me." Dan smiled cryptically. "With the Coil, space is moldable." He slapped his best friend on the shoulder. Flipping open Lisa's laptop, he then spent a few moments furiously tapping at the keys, his fingers a blur. "There … Christine, this is the venue. Take the long way around to give our audience a chance to make the show. Socks, here's what I want the broadcast to say …"

--

Christine dropped out of drive and edged her way into the at-mosphere slowly enough to not develop any significant reentry heat. Pony kept the shield tuned to absorb any thermal, radar, or micro-wave scans, and they managed to reach ten thousand feet above sea level without alerting anyone.

Dan and The Misplaced set up on the top of the bus, the portable stage visible from every angle as Bobbisocks floated about. "The au-dience should be arriving at any moment, and the navy is right behind them. I sure hope this plan of yours works. You're cutting it awfully close."

Wind tossing her hair, Lisa tuned her guitar and tried not to think about the drop when the bright clear sky fell suddenly dark as tens of thousands of ships arrived in orbit almost simultaneously. Completely encircling the Earth, the crowd blotted out the sun, a claustrophobic stillness drawing every living creature's eyes toward the suddenly crowded heavens. Absently, as if the distant audience could all see her clearly, she waved to the sky above and thought, *Yes, Dan, this is 'very discreet and very quiet!'*

--

The director paced back and forth in agitation. The large monitor displayed the simulation of The Misplaced ship, and the timer now read that they were only a minute or two behind.

The clone was sweating as the ship followed the twisting FTL corridor, and a planet swung into view. The display read "Pangaea," and they were only minutes away and closing fast.

The colossal wall monitor suddenly came alive as many, many vessels began appearing, all on a course for the planet, and all a minute or so ahead of them. He watched helplessly as the globe was entirely encircled by spacecraft just after The Misplaced made planetfall.

The director waited until they were past the orbital path of Mars before he pitched his voice to that of command and ordered, "Decrease speed to the maximum attack velocity—we don't want to outrun our guns." Intent on blasting his way through the blockade, the director ordered, "All ships, pick a target and fire when ready."

--

Dan gave Bobbisocks the signal, and the Hive ship easily commandeered Earth's entire satellite and cell communications grid, while simultaneously transmitting the scene via a live feed.

In the artificial twilight provided by the interstellar audience in orbit, the lights illuminated the stage. Dan stepped up to the microphone and said into the stunned eyes and ears of the entire planet, "Hey everybody. Don't panic! It's cool! It's cool. I'm sorry to barge in like this, but we just returned from a little road-trip and brought some guests back with us to watch a show." Dan pointed up to the choked sky. "But, uh, before we go on, I would like to introduce my fiancée: Miss Blixa Altabatt, from the planet Canabrea, and our manager, the Hive mind, Bobbisocks, from a planet whose name I can't begin to pronounce."

Bobbi ran the preset video of them all smiling and waving on the paradise world with three golden moons in the background.

"On guitar, we have Dr. Lisa Parks, and on percussion, Dr. Anthony 'Pony' McCormick ..."

Lisa couldn't believe Dan was going to do a standard intro again at a time like this, excluding himself, as always, and then Dan added proudly, "And I'm Dr. Dan Towne on bass and vocals, and like or not people, we are *The Misplaced!*"

Lisa's heart soared, and the band blasted into the anthem.

--

The massive Altabatt Navy was nearly within the maximum range of its weapons. The commander of the lead liner sat in his comfortable chair and focused all his attention on each second before he could open fire when the Administration vessel dropped out of FTL.

The black ship, a massive shadow against the pristine starscape of space, snapped into being directly in the path of the armada.

Cal'dreem Altabatt had only a fleeting moment to react, centuries of perfection and the genetic integration of a multitude of reactions giving him a powerful perspective of perspicacity. Walled up within his mental machine, he worked at the controls and came to a rather startling revelation. The awareness of which was most unsettling.

To his nearby attendant he said, "We've been crushed."

Opening a set of enormous doors, the Administrator vessel swallowed the entire navy and like a gigantic whale, swam off into the stars just as Dan began to sing.

We've been all around this galaxy
From the Belt of Orion to planet Wildrahnae
And on all these worlds, we set them free-
with the power of rock and roll

Riding the light highway through the endless void past Mars
Meeting aliens, while playing in far off bars
They ask me the name of my home world

And I shout-out to the stars, Pangaea!

Pangaea, our home in the Milky Way
Third from our sun, we call Sol.
The galaxy meets us all today
Once called Earth
that name is now passé
forever we are Pangaea
and for the future, it's here to stay.

Now let's give a welcome- to our friends from beyond the stars
They've traveled quite a distance- to this lonesome home of ours
They've come for the power of rock and roll-
Something found only in this place-now called… Pangaea!

Pangaea, our home in the Milky Way
Third from our sun, we call Sol.
The galaxy meets us all today
Once called Earth
that name is now passé
forever we are Pangaea
for the future is here to stay.

--

"Ladies and gentlemen, it is my pleasure to introduce the Hive mind, Bobbisocks, on tonight's show. The Hive mind, as you may know, is the manager for the intergalactic traveling band, The Misplaced. The very same group of individuals responsible for building—and piloting—the first starship that subsequently opened our world to the galaxy! Bobbi, it is a pleasure to have you."

"We are thrilled to be here!"

"There are a million questions people are asking, so let's just field a few. For starters, the new name 'Pangaea' is taking a bit of getting used to."

"We can well imagine." Bobbi's voices carried the emotions ranging from sympathetic to mildly amused. "Just the simple arrival of a few billion excited fans nearly threw your entire planet into chaos. I can see how needing to adjust to your noisy neighbors would be a bit of a strain—especially if they kept referring to your home by what you would consider the wrong name."

The announcer was silent for an impolitic moment as he swallowed his own personal outrage and continued, "Well ... ahem, yes. But, I would hardly consider planet-wide riots and wars as just a strain. People have died!"

The Hive's tone was dismissive. "Get over it. The galaxy is a big place, and you have finally been drawn kicking and screaming into it. And here's the really important part: stop all this nonsense and figure out a plan—nobody out there cares if you kill yourselves. We only care if you start in on others."

"Ah, and that brings us to the mysterious Administrators and their so-called laws." The host sat back in his chair with a smug expression. "What are they—rulers of the galaxy?"

"They don't rule anything. They administrate policies that were old before your little star—uh, Sol is it?—was born. We think they have a handle on things."

"That remains to be seen." The host sat back and looked at his prompts with a smug expression.

Bobbi almost had an internal riot itself when it heard the Pangaean's arrogant reply. So far, with the exception of their friends, everyone the Hive had met on this backward planet was so unbelievably condescending that it bordered on irrationality. It was as if their precious sanity depended on their maintaining their illusion of racial superiority.

The Hive had a quick debate and elected to say, "There are hundreds of thousands of planets out there, all united together and all functioning quite smoothly. You are only one tiny," Bobbi resisted adding the adjective *insignificant*, "planet. Show everyone you are up to the challenge and get your act together!"

"Well, um, thank you for that advice Bobbi. Alright then, on that note ... people all around 'Pangaea' have been asking another question: What defines a world as 'civilized' to the rest of the galaxy?"

"You mean aside from not rioting and killing yourselves at the first contact?"

"Yes." The announcer's contrite tone finally contained some respect.

"That's simple," replied Bobbi allowing a large portion of the Hive to speak cheerfully. "Traffic; or more precisely, a lack there of."

"Traffic?!"

"Yes, traffic," stated the Hive emphatically. "Civilized worlds do not have vehicular congestion. To be thought of as truly civilized, forget about eliminating money, poverty, war or religion, one must solve one's traffic problems, especially now that you have easy access to inexpensive interstellar transportation."

"Ah, yes—a starship in every garage, so-to-speak."

"Precisely," agreed the Hive, in a happy chorus.

"And how have these so-called 'civilized' planets accomplished this?"

Bobbi floated around, turning its face to the cameras. "It wasn't easy. Galactic history is filled with lurid tales of wars being fought over this matter. Nevertheless, in the end, after hundreds of worlds debated the issue, a conclusion was finally reached."

"And that is?"

"Intelligent beings do not tailgate!"

--

Blixa sat in the boardroom and watched the members of the Altabatt Trans-Galactic Conglomerate. The expressions of her subordinates were grim as they filed in and took their seats.

She didn't wait for them to get comfortable. "Now that directorship of the family business has passed on to me, following the Administration's 'reeducation' of my father, I wish to instigate a new breeding program."

Blixa smiled at the mixture of shock and indignation that flowed across the faces of those present. Not a single antenna was at half-mast.

"When she returns from tour next week, Dr. Parks will direct the medical facilities in preparing for the natural birth of Canabreans. And I want my husband's recently established Pangaean educational programs to reflect the goal that perpetuation of our species is no longer to be controlled by machines, but by free will."

"Director!?" Of course, the objection would come from the manager of Vat-masters; she was essentially putting the man out of a job. "Surely you wish to give this matter a little more consideration?"

She was prepared for his objection with a simple statement. "Nature grows a vat in every Canabrean woman." To emphasize her point, Blixa stood up and stretched her tired back. She was round and due to deliver within a few weeks. She added, "Your services are no longer required. I believe we can handle it from here."

--

The New York skyline was alive like never before in history. Bristling with a magnificent energy fueled by interstellar contact, the neo-renaissance, brought about by the influx of galactic ideas, had propelled the already thriving metropolis into economic and social overdrive.

The lights of the air traffic flowed like three-dimensional streets across the city, and Christine had to tear her eyes away. All her life she had dreamed of flying cars and now … the sky was full of them.

A slight moan came from the direction of the bed. Christine turned to the noise and said, "You've been a bad girl."

Lisa struggled against the ropes that held her wrists and writhed seductively. Between her legs, there was a gigantic ache and the dampness sent a delicious shiver up her body when she let her thighs drop apart slightly.

"I know …" replied Lisa weakly, a slight sob on the edge of her voice. "It's just that,' she twisted her wrists against the ropes in frustration, "I love you!"

Christine stomped her bare foot on the plush penthouse apartment carpet. "That's no reason to be such a bitch to everyone who looks at me!" She dropped on top of Lisa, gripped her wrists and pressed her firmly to the bed, as she whispered, "I'm sick and tired of you getting jealous for no reason!" She emphasized the words with gentle kisses.

Lisa felt how moist Christine's right hand was where it squeezed her wrist, and let a little groan escape her lips followed by a tiny sob. "I know, I know … I'm sorry."

With a little pretend sigh of concern, Christine smoothed back a stray strand of hair that had entangled itself near Lisa's mouth and purred, "You have never had any reason to be jealous of me and do you know why?"

Lisa sniffed and said petulantly like a spoiled child, "No … why?"

"Because we have always been in 'The Zone!'"

--

Tiny Gigantic was checking over his latest acquisition, a group of Korvekeain Gut Wasps that he had taken months to get hooked on a rare drug from a little known planet called Burkeralia, when all his defensive alarms went off simultaneously. Initial indications were that something had just created a miniature wormhole, similar to the one employed by the Administrators, directly into his command center.

Obviously, the unifiers were in error, thought the Gel. While Tiny frantically began searching for the source of the problem, the door to his operations center pin-wheeled across the room, neatly crushing several of his newly acquired—and very expensive—Berakean mercenaries into something less appetizing than paste.

"Knock, knock!" called Lisa from within her newly painted black and red power-armor.

Dan stepped up, leveling his hailstorm. "Seeing as we were interrupted last time, we thought you might like a 'private concert.'"

"And Tiny ..." said Pony displaying the massive battle hammer he had used to open the door. "*This* is what we call *Heavy Metal!*"

AUTHOR BIO

Raven c.s. McCracken currently lives in Seattle, Washington, with his Welsh corgi Bannor. In his spare time, Raven enjoys wombat training, untying and retying his shoes, and terraforming the sun with dehydrated water.

Raven c.s. McCracken is perhaps best known for his creation The World of Synnibarr. For which he has sincerely apologized, except for the Flying Grizzlies.

He offers these explanations: Choose one:

A: "There was no INTERNET!"

B: "I had a spare decade lying around."

C: "It takes a lot of paperwork to play god."

D: "I was thrown in a small cage, sent forward in time via the astral plane, and forced to create Synnibarr for a bunch of inbred hillbilly … uh …Viking chess masters, yes …! No wait …! Myopic alien Viking vampire speed-readers, on steam-powered robot ninja dinosaur ghosts, secretly protecting Area 51 and the Holy Grail from the wicked hovertank riding pan-dimensional hypoglycemic mutant werewolf conservative shaman strippers in mystic leather tube-tops! They made me do it! If I failed, they said that the fate of every extension cord in Indonesia was at stake!"

E: "All of the above."

For more information on the author or his books, go to www.ravencsmccracken.com

www.ingramcontent.com/pod-product-compliance
Lightning Source LLC
Chambersburg PA
CBHW050938120626
46552CB00001B/265

*9 7 8 0 6 1 5 5 6 0 5 3 3 *